# THE
# OLD GUY
## IN THE
# CLASSROOM

ROBERT LIVINGSTON

# Contents

# OTHER BOOKS BY ROBERT LIVINGSTON

THE SAILOR AND THE TEACHER

TRAVELS WITH ERNIE

LEAPING INTO THE SKY

BLUE JACKETS

FLEET

HARLEM ON THE WESTERN FRONT

W.T. STEAD AND THE CONSPIRACY OF 1910

TO SAVE THE WORLD

IN THE WAKE OF THE EMPRESS OF CHINA

THE FORGOTTEN CHAPLAIN

AXIS SALLY

THE TARNISHED ROSE

AMERICAN STORIES 1940 - 1960

THE ANCHOR AND THE JOURNALIST

TASTE THE WIND

A DEAN'S LIFE

# Dedication

*TO THOSE WHO TEACH HISTORY UNDETERRED
BY THE ANGRY DEMANDS TO CLEANSE THE
PAST FOR PARTISAN PURPOSES. THEY ARE
THE STRENGTH OF OUR REPUBLIC.*

# PROLOGUE



See that vintage VW Camper exiting the 405 Freeway at Devonshire Street in the San Fernando Valley? That's where our story begins in California. The old guy driving the rig will be 65 years old in a couple of weeks. He's also within three months of finally retiring from the Los Angeles School District. By July of this year he'll have racked up 40 years in the classroom, as a high school Social Studies teacher and as a part time history instructor at the local community college. It was time, he understood, to spend time with his wife and grandchildren, and maybe write still another book lurking in the back of his mind.

If we had been able to eavesdrop on the driver we would have heard him say, "Well Pomp, just a few more trips to your old parking place at the school and then only our driveway. With over 280,000 miles on your odometer you're entitled to a little rest. I guess I am, too. How many hundreds of classes have I taught? How many thousands of assignments have I graded? How many happy and upset parents have I met over the years? More than one, that's for sure."

The old guy was in the habit of talking to Pomp, the name he had given to his 4-cylinder, air-cooled, 25-mpg rig. Pomp! It was the name Sacagawea gave to her son when America was only thirteen states clinging to the eastern seaboard. Never heard of her? Well, what about the Lewis and Clark trek from the Mississippi River to Astoria, Oregon in 1806? Still unsure, are you? I guess you need to be in my history class. Anyway, let's get back to the old guy and his conversation.

*"Pomp, you've held up well."*

*"A new transmission and an excellent paint job helped."*

*"As did regular oil changes and new tires along the way."*

*"And taking me to Leo's Repair after that inebriated, off duty police officer rammed us. My fenders still ache from that one."*

*"Well, here we are, Pomp. About six months to go and we're out to pasture."*

*"I hope the cows will like me."*

*"Not to worry, old friend."*

**1968 VW CAMPER**

Of course, the old guy also talked with his wife at breakfast each day before heading out to Monroe High School in lovely North Hills, California, and a postal zone suburb just north of Los Angeles. They talked about everything, but especially politics. She was an unredeemed liberal. He was a moderate. Their discussions were at times heated, but always respectful, and never personal. She had retired a few years earlier. Teaching English was her thing, especially Shakespeare and American Literature. Somehow she was able to reach even the most reluctant student. In her husband's eyes, she was a miracle worker in the high school classroom. Anyway, she always got him off to a good start two-eggs, some potatoes O'Brien, and a muffin, a glass of prune juice to maintain his regularity, and his decaf coffee in a mug he bought in Mainz, Germany years ago. She always placed his lunch in the battered old leather briefcase he'd carried around for decades. And then it was a goodbye kiss, and a stern warning to watch his blood pressure in dear old Monroe High. In response he would say, "Go Vikings."

## MONROE HIGH SCHOOL VIKINGS

More by force-of-habit the old guy parked his van, set the brake, and locked the van's doors with an old-fashioned key. Then, briefcase in hand and often with a copy of the *Los Angeles Times* tucked under his arm, he sauntered into the Main Office, there to sign in before checking his mailbox for the latest administrative edicts and the ubiquitous school bulletin. At that point he always checked his watch: 7:20 a.m. Right on time. He was fastidious about that sort of thing. That routine out of the way he would head to the teacher's cafeteria for a sinful plain donut and a joyous cup of hot chocolate. As was his nature, he always flirted with the charming Hispanic lady from Peru who served the early arrivals.

"Maria, as lovely as ever. How are you today?"
"Mr. Goldman, quite well, and you?"
"Always better when I see you."

The exchange always brought a shy smile to Maria's face before the old guy sat down and repetitiously dipped his donut three times into his hot chocolate as he checked out, as he always did in a precise order, the funnies, the sports page, and the vital statistics page before afflicting himself with the editorial/opinion sections of the paper. That part of his ritual was a necessity. He needed to be aware of diverse views, he always told himself, in order to better serve his students

At precisely 7:40 a.m. he made a beeline to his classroom, Room 313. Once in his room he entertained other rituals. He made sure the day's date was on the new white smart board, the theme for the day, and a short outline for his first period class. This he needed to do this each day and for each class, since it was embarrassing to confuse a US History class with US Government. He had done that once to his everlasting astonishment. He vowed never to do it again.

The old guy knew what was ahead of him today. Five trains were about to pull into the station where he was the chief engineer. First would come US History, periods 1 and 2. They would be followed by US Government period 3 right after nutrition, which he usually took in his classroom with wayward students seeking shelter from the rest of the adolescent world. Then came period 4. He looked forward to that time slot. It was his conference period when he could grade papers, call parents, fill out required district forms, and perhaps talk to a grade counselor about a troubled kid. Then came lunch, which he usually enjoyed in his room, along with two clubs he sponsored, one a chess group (a game he didn't play), the other for young people interested in collecting stamps (which he did). The last two periods, 5 and 6, were World History classes and then he was done. Well, almost. We'll get to that in a moment.

Of course, all that was before the pandemic hit and testing, masks, distancing, and zooming entered his world, and forced him to become a hybrid teacher. Three times each week he reluctantly zoomed his way through the day, attempting to reach his students by way of the Internet from his classroom. The kids showed up on the off days, those who were well, masked, stressed, and resistant to this kind of educational purgatory. In that they mirrored their teacher's feelings.

Twice a week, however, he met after school with a US Government class sponsored by the local community college. It was a concurrent class. Students passing the class received both high school credits and college units. It was an optional class. Students opted to be in it. It met on Tuesdays and Thursdays, 3:45 to 5:15 p.m. The old guy looked forward to this class. He had taught it many times before. The extra pay was nice. Being with bright seniors about to depart for the collegiate world was a joy. Today would be the first meeting of the class. He would go from being Mr. Goldman to Professor Goldman. He kind of liked that. After all, he had earned a doctorate in history from UCLA. Twice a week it was a nice way to end the day, and for a guy retiring at the end of the semester, a delightful way to conclude his teaching career.

Naturally, all that was no longer completely possible, at least as he had envisioned his last days as a teacher. The virus had seen to that. Because of the virus and heightened student absences, the semester was extended two weeks into July. Only rarely now could he flirt with Maria before school and enjoy dunking his donut. Daily meetings with all his classes were out. Of necessity, he zoomed on Tuesday with his concurrent students and taught in person on Thursdays, constrained only by CDC's edicts and District policy. As with his students he detested what Covid had wrought. He wanted debate and discussion, not an easy thing to do when zooming. Though he was good at it, he didn't want to just lecture. He wanted students doing group projects up close and personal, but that was no longer possible. He wanted guest speakers representing a variety of political views. That was still possible, but difficult to arrange. But most of all he wanted and needed the human contact. Politicians might call it "touching the flesh."

As he sat alone in his classroom staring at his lecture notes, he of course, couldn't have known what was about to transpire. Over the next few months he would be the focus of an unintended controversy, which would consume his last days as a teacher, zooming not withstanding. He could not anticipate that soon he would be jousting with Mothers Against Guilt (MAG), who wanted his head on a platter (that is, his teaching credential). Nor did he think the Congressional Black Caucus might enter his life big time in defense of his controversial lectures. And beyond all that this mild mannered old teacher could not conceive of ruffling a staunch, partisan group, Citizens Allied with Trump (CAT).

But, of course, there was more. His name would be plastered all over the *LA Times, USA Today,* and the *New York Times.* The community college president would be on his case, as would his high school principal. The Superintendent, acting on behalf of the school board, would question him to no end. The teacher's union would get involved in his life, demanding "due process" for one of their own, and, on a larger scale, resisting the efforts of parents to censor a classroom instructor. On a personal level his wife would receive threatening, disrespectful phone calls. The Internet would be ablaze with scurrilous, repugnant allegations about his relationships to his students. That this would happen to him was beyond his comprehension as he prepared for the new semester.

<u>Later in the Day</u>

The old guy checked his watch – 3:43 p.m. Alone in his classroom and standing before a sea of vacant chairs the old guy prepared to teach. The class would begin in two minutes. His Apple computer was turned on and tuned in, now ready for zooming. He got up from his desk and walked to the inert smart board. There he wrote the few words that would seal his fate.

*US Government*
*Teacher: Professor Goldman*
*Focus: The Reconstruction Period 1865 – 1876*
*Major Emphasis: Race in America: A Comparison - The Impeachments of President Andrew Johnson in 1867 and President Donald Trump in 2020.*

# CHAPTER 1

# COMBUSTIBLE E-MAILS

<u>Tuesday, January 13, 2022 – Late Afternoon</u>

The old guy walked into the Main Office. He nodded to the principal's secretary before saying, "The boss wants to see me."

"She's waiting for you and, as always, you're punctual for these recurring meetings, at least one every school year."

"It must be my enchanting personality, Mrs. Jones."

"Well it's the first time with this new principal."

"And the semester has hardly started."

"Try to be cordial."

The old guy knocked on the door, twisted the handle and entered, thinking under his breath, "Here we go again, once more doing battle in the Star Chamber."

"I received your *'See Me Note,'* Mrs. Lopez."

"Dr. Eleanor Lopez, Mr. Goldman."

"Of course."

The old guy was silent for a moment, wondering if he should reply in kind. He gave into the inevitable.

"And I'm Dr. Harold Goldman.

It was the principal's turn to consider what she would say next. She responded in a sagacious way.

"If you insist?"

"I do."

As the old guy sat down on a hard, very comfortable wooden chair, he looked around the room, noticing an abundance of USC paraphernalia in the office: a USC pennant, a photograph of the last Trojan unbeaten football team, and a coffee cup sporting the schools logo --- "Fight On." Given all that he felt the USC school band might come marching in at any moment, along with the thundering hooves of *Traveler*, the university's mascot.

"You're a Southern Cal graduate, I take it."
"BA in English, MA in American Literature, and a doctorate in Education."
"Expensive school."
"Full scholarships helped."

The old guy couldn't resist what he said next. "Nothing so pretentious in my background as you know from my file. An AA from City College of San Francisco, a BA in history from San Francisco State, an MA in the Humanities from Cal State Northridge, and a doctorate in history from UCLA. No scholarships."

"Pretentious?"
"Comparing parchment initials seems that way."
"I was told you could be irritable."
"I would prefer feisty."

Dr. Lopez gave Dr. Goldman her best intimidating administrative look, which she had first cultivated as a classroom teacher years ago. He returned the look in kind. Had they been bullets, the looks would have collided with a resounding "bang." Instead, however, silence reigned as each took the measure of the other.

The old guy couldn't help but notice the principal's physical assets. She was tall, almost six feet in height with dashing black eyes, and equally dark hair cascading to her shoulders. She was by all accounts a beautiful woman. Her tailored dress was both attractive and appropriate for her status, and certainly not from a discount catalogue. An exquisite diamond ring suggested she was married and had good taste in jewelry. Her age, he thought, was somewhere in the mid-thirties. He chose not to ask her about that. But, as always, he gave into curiosity about something else.

"You played basketball at SC?"

"How did you know?"

"Three things. You're tall. You received scholarships to USC. And behind you is a photograph of the Trojan women's team. You're the third person from the right in the second row."

"You do notice details."

"An affliction I've never been able to jettison."

"You played sports?"

"At 170-soaking wet pounds my high school football coach rejected my ambition to be an offensive tackle. I shifted to soccer and was a backup goalkeeper."

"Really?"

"Really."

It was quiet for a moment. The preliminaries were history. The principal held up a piece of paper, saying, "Do you know what this is?"

"I'm no Sherlock Holmes but again I can deduce three things. First, that flimsy refers to me or why would you show it to me, am I not correct? Second, it's probably a hot note from an upset parent. I'm seldom summoned for notes of commendation, isn't that so? Third, as a new principal, you're on the spot to do something about it. That's the case, is it not, Dr. Lopez?"

"You've been through this before?"

"It's a yearly ritual."

"Why is that?"

"Over the years different principals have had various answers to that question, but since you have my file in hand you know that."

"A rebel was a common theme."

"Or a contrarian. Many felt I was ill suited for institutional life."

"Working in a large school district?"

"Being a cog in the bureaucratic education business."

"Following the rules?"

"My proclivity to bend them a bit was often at the root of the problem."

"You strayed from the tried and true, Dr. Goldman?"

"Yes, but with justifiable cause. Beyond the vagueness of the instructional guides and the incipit textbooks, I wanted my students to know what really happened in American history and to think seriously about what they've learned."

"As you saw things?"

"Of course."

"Even if parents got upset?"

"That was sometimes the case."

"I was told you could be difficult."

The old guy responded with an agreeable nod, nothing more and waited for the next shoe to drop, so to speak. It did.

Dr. Lopez handed him the note, quietly saying, "Please read the note, reproduced from the E-mail I received two days ago."

~

Dr. Lopez,

"I want you to do something about Mr. Goldman, my son's US Government teacher. I taped his first zoom comments. He's going to discuss the impeachment trials of two presidents and something called the Reconstruction Period, whatever that is. I thought my son would be learning about the US Constitution and our great leaders. I've talked to other parents and they think he's going to focus on racial issues. We think he has a hidden agenda to incite the students by talking about institutional racism. Is that the case? We want to protect our children from discomfort, guilt, even aguish. We don't want our children suffering from any form of psychological distress on account of their race. We don't believe their cultural heritage, religion, or political beliefs should be called into question. You must do something about this teacher. If not, we're considering removing our children from the class. Please check this out. I have included a tape of what he said to his class.

Mrs. Sharon Reilly

~

"Well, Dr. Goldman?"

"Well, Dr. Lopez?"

"Your response?"

"You're checking me out, Dr. Lopez?"

"Yes."

"Predictable and I don't blame you. Parent pressure always equals a not so subtle conference with the offending teacher. Assumptions reign: (a) the parent is right; (b) the teacher is wrong; (c) even if the teacher is right he is wrong; (d) protect the system from public embarrassment; and (e) consider the ramifications for your career."

"You are harsh in your assessment."

"Not harsh, just experienced. I've been around this tree many times."

"You are insufferable."

"You've been talking to my wife."

"We must be serious."

"I agree. Isn't it time to play Mrs. Reilly's tape? It's all set up, isn't it?"

"How did you know?"

"Why else would you have a recorder on your desk?"

~

Good morning seniors. I'm Professor Harold Goldman. First, let me say I detest zooming. However, given the pandemic and the unreasonableness of many of our citizens to wear a mask and produce an arm for a shot, this plague continues to bug us. Therefore, we can't meet in person as a class. CDC rules, Board of Education edicts, and Sacramento's requirements restrict us to zooming. That being the case we must forge ahead as well as we can.

This, as you know, this is a US Government concurrent class. You'll receive high school credits and college units at no charge to you. It's the best deal in town. If you pass you get a jump start on college. That's one benefit. The other this: you will gain the ability to think critically about the issues facing our country and will, I hope, do what you can to improve things. In other words you will be a productive citizen and take your rightful place in our body politic. If you're not interested in doing this you're in the wrong class. Give some thought to what I've said.

After this introduction I will post a syllabus on-line. It will indicate what we will cover, your assignments, and when, if you choose, to meet with me personally instead of just zooming. If the pandemic restrictions are lifted during the semester we will meet on a more conventional basis. Any questions?"

"There's a final for the class?"

"Your name?"

"Tim Anderson."

"Tim, there will be 150 multiple choice questions covering the entire curriculum for this class as determined by the district course of study."

"It will be difficult, Dr. Goldman?"

"And you are?"

"Sandra Diaz."

"It will be appropriate for college students, Sandra. However, and in addition, there will be one essay question on the final, to be answered in no more than three typed pages."

"When do we learn what the question is?"

"Today, right now.

*Thomas Jefferson once said that an educated populace was necessary to protect our Republic.*

"Given the social and economic issues facing our country today, I'm requiring you to defend or challenge Jefferson's contention. Write in the first person.

"That seems straightforward."

"And your name?"

"Marie Song."

"Perhaps not as much as you might think."

"What's this business about Reconstruction and impeachments, Dr. Goldman?"

"Tim, good question. In the process of learning about our government and related but necessary history, we will also focus on a relatively unknown period in American history, which you should know something about given our efforts to improve social justice in our society. That history is known as the Reconstruction Era (1865-1876). The two impeachments tie two American presidents together, Andrew Johnson and Donald Trump. The two impeachments noted, though years apart, will enable us to understand past race issues and current ones still troubling our society. All this will become obvious as we get into the course material. And one other thing... Some of the material we will cover will challenge your sensitivities. Some of the information will throw into question what you've learned already or thought you knew about our government and the history we all share. That cannot be helped. I cannot sanitize the past or ignore questionable policies in the present. Past experience has shown that most students are up to the task, both intellectually and emotionally. Okay, that's it. We'll zoom again in two days. Stay safe and well."

～

"You said all that?"
"Dr. Lopez, I cannot deny the undeniable."
"Still feisty."
"My DNA."
"What am I to do with you?"
"If you have an additional mug, I could use a cup of your administrative coffee, black and hot, no sugar, please. I need a jolt. After that, I explain why I approach the course as I do. That will, I trust, assist you in responding to the parents, and possibly the downtown administration. Deal?"

Dr. Lopez stifled a frown, forced a smiled, and got up. A few moments later placed a hot, steaming cup of black-as-the-night coffee before the old guy. He sipped it, smiled, and nodded approval.

"Thanks."
"Well?"

"As to why I do things. In a word to avoid boring my students to death. Include me in that. The text is a volume only good for two things: it could be a paperweight or a cure for insomnia. Take your choice."

"In your opinion?"

"Naturally. Government is not an abstraction. It is a living, evolving entity replete with all the characters, emotions, and ambitions are any sit com. This is especially true of our constitutional form of governance and the pronounced rule of law as opposed to authoritarianism and top-down edicts. It invites diverse opinions and accepts passionate partisanship. It can be at times very messy, even at times seemingly ineffective, demanding negotiations and compromises. Textbooks lack these dimensions. It's my job, as I see it, to breathe life into the study of government. That is what I do. That is what I am doing now."

"You're an idealist?"

"Hardly. I see the world the way it is. I have no misconceptions. I am, if you will forgive me, a realist. But I also see how government, as an instrument of society, can improve social justice, and that is the key to everything."

"You are a liberal in your political affiliations?"

"I am an independent. I am not saddled to any political party. I focus on policies, not the political posturing of those seeking office or the inane talking points of mouthy politicians who will say anything for a vote."

"You would consider yourself a progressive?"

"You continue to type cast me. I'm for social and economic progress, whether from the dissatisfied left and or the angry right. Good ideas are not the monopoly of any one political party."

"You're really nonpartisan?"

"You continue to read me wrong. I'm can be partisan as hell when it comes to social justice issues. I'm not, however, an ideologue. I refuse to give either political party my unconditional support."

"You're registered as an independent?"

"I am. Party politicians have to earn my vote."

Mrs. Lopez wasn't sure what to make of this iconoclast, the only word that came to her mind about this teacher. It was time to change the topic slightly."

"Dr. Goldman, I need to show you something."

Dr. Lopez walked over to one of her file cabinets, shuffled through a number of folders before pulling one out and placing it before the old guy.

"Do you know what this is?"
"Given that my name is stamped on it, it's my dossier, is it not?"
"Yes. Very thick as you can see."
"Well, I'm not surprised. I've been around a long time."
"About thirty-eight years with yearly crises."
"I would select another word, perhaps differences of opinions."
"That's three words."
"Literary inflation."
"I am not amused. In a conservative profession you seem to be an unredeemed rebel, is that not the case?"
"If you say so."
"I do, right down to this meeting."

It wasn't quite an impasse. It was more like a lull in a potentially violent storm. Both the principal and the teacher knew that.

"What is it you want, Dr. Lopez?"
"The critical notes in your file indicate again and again that the word comparison is used by you in explaining your instructional goals. However, there is no real amplification. Perhaps you might clarify the situation."
"The word refers to the concurrent government class for the most part. Over the past decade I added spice to the course by twisting history a bit to keep my students from dozing off. If my memory doesn't fault me here are some examples:

Compare the:

- American, French, and Russian Revolutions
- War of 1812 with the Mexican War of 1846
- Jim Crowism with South African racial policies, and our treatment of Native Americans.

- Red Scare of 1919 with McCarthyism in the 1950's
- Muckrakers of the 1920's with Contemporary Social Critics

Dr. Lopez considered what she had heard as she reappraised the old guy sitting before her.

"The War of 1812?"

"A land grab. In this case take control of Canada."

"The Mexican War?"

"Same motivation. Gain control of Mexico's provinces in the southwest."

"These comparisons landed you in the principal's office?"

"Seemingly."

"Still, you persisted?"

"It's a matter of record, is it not?"

"It is."

"That being the case do what other principals have done."

"Which is?"

"Tell the parents who criticize me that you're not into censorship. Do that in no uncertain terms. Tell them you're not a fascist who burns books and jails the author. Tell them that high school and college is a place for diverse ideas, not for thought control demanded by insecure parents. Tell them that I competent and that they are off base."

"Other principals did this?"

"Of course not. They weren't certifiable. They wanted to keep their jobs. They muted the controversy as best they could, hoping that it would just go away. They played for time. In this they were sincere in their intent to satisfy parents, while protecting a faculty member, and safeguarding their own careers in administration."

"That's not always an easy thing to do."

"And that's why you're paid the big bucks."

"We are living in difficult times with a society split down the middle with partisan views stressing emotionalism and assumed grievances, and brooking little dissent."

"I couldn't have said it better, Dr. Lopez."

"I may not be able to keep the hounds from biting you."

"My backside has a thick hide."

"Then perhaps we can reach an understanding?"

"Such as?"

"Do what you do but tone it down a bit."

"A difficult thing to do. I will do what I can and that being the case, here's some ammunition to safeguard your backside."

The old guy opened up his battered old briefcase and pulled out seven sheets of paper, nicely stapled together, along with an additional page. He passed the papers to the principal.

"What's this?"

"Two items of interest to you to be used, if necessary, in my defense. Consider them bureaucratic ammo to slay the barbarians at the gate."

"Barbarians?"

"Those who seek conformity and detest dissent, and would use the power of government to enforce their views by stifling the free exchange of ideas. Hopefully, what I give you keep them at bay. The larger bundle of pages is the final examination I alluded to earlier. Again, it covers every topic in the college's curriculum guide for the course as well as District requirements. Perhaps you would like to peruse through it or even take it. The answers are on the last page. No peeking is allowed."

"And the second item?"

"The syllabus for the course noting every lesson and assignments, the architecture for the course. Handouts can be useful in defusing some of those parents who have gone astray."

"This has worked in the past?"

"To a degree."

~

Dr. Lopez gave the old guy a long look before asking, "You intend to retire at the end of the semester?"

"Yes. The necessary forms are completed, only awaiting my signature. I will submit them to you in June."

"Some parents may seek an earlier exit."

"I am what I am. I cannot change my spots at this point. I stand with Jefferson. An enlightened public is our only hope in preserving our constitutional government."

"You're an idealist, your claims to the contrary notwithstanding."

"I envision a more humane world based on social justice and an expansion of economic opportunity for all our citizens. That is why I went into teaching, and why I teach as I do. Your presence in this office is a realization of what I've continuously stood for throughout the years."

"What are you getting at?"

"You are a woman, a Hispanic administrator. This, as you know, has not always been the case."

"You are, as I was told, conniving and enchanting, difficult to deal with, yet with a charm that is hard to resist."

"Then we are possibly mirror images, Dr. Lopez."

"Possibly, Dr. Goldman."

"If our business is concluded, I should take my leave. My semi-gluten-free dinner awaits me."

The old guy stood up, grabbed his briefcase, and left the office, saying, "Until we meet again."

The principal smiled, acknowledging the inevitability of his comment.

# CHAPTER 2

# ROSS AND RECONSTRUCTION

<u>January – A Few Days Later</u>

"Good morning, Mrs. Jones."

The principal's secretary didn't say a word. She merely held up two fingers and pointed toward Dr. Lopez's door. Two fingers… That was code for "be on your guard, Dr. Goldman, the odds are against you today." Over the years the secretary had become something of a guardian of the old guy, alerting him to dangerous waters. She wasn't sure why she was so protective. Maybe it was because he always remembered her on *Secretary Day* with a bouquet of spring flowers, or at Christmas when a little token of affection found its way to her desk. And Valentines Day… He never forgot her, always giving her a heart-shaped box of soft chocolates. And perhaps most of all, he always said, "Thank you."

The old guy entered the office. Dr. Lopez, as always, was a pleasant sight to see. Today she was wearing a beautiful dress with dazzlingly red and blue colors that any member of the British royal family might envy. Already seated was another woman. She appeared to be in the last stages of middle age. Her salt and pepper hair was pulled back severely. That seemed appropriate for the dark pants suit she was wearing that reminded the old guy of a mortician's apparel.

"Dr. Goldman, this is Dr. Florence Williams. She is the District Administrator for Secondary Education. Please sit down."

Not knowing what to say, the old guy ad libbed. "Well with three doctors in the room, we could start a clinic."

The women didn't smile.

"Mrs. Williams will explain why she's here."

"There's no need for that. I know perfectly well what's up."

"He's feisty, Mrs. Williams, especially before the 8:00 o'clock bell and before he's had his cocoa and donut in the cafeteria."

Mrs. Williams stood up and gazed at the old guy with her most penetrating downtown, intimidating look. The old guy had seen it numerous times. It no longer had any impact on him.

"Dr. Goldman, the Superintendent has asked me to speak to you. I think you know why."

"More love letters from fawning parents?"

"If only that were the case. A member of the Board of Education received a most critical letter concerning your US Government class. He in turn called the Superintendent."

"Who in turn asked you to scoot over to Monroe High and put out the fire, is that not the case?"

"That is so, but only after a contingent of MAG parents visited him demanding that something be done."

"MAG?"

"Playing innocent, Dr. Goldman, doesn't suit you. MAG, as you perfectly know, stands for *Mothers Against Guilt.*"

"And they want what?"

"No repeat of your first zoom lecture."

"Well then there's no problem. I don't repeat my lectures."

"Or any similar discussion of slavery."

"That's not possible."

Dr. Williams chose not to respond, saying only, "We'll discuss that statement after reviewing the lecture in question."

"You have a tape, I assume."

"The parents recorded everything you said."

~

Lecture #1:

"Good morning class. Today's topic is the Reconstruction Era in our history, approximately 1865 through 1877. As you will note it immediately followed the Civil War (1861-1865). In rummaging through the past I will introduce you to an unknown American, Edmund G. Ross, the man who many historians credit with saving our constitutional form of government in February 1868. Who, you must be asking, was this man?

"A few sketchy images: he took his family from the safety of Wisconsin into what was called *Bloody Kansas* in 1858. There he sided with the anti-slavery forces. They wanted the territory inducted into the Union as a free state. Once the Civil War began he enlisted in the Union Army and was highly decorated. After the war he entered the US Senate, replacing a distraught Kansas Senator who committee suicide. Once in Washington he was an eyewitness to the struggle between Congress and the President to determine the nature of Reconstruction, that is, the process by which the Confederate States would rejoin the Union. He also participated in the impeachment of President Andrew Johnson, casting the final dissenting vote that saved the delicate balance between the White House and Congress. By a 35 to 19 vote the President was not found guilty of the charges brought against him.

**ANDREW JOHNSON**

Because of his vote his political career was destroyed, his life threatened, and his newspaper business almost ruined. Ross, as you will see, lived through interesting times. Fortunately, he recorded that history and published a book late in life, around 1896. I will quote from this book today and in future lectures. The book was entitled *The Impeachment of Andrew Johnson, President of the United States by the House of Representatives and his Trial by the Senate for High Crimes and Misdemeanors in Office 1868.* That's quite a mouthful wouldn't you agree?"

**EDMUND G. ROSS**

"Ross' understanding of the period will, I hope, engage you."

*The close of the War of the Rebellion, in 1865, found the country confronted by a civil problem quite as grave as the contest of arms that had been composed. It was that of reconstruction, or the restoration of the States lately in revolt, to their constitutional relations to the Union.*

"It's Mario, isn't it? Thanks for having your name tag on. And same to all of you out there… It helps the recall of an old guy. You have a question, Mario?"

"Mr. Goldman, the language… It's so different."

"Dr. Goldman, please. And yes, the literary construction of words was different. You'll get use to it; it's like acquiring a taste for music beyond hip-hop, or reading Othello for the first time. You adapt. Shakespeare grows on you. Hopefully, Ross will do the same. Now, if I may. Ross saw the connection between reunifying the Union and the whole question of slavery. I quote:

*The institution of negro slavery, the basis of the productive industries of the States of the South, which had from the organization of the Government been a source of friction between the slave-holding and non-slave-holding sections, and was in fact the underlying cause of the war, went under in the strife and was by national edict forever prohibited.*

"Now what was Ross saying? Any volunteers?"
"Slavery was important to the Southern economy?"
"Not only important, Louis, but essential."
"Slavery was the cause of conflict between the North and South."
"Excellent, Maria, and from when?"
"Since the Constitution was written?"
"That's it. Anyone else?"
"Slavery was the key cause of the Civil War."
"Ralph, question or declaration?"
"Declaration."
"Right on. Now let's see what Ross said about slavery."

*The struggle being ended by the exhaustion of the insurgents, two conspicuous problems demanding immediate solution were developed: The status of the now ex-slaves, or freemen --- and the methods to be adopted for the rehabilitation of the revolted States...*

"Ross, as you can discern, summarized the whole problem. What would be the lot of the ex-slave? Would he be a citizen? If so, would he be able to vote? Did the ex-slave enjoy the same civil liberties as whites? Was he to be in every way the equal of whites? How would a non-slave South economy function? What would be demanded of the former Confederate States before they could rejoin the Union? These questions were the impulses behind the Reconstruction Era. To resolve these questions was the challenge facing the country."
"Sort of like the racial issues we face today, Dr. Goldman?'
"Right on point, Jasmine."

The old guy paused. He had to. Zooming just wasn't his thing. He needed to catch his breath.

"Some historians believe these questions still confront us today, as Jasmine pointed out, especially in the realm of civil liberties. Ross understood the gravity of the situation and the immense task of dealing with these questions. He pointed out:

*As history had recorded no similar conditions, and therefore no demand for the solution of such a problem, there were no examples or historic lights for the guidance of those upon whom the task had fallen.*

"You can see what Ross was getting at? There were no precedents to follow. To a degree his country was flying blindly into the future, one that we've inherited. Ross alluded to this:

*Never had a nation or party thrust upon it a more delicate duty... It was that of leading a conquered people to build a new civilization wholly different from the one in ruins. It was first to reconcile two races totally different from each other, so as possible to remove in harmony in supplanting servile by free labor...*

"Reconciling the races, class... Is that not a challenge we continue to face today? Ross summed up the whole business, stating:

*The transition was sudden, and the elements antagonistic in race, culture, self-governing power --- indeed, in all the qualities which characterize a free people.*

The transition, as Ross pointed out, was abrupt for both races. This was most certainly the case in respect to voting rights for the former slaves. Would the white community accept equality at the ballot box? Would the black vote, supported by the Republican Party, be perceived in the South as another form of Northern oppression? A difficult question then, as is for some today.

"The Reconstruction Era attempted, no matter how imperfectly, to deal with these questions. There were major accomplishments. First, the Confederate secession in the South ended. The rebellion, so costly in blood and treasure, was over. Second, the Thirteenth Amendment ended slavery once and forever. The power of the plantation class benefiting from slavery was broken. Third, the Fourteenth Amendment defined citizenship for all Americans, including the ex-slave. If born in the United States you were a citizen. Previous servitude --- that is, slavery --- was gone with the wind, no longer to be an obstacle to citizenship. Fourth, the Fifteen Amendment extended suffrage to all male ex-slaves. In all this, at least in the abstract, the white and black population now shared the same constitutional right to vote. This proposition, as you may know, is still being worked out today."

**BLACKS VOTING**

~

Dr. Williams turned off the recording. She turned to the Old Guy and said, "This is what MAG is opposed to."

"I'm at a loss. Exactly what is the group opposed to?"

"The racial questions you raised?"

"What Ross said?"

"No."

"Then what?"

"Your attempt to connect the past to the present."

"Race relations, is that it?"

"In a word, yes."

"We're not still working things out, Dr. Williams?"

"We are but MAG doesn't want it a topic of discussion in the classroom. That's the long and the short of it."

"As I stated them do these parents disagree with the facts?"

"No."

"Have I stated untruths? Did I distort the history under discussion? Did I take a partisan stance in any way?"

"No, but that's not what the parents are concerned about. They simply do not want racial issues raised in the classroom. They feel their children will be upset by these topics, causing them to feel guilty about the past and possibly what's going on today."

"But it's a college class."

Dr. Lopez now interjected. "It's a hybrid class offering high school and college credits. The class is sponsored by the Community College System, but is taught by a district teacher in a public school facility. It is a unique situation with both parties not independent of the other. You do understand this?"

"I do. So Dr. Williams, but where do you come down on this?"

"I'm here to quiet the waters which you brought to a boil at the end of the first lecture."

"The Memphis Riots? The New Orleans Massacre?"

"Yes."

"I only stated what happened."

～

## The South in Ruins

"It's hard for us to imagine what the Confederacy was like at the end of the war. The best analogy I can give you is Nazi Germany and Imperial Japan at the conclusion of World War II. Total destruction... After General Robert E. Lee signed the papers of surrender at Appomattox Courthouse, he returned to a South in total ruins. The farms and plantations were no more. The animal stock was greatly reduced by the war --- horses, mules, and cows. Some 40% of the livestock was destroyed by some estimates. The train transportation system was nonexistent. Bridges were down; the rails were torn up and bent, and repair shops and rail yards were hardly functioning. There was almost no rolling stock. The Union Army had systematically destroyed the infrastructure of the South and with it the region's economy."

"How could the South survive?"

"Good question, Harlan. The answer was the crop-lien system."

"Which was?"

"The plantation owners divided up their land into smaller sections. The freed Negroes were provided with seed, equipment, fertilizer, and draft animals to plant and harvest cotton and other crops. The landowners used their own capital or borrowed money to fund the operation. The future crops were used as collateral. That is, there were liens against the borrowers. In other words the crops were mortgaged in advance of the harvest. By the time all credits were paid off, white tenant farmers had a fair return on their investment and black sharecroppers were still in debt, and the vicious cycle of perpetual debt continued. It was a form of indentured servitude and continuous impoverishment, especially for the former slave.

"Into this extraordinary economic situation there were violent push-backs against the dramatic changes taking place."

~

Riots

"The Memphis riots of 1866 illustrated how difficult it was going to resolve racial tensions in the post-war South. The riots in the city took place between May 1st and 3rd. The known facts are these as later reported by a joint Congressional Committee:

- A shooting altercation took place between white policemen and black veterans who had fought for the Union. The exact cause of the confrontation remains unclear.
- Mobs of white residents and police entered black neighborhoods and the homes of freedmen.
- The mobs attacked and killed black soldiers and civilians.
- The mobs also committed many acts of robbery and arson.
- 46 black and 2 white people were killed.
- 75 blacks were injured and over 100 blacks were robbed.
- 5 black women were raped.
- 91 homes, 4 churches, and 8 schools were burned to the ground.

• In current dollars there was over $100,000 in property damage.

"The Congressional Committee noted that competition in the working class between blacks and whites, especially newly arrived Irish immigrants seeking a better life, lay behind much of the animosity between the groups. The Irish had left their homeland because of the Great Famine of the 1840's. The two groups competed for housing and work. Things came to a head on April 30, 1866. Many of the former black soldiers were awaiting their discharge pay in the city. The record indicates a street fight broke out between black soldiers and Irish police officers. There were injuries on both sides. The combatants left the scene. On May 1, 1866 a large group of black soldiers, women and children were having an impromptu party in a public square. White police officers tried to break up the gathering. The blacks refuse to disperse. Reinforcements were called in and things got out of control. Many in the attacking mobs wanted to drive the blacks out of the city, or back onto the plantations.

**THE MEMPHIS RIOTS**

"The local newspaper, *The Daily Avalanche,* summed up the situation from the mob's perspective:

*The chief source of all our trouble being removed, we may confidently expect a restoration of the old order of things. The Negro population will now do their duty… Negro men and Negro women are suddenly looking for work on country farms… Thank haven, the white race are once more rulers in Memphis.*

"News of the riot influenced those in the North who wanted the Southern states to be under military control in order to protect the former slaves. As a political group they were known as Radical Republicans. You will learn more about them in time. They were at odds with President Andrew Johnson who favored a less harsh treatment of the former Confederate states. That conflict would eventually lead to an impeachment trial of the President. In any event the Memphis Riots indicated how difficult the Reconstruction Era would be."

**PUBLIC ACKNOWLEDGEMENT**

~

"Was it necessary, Dr. Goldman, to show illustrations of the riots? The parents were most upset about this."

"I don't know how to answer your question. Without a photograph how do you indicate the destructive power of the Hiroshima bomb? How do you show Pickett's charge at Gettysburg? How do we show the desperation of hungry, jobless men during the Great Depression? Words alone are insufficient, are they not?"

"These parents can't handle it!"

"My students can!"

"They think you're overstating what happened."

"The state of Tennessee would disagree."

"That doesn't faze them."

Dr. Lopez remained silent during this exchange before interjecting, "Let's continue this after listening to what Dr. Goldman said about the New Orleans Massacre."

~

As substantiated by newspaper reports, later investigations by Congress, and eyewitness reports, the following facts relate what happened on July 30, 1868 in the city of New Orleans.

- A mob of ex-Confederate soldiers attacked peaceful black marchers outside of Mechanics Institute.
- It is not known who fired the first shot.
- The black unarmed marchers were unprepared for the attack.
- Many of the blacks also war veterans who had recently fought for the Union.
- A total of 38 people were killed and 146 were wounded.
- 34 of the dead were black; 119 of the wounded were black.
- Some estimates open to question state as many as 200 blacks were killed.
- The mob was opposed to abolition and to black suffrage.
- The mob favored white supremacy; it wanted to maintain its political and economic power in the city.

It's fair to ask what was going on in the Mechanics Institute? Organized by the Republican Party, a reconvened Louisiana Constitutional Convention was in session because of the State Legislature enactment of Black Codes, which essentially permitted legal discrimination and segregation of blacks, while also denying them the vote. The Convention meant to override these actions. This was a mini-civil war between Lincoln's party of emancipation and suffrage and the last vestige of the Southern Democratic Party's effort to maintain power. All that led to a massacre. As described by one historian:

*The white stomped, kicked, and clubbed the black marchers mercilessly. Policemen smashed the institute's windows and fired into it indiscriminately until the floor grew slick with blood. They emptied their revolvers on the convention delegates, who desperately sought to escape. Those lying wounded on the ground were stabbed repeatedly, their skulls bashed in with brickbats. The sadism was so wanton that men who kneeled and prayed for mercy were killed instantly, while dead bodies were stabbed and mutilated.*

**THE MASSACRE**

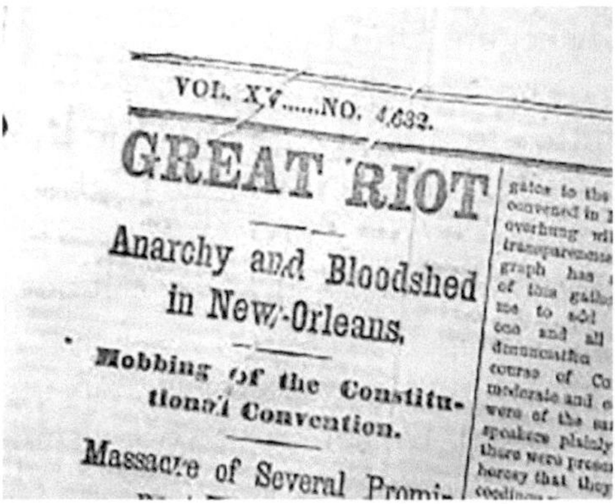



**REPORTING THE EVENT**

"The Northern response, as in the case of the Memphis riot, hardened the Radical Republicans who, now more than ever, demanded a military occupation of the former Confederate states. In time this led to Louisiana becoming the Fifth Military District. All ex-Confederate soldiers and leaders were temporarily disenfranchised, while the right of suffrage was enforced for free people of color. Those politicians associated with the riot were dismissed from office."

~

""More photographs were necessary, Mr. Goldman?"
"Words can only convey so much."

"I must make a report."

"Of course, Dr. Williams."

"It will not sit well with the Superintendent."

"A predictable outcome."

"Which might mean you'll be replaced."

"Fired?"

"No, only relieved of your duties for this class."

"Pruning the weeds, sort to speak?"

Dr. Lopez felt like she was at a tennis match as volley after volley was exchanged. Though she didn't know if it would do any good, she timidly entered the fracas, seemingly about to get out of hand.

"Dr. Goldman, we must try to avoid a crisis."

"It has already begun, Dr. Lopez."

"Meaning?"

"I am committed to a short line from the King James Version of the Bible, John 8:32, I believe: 'And the truth shall set you free.'"

"As you see it?"

"That's the way it works with all of us, is it not, Dr. Lopez?"

"You digress."

"Well, then let me put my cards on the table. Dr. Williams, as you say, I can be relieved. But let me show you something."

The old guy reached into his briefcase and brought out a folder. These he handed to the two women.

"What this?"

"Dr. Lopez, this is my defense. Please open the folders. You will find a list of 1173 names, all past students from my Honors US Government and Economic classes through the years and, of course, those who were in the hybrid course. You will notice the e-mails for each name."

"So?"

"Dr. Williams, I am in yearly contact with these former students. You know Christmas and birthday greetings, an occasional get-well thought, even advice when requested. In a few cases I provided a small loan to get them over a financial 'hump.'"

"Your point?"

"Just this, Dr. Williams. Once these former students hear that I've been relieved or fired, and they will, they will come out of the Internet cloud, demanding to know what's going on?' The digital world will be alive with questions. The local newspapers, radio, and television stations will get wind of it. The students will be interviewed. MAG will not be immune from inquiries. The teachers union will get involved. Talk shows will bristle with commentary. Fox will condemn me as an agitator at best, a disloyal, and unpatriotic American in league with our enemies, whoever they are. CNN will take, as it always does, a problematic neutral stance, while CNBC will declare me a defender of our First Amendment Rights. There will be street demonstrations, some even organized. Opposing parent groups will converge on the School Board demanding that something be done, or that the Board members will hear about it at election time. It will be a bloody mess. All this I see, as if it has already happened."

"You are threatening us?"

"I'm merely asking you to consider the implication of your actions, Dr. Williams. Once these dogs of war are released all of us may feel their bite."

No one spoke. An impasse had been reached.

"What did you propose, Dr. Goldman?"

"Delay. Provide a bureaucratic wall of cotton, suggesting the District is dealing with the problem. Delay until the semester ends and I retired into the winter. Delay taking drastic actions; write me up, call me in for a verbal spanking, and just help me get through the semester."

"Winter, an interesting choice of words."

"But appropriate in my case, Dr. Lopez."

"You wouldn't care to elaborate?"

"Correct. I wouldn't."

"That being the case we've gone as far as we can. Dr. Williams and I will review all that's been said."

"Then I will take my leave. We all have much to consider."

# Chapter 3

# STAR WARS

<u>January – Later in the Month</u>

The old guy was looking forward to today. If he could get through today the weekend beckoned. Clear the decks… Collect homework, administer tests, and make sure things were in place for the next week. Stay late and grade as many assignments as possible. Avoid taking stuff home. It was a routine he had followed for years, and at the looming age of 65 it still worked for him. This Thursday, however, was unique. He would meet with his high school/college class for the first time in person. No zooming today. Finally, flesh and blood students. No longer just names on the digital computer roll book. All these thoughts crossed his mind as he looked at his mail in the Main Office. A nondescript envelope caught his eye. Only his name was on it. Years of survival in the District alerted the hairs on the back of his head. Even before he opened the envelope he knew the probable contents.

*Dr. Goldman,*
*I will be joining you today for the college class.*
*Dr. Lopez*

Succinct and to the point, as was her way. But behind the scenes the old guy understood the plot line to this decision on her part. Mrs. Reilly had made her report to the Superintendent. Various options were considered as to what should be done. The ramifications of possible actions were considered. A bureaucratic compromise was reached. Parents would be told that Dr. Lopez or another administrator would supervise all future class meetings held in the school. In addition, whether on zoom or in person, all meetings would be taped. Written records would be made available to parents and/or MAG.

Essentially, thought the old guy, the District was buying time with the appearance of controlling what went on in the classroom. That being the case, the old guy murmured under his breath, "Well, I'm buying time too." He then broke into a half smile as he remembered what today's topic was: *Slavery in the United States*. That, he thought, should make for an interesting day.

~

The students, all wearing their masks, entered the classroom and took their seats, mostly in an unorganized random fashion. The turnout was good, 24 of the 25 students were present. Their attention was immediately focused on the smart board where they read the teacher's name, the date, and the topic for today. As they peered at their teacher in front of them, they hardly noticed Dr. Lopez quietly entering the room and sitting in the back row where the overhead florescent lighting seemed dimmest.

"Good morning. I'm Dr. Harold Goldman, the old guy you've been zooming with this semester. It's a pleasure to finally meet you in person. I trust you're all healthy, as are your families. A few pedestrian tasks before we get started today. First, you've reviewed the syllabus and you've picked up your text. Second, as necessary, you can E-mail me if there are any questions. I'll get back to you as quickly as possible. And now a time-honored question… Are there any questions?"

Teachers always ask this question, and always dread the possible responses.

"Dr. Goldman."
"Yes?"
"I'm Philip Reilly. My parents are concerned about the subject matter."
"Meaning what, Philip?"
"They think you have a hidden agenda to inculcate us with Critical Race Theory."

"Inculcate…Good SAT word, Philip."

"And?"

"Let me respond this way, Philip. First of all, parents should be interested in what transpires in this classroom. Second, due to zooming they are in a unique position to monitor the course material. Third, they have every right to discuss issues with me, or any teacher. As to the question of CRT I can say this. Racial issues will emerge as we discuss the Reconstruction Era. That cannot be avoided. We will relate them to today's society as we learn about the structure and policies of our government. I hope my explanation suffices."

"My parents think you want us to feel guilty about the past and the terrible things which were done to blacks."

"And you are?"

"Claudia Jenkins."

"Well Claudia, permit me to answer your question this way. I have a grandson who was born after the Vietnam War ended. Is he guilty of what took place in Southeast Asia before his birth? In the same vein young Germans are not responsible for what took place under Nazi Germany. That means, of course, that no one today is responsible for slavery in this country. But all this is only half-the-glass. As concerned citizens we are all responsible for dealing with the lingering baggage of our history and continuing unresolved race-related questions."

Listening to all this, Dr. Lopez found herself admiring Dr. Goldman. How he could dodge and dance, always pleasant and considerate of his students and their parents, yet fiercely making his point. She also realized she had forgotten his age. He really was an old guy.

"I don't know what CRT is," another student interjected. I often hear my mom talking about it. Just what is it, Dr. Goldman?"

"And you're?"

"Harlan Wilkinson."

Long ago the old guy had learned an important lesson, never to be forgotten in the classroom. Always, if at all possible, follow the Star War mantra enunciated by Obi-wan Kenobi: *May the force be with you.* Translated for the classroom the words meant this: if the students are interested follow their lead. Take advantage of their desire to learn more.

"Harlan, I'll share what I know. Please understand I'm no expert. Okay?"

From her somewhat secluded perch, Dr. Lopez thought, Oh my god, what will he say?

~

"Civil rights scholars see a relationship between our laws and the notion of race. They seek a critical review of our institutions that perpetuate racial prejudice that leads to social inequality. That's the theory. How does this play out in the real world? One example cited is this: the courts often give more lenient punishment for white drug pushers than black drug dealers. Whites can purchase a home anywhere. This was not always the case for blacks. University law schools were always open to competent white applicants, not necessarily to other people of color. Professional football assistant coaches are seldom chosen to be the head coach. Is it just personal bias and individual prejudice at work, or is all this built into the structure of our society, reinforced by our laws? Related to this is the view that institutional racism favors certain groups, while disadvantaging others making racial equality almost impossible."

"Does the system favor whites?"

"Louis, isn't? Yes, some would say that, though I think the situation is more complicated than that. For example, there can be divisions within the Hispanic community between those from Mexico and Peru or Cuba. The same is true within the Asian community with Koreans, Japanese, Chinese, and Vietnamese cultural groups.

Historically, however, the system has favored whites over blacks, and always the wealthy over those with less regardless of race."

"Does that lead to white privilege?"

"You are?"

"Evelyn Gonzalez."

"Well, Evelyn, where did you hear about this?"

"On the Internet."

"What did you hear?"

"That people of color are trying to take away things from whites. Is that true?"

Dr. Lopez swallowed hard. What would Dr. Goldman say? What would she say if asked the same question?"

"Evelyn, let me say this. No, that is not the case. In every society there are those who have a degree of political or financial control over others. Tied more to our country it works out this way. According to many sociologists, societal privilege benefits white people over non-white people in our country. But again, we must be careful since there are, as already noted, divisions within all groups leading to inequalities. As to the source of white privilege many would point to European colonialism and imperialism, and the Atlantic slave trade leading to the notion of white superiority. This view justified creating colonial empires around the world. The British did so in India, the French in North Africa, and the United States in the Philippines. Aspects of this are comes to mind, of course, in our relationship to indigenous natives. The story of Chief Joseph is a classic example. The Battle of Wounded Knee symbolizes the violence often associated with this mindset. The near extermination of the Mexican culture in the Southwest after the Mexican War of 1848 provides still another example. And, of course, the slave system in the South and the post-Civil War rise of Jim Crowism; that is, discrimination and segregation backed by law and too often violence to maintain white control. Some would argue this attitude still motivates some to limit access to voting by people of color. I hope this partially answers your question."

"Can you make it more personal. I'm having trouble relating."

"Fortunately, you are persistent, Evelyn. I'll try."

This will be interesting, thought Dr. Lopez. He's like a man in the circus trying to walk on a high line. Can he keep his balance?"

"Evelyn, when I was growing up I never thought about white privilege, or, for that matter, anything to do with CRT. Living in San Francisco, I never thought about our family's ability to buy a home, or where we could live. I never thought about what jobs were open to me, or what schools I could attend. I was just a kid. I didn't know about secret housing covenants to keep Jews and people of color from moving into a neighborhood. I didn't know why blacks were concentrated in the Fillmore District of the city, or the Chinese in what was called Chinatown. When I went to grammar school, I just walked up the street to George Peabody Elementary. No big deal. Roosevelt Junior High was next and then George Washington High School. These were my neighborhood schools open to all students if there was room. I didn't realize that in other locations in the country black children were bussed past white schools to black schools that were inferior by almost any measure. I didn't consider myself advantaged, though others might. It was just the way things were. Naturally, all this was before the Civil Rights Movement of the 1960's and Black Lives Matter campaign of recent times. Certainly, there was no social media influencing my views."

"You didn't feel privileged?"

"Privileged, no. I did note that my dad's wallet was smaller than other dads on the street. Cars were expensive. We didn't have one. We used the buses and trolley cars. Other families went on longer, if not more expensive vacations. Some kids had newer clothes, not hand-me-downs. Others had private tutoring lessons. I learned early that money makes a difference in this world regardless of your race, ethnicity, or social class. Education, I came to understand, was the key to getting a good job. Hard work pays off. In the parlance of today the minimum wage is not the basis for a middle class lifestyle. It's okay to work at *Burger King* now as a student, but not forever."

The old guy paused, then reached into his briefcase to pull out a large folded sign, which he held up for all to see.

"I think these words explain the complexity of achieving social justice in our country. Consider these words when the CRT and questions of white entitlement come up again. Perhaps they will help. Now, I see that our time is rapidly running out. Maybe I can bring this discussion to an end with a more personal story. Okay, Evelyn?"

"Okay."

"Years ago when the dinosaurs were roaming the world I dated a beautiful black woman while attending college in Pennsylvania one joyous summer. This was in the early 60's. On one occasion I asked her how she traveled from her home in Mississippi to the Quaker State. I can still hear here words:

*Well, unlike you who just drove across the country from LA in your old Plymouth and then stayed in any motel you liked, I had to do things differently. I had to carefully plan out my trip. I needed to know that where I stopped there would be accommodations for a Black woman. I needed to find a restaurant that served Blacks. I had to be very careful.*

"What she said really got to me. I had driven across the country. I wasn't concerned about where I would dine or sleep. What I was told was a wake up call for me. Does this make sense to you?"

The old guy stopped talking. The class was quiet, subdued. Finally, he said, "Our topic for today was going to be Slavery in the US. We can't get to it today. Planning ahead for this eventuality, I've typed up my long hand notes. Please take a copy on your way out. We'll discuss the institution of slavery at our next meeting. Be prepared. And one more thing… What you will read is difficult to deal with as a young person. Indeed, I'm a bit older and I have trouble handling the topic. If you feel you don't want to be part of the discussion I'll understand, but at least read the lecture notes. Well, that's it. Enjoy your weekend."

The students exited the room. The old guy sat down behind his desk. He leaned forward placing both of his hands against his face. He remained that way for a few minutes. He didn't hear Dr. Lopez approach him.

"Are you okay?"

The old guy sat up, almost as if he were awaking from a deep sleep. He stared at her for a long moment, then rubbed his eyes before almost whispering, "It's been another long day, probably for you too."
"Yes."
"I wasn't quite prepared for those questions today. I should have been."
"We were both caught off guard, Dr. Goldman."
"I should have anticipated their questions."
"You did fine."
"Let's hope the parents agree, and especially Mrs. Reilly."
"Well, I was here and I will vouch for you."
"In which direction?"

Dr. Lopez, perhaps for the first time, really gazed at the old guy. His years were showing. He seemed frail, physically and emotionally vulnerable, a tired old man running out the clock before retirement. She watched as he opened his briefcase and took out a baggie and a plastic bottle of water. He opened the baggie and took out two pills, which he quickly swallowed.

"Dr. Goldman, I will not side with MAG."
"Thanks."
"But I do have one question. You have two black students in the class. They never said a word and you never called on them."

"Oh, they were involved. They were a quiet reminder of what's at sake. They'll speak out when they're ready. These things can be pushed."

It was time to go. They turned off the lights and closed the door. Outside the old guy said, "Did you take the final examination?"
"Yes."
"You passed?"
"Ninety-three percent."
"Cool."
"Just cool?"
"I wouldn't want you to get a swelled head. And by the way…"
"I know. Do my homework. I will read your lecture notes, though I would prefer a good mystery."

C H A P T E R  4

---

# A FIRE IN THE NIGHT

<u>February – Early Evening</u>

Encino, California is a neighborhood in the San Fernando Valley just north of Los Angles. It was first explored by the Spanish Portola expedition in 1769. For two nights the Spanish camped near a native village after traveling through what is now called Sepulveda Pass. Today approximately 45,000 people have residence in the area. Flanking Encino is Reseda to the north and Lake Balboa. Sherman Oaks is on the east, and Tarzana is to the west. To the south is Brentwood. Running through the "Valley" is Highway 101, a north-south road extending from Los Angles to Tumwater, Washington after passing through Oregon. The "101" is often called the Ventura Freeway. The Ventura Boulevard parallels the highway that is simply known as the "freeway" by many motorists. On the southern side of the street are many upscale homes, all of which grow more expensive as elevation increases on the hillside and views of the Valley expand.

Slightly above the boulevard is a ranch-style home with a delightful French window facing northward. From that perch a rather remarkable building can be seen if one enjoys unique architecture. The building is Valley Beth Shalom (VBS), a Jewish synagogue.

As fate would have it Mr. Jaime Lopez and his wife, Dr. Eleanor Lopez, owned the home with the great view. Again, as decreed by the serendipity impulses of fickle fate, one member of the "VBS" congregation was Dr. Harold Goldman. That's right, the old guy. Our two protagonists were linked by proximity though, of course, each was unaware of this. And that was somewhat unusual since on

37

**VALLEY BETH SHALOM**

more than one occasion they mingled and mixed in the synagogue. Since Dr. Lopez was a pious Catholic an obvious question comes to mind; what had brought them together? The answer: the local parish needed a place for worship for three weeks after a fire burned portions of Our Lady of Lourdes. The synagogue stepped into the breech, and church services were held in sight of the tabernacle containing the holiest of scriptures for Jews, the Torah. Father Joseph Donovan and Rabbi Sam officiated. The two choirs merged and all present sang out to God their prayers of love and hope."

*Amazing grace*
*How sweet the sound*
*That saved a wretch like me*
*I was once lost but I'm found*
*I was blind but now I see*

On behalf of all in attendance Rabbi Sam quoted from Micah 6.8:

*He has shown you, O man, what is good. And what does the Lord require of you but to act justly, to love mercy, and to walk humbly with your God.*

Dr. Lopez had attended the service and two more over the ensuing weeks. Dr. Goldman, as an elder in the temple, helped organize the gatherings and was also present. They never recognized each other in the very crowded synagogue. Perhaps they, upon reflection, thought to themselves, if Jews and Catholics can honor their faith and extol brotherhood (and sisterhood) for services, why can't this feeling inculcate our society? They witnessed theological differences and metaphysical debates shunted aside as a common humanity was forged. Dr. Lopez was surprised to see blacks wearing a yarmulke (skullcap). It had never occurred to her that there were black Jews. She had always thought of Jews as white and from Russia, Poland, or Germany. In time she also saw a few Asians and Hispanics who were also pious Jews. She had always equated Hispanics as Catholic and Asians as Buddhist. Obviously, her earlier perceptions were open to question. Diversity, she now understood, existed in the synagogue beyond the sectarianism of Christian and Jew. That realization she silently applauded.

~

"A refill?"
"Please."

Dr. Lopez and her husband were enjoying a quiet evening after an appetizing salmon dinner with sweet potatoes and salad. A nice red wine from Napa County was had with their meal and after. Their two children were with their grandparents for the weekend. Precious time for mom and dad was at hand, but..."

"Eleanor, what's on your mind?"
"What...?"
"You keep looking at that folder on the side table."
"I..."
"Come on, fess up."
"Jaime..."
"Let me take a wild guess. It has something to do with that teacher?"
"You are discerning."
"I'm your husband. What's up?"

Dr. Lopez liked to keep business in school. That is, when she came home she wanted to focus on her family. Given the whirlwind responsibilities of a high school principal, this was not always possible. If nothing else, the night football games required her presence, as did the drama and music shows, and senior activities, including the yearly prom. And, of course, there were the night meetings with the parent counsel, twice per month. All that wore on her.

"Dr. Goldman has given me a homework assignment."

"Be a good girl and tell him your dog ate your work."

"We don't have a dog."

"The folks next door do. They owe us a favor. I'm still waiting for them to return our power drill."

"I…"

"What's the assignment? Maybe I can help. Don't think of it as cheating. It's consultation."

"I have to read his notes for two lectures not yet given."

"So, why the hesitation?"

"The topic is repugnant."

"It can't be that bad."

"Slavery in America. Bad enough?"

~

Lecture Notes – By the Numbers

The slave trade reached its high point between 1700 and 1850. The years from 1825 to 1830 saw 80,000 people each year brought to the Americas, namely the United States and Brazil, as well as islands in the Caribbean. Between 1830 and 1850 approximately 1.6 million slaves were transported to the New World. Those are the statistics. They are a matter of historic record. But what do they represent beyond numbers in a leger of atrocities? Each slave-to-be had to be hunted down, captured, and held against his will in Africa until he was sold to a slave trader, who might be Arabic or white, or even another black tribal leader. In many cases families and clans were broken up to expedite the trade.

The numbers astound us, even today. In the 1820's 4 out of 5 people migrating to the Americas were Africans. Approximately 80% of those crossing the Atlantic were blacks violently removed from their homeland. They far outnumbered the Europeans who made the same journey. Alarmingly, 12 to 15% of those who departed Africa did not survive the voyage. They died ignominiously at sea.

**CAPTURED AFRICANS**

Considering the figures cited it is telling to remember what Joseph Stalin, the dictator of the old Soviet Union, reportedly said: "The death of one person is personal; the death of millions is a statistic." It is our job to look beyond the statistics.

## Lecture Notes – The Triangular Slave Trade Routes

What we are talking about here was the removable and transportation of enslaved Africans to the Americas facilitated by the Triangular Slave Trade System. How did this work? Ships departed from Europe with manufactured goods and other items in demand. That was step #1. The ships went to Africa, where goods were traded for slaves. That was step #2. The ships then departed Africa for the Americas. That was step #3. Once in the New World the slaves were sold for cash and/or agricultural products, such as cotton, tobacco, and sugar or rum in the Caribbean. The slave ships then returned to Europe, which really meant England and Portugal, to continue the contemptible but profitable cycle.

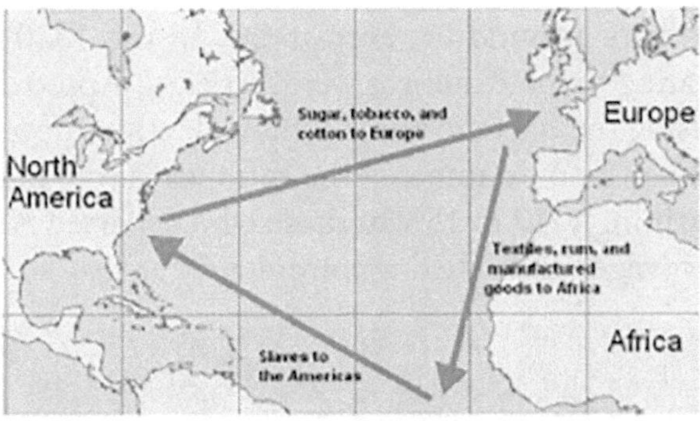


Funding was needed to maintain this system. Groups of individuals, what we would call investors, provided the needed capital. Larger companies were established to purchase or build ever-larger slave ships, which in turn eventually produced greater profits. Crudely put, New England ships from the North sailed to Africa to fetch slaves for the auction blocks of Charleston, South Carolina. The black slaves were considered at best merely property, at worst, a dehumanized commodity.

In 1860 a male slave of 25-years in age sold for $800 to $1200 on the auction block. Why 25? At that age the slave was at his peak physically and had many years of life ahead of him. The amounts noted would be $32,000 to $48,000 in today's dollars. Most of the profits went to the wealthy individuals and large companies that sponsored the trade. The slave ship captains also prospered but not the crew, who in many cases were impressed sailors and poorly paid, and often treated harshly.

Lecture Notes – The Middle Passage

The Middle Passage referred to that stage of the Triangular Slave Trade, which brought captive African people to the Western Hemisphere. The numbers quoted here are only estimates based on the best records available. Between 1500 and 1860 as many as 2,000,000 slaves died at sea, and possibly another such number in Africa. As to how many slaves were transported by way of the Middle Passage, the most reliable number is 12.5-million people.

What accounted for such loss? Disease was a primary culprit: scurvy, smallpox, syphilis, measles, malaria, and yellow fever ravaged the slave ships, killing both slaves and crews. Due to a lack of nutritious food and clean water, and because they were stacked together in humid quarters below deck, the slaves were easy prey for diseases. Food consisted mainly of beans, corn, yams, rice, and palm oil. There was one meal per day with water. If food supplies and water ran low, the crew had priority over the slaves, who were viewed as cargo. As you can imagine, there was only squalor below deck. There was no privacy. No showers, or baths were available for personal needs. Waste material, diseased slaves, and surviving slaves occupied the same space. Consequently, all this led to a high mortality rate. Only as necessary did the crew venture below deck.

**DIAGRAM OF A SLAVE SHIP**

A typical slave ship had a crew of 30 and carried as many as 200 Africans, sometimes more in order to ensure greater profits. To keep the slaves under control during a typical six-week voyage from Africa, the males were chained together in pairs to save space. The right leg of one slave was attached to the left leg of another, and both were chained to a post. The chains, ankle restraints and handcuffs were known as "Bilboes." There is evidence that these restraints originated in the Basque Country of Spain and found their way to England because of the Spanish Armada. Madrid hoped to use them on captured English prisoners. Only periodically were males brought on deck for fresh air. Women and children were treated only slightly better. The whole purpose of the restraints was to avoid a slave revolt at sea.

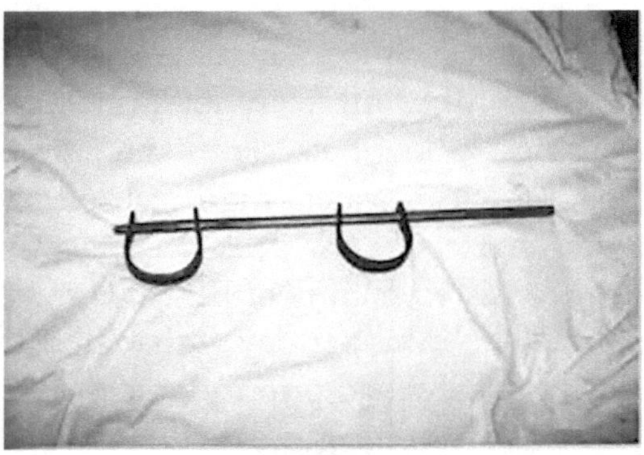

**BILBOES**

~

Dr. Lopez had enough. She thrust the lecture notes down on the coffee table in front of her. A resounding smacking sound broached the air, startling Jamie.

"I take it you've had enough for tonight?"
"I had enough two hours ago."
"What's taking you so long? You're a fast reader."
"The reading isn't the problem. It's what I'm reading that affronts me."
"Care to share?"
"No!"
"I'll take that as a yes."

The truth was Dr. Lopez needed to share. She needed to give voice to the anger raging through her. She wanted to hit something. Not the God Captain Ahab thundered against during his journey to kill Moby Dick. Nor the God that Noah questioned. No, she wanted to slam a fist at the threads of history that cursed the world with slavery. But history, much like God, was too distant, and upon reflection, not the cause of this inhumanity. All she could do was scream into the night knowing full well that the past was immutable to change.

"Talk to me, Eleanor."

So she did. Later he said, "You will continue reading?"
"Yes. Tomorrow. That will be soon enough."

# Chapter 5

# ATROCITIES AT SEA

<u>February – The Next Morning</u>

Dr. Lopez was up early, competing with the roster to welcome the sun. Her husband, as was his way, slept in on Saturday. That being the case, potent Columbian coffee in hand, along with two juicy chocolate donuts, she was fortified for the literary ordeal ahead.

<u>Dr. Goldman's Lecture Notes</u>

We must begin with word *atrocity*. You've heard it already and have some sense of its meaning. Let's now look at it with clear eyes and a heavy heart. The word refers to an action that is shockingly bad. The action in question is extremely cruel and of necessity violent. Brutality, savagery, and barbarity are the hallmarks of an atrocity that is in a legal sense, a crime against humanity. But it is more. It indicates a lack of empathy to the terrible suffering inflicted on another human being, whether for political, economic, or merely personal reasons. It is emotional and irrational and, worst of all it is not inhibited by the norms of a civilized society. That is the theme we're dealing with today.

Recall, if you will, that the Middle Passage referred to the voyage from Africa to the Americas. Slave ships usually made the trip in six to eleven weeks, times enough for atrocities. There were two methods of storing slaves. The first was called *tight pack*. This method tried to pack the ship with as many slaves as possible. The ship's hold was dark and cramped. It was only five feet high. There was a shelf running around the edge of the old for additional slaves. One contemporary described pack slaves as being "like books on a shelf." The *loose pack* method packed fewer slaves in the hold. This provided them with more space and more slaves survived the trip. Regardless of the method used they were cramped in the hold.  As noted earlier, the slaves were chained together. If a slave died, he remained chained to another person. There was no toilet and the slaves had to lie in their own waste. The hold was a stinking, dark, and stuffy place to be. The air was foul. It was reported that there was little oxygen in the air, so little that not even a candle could burn.

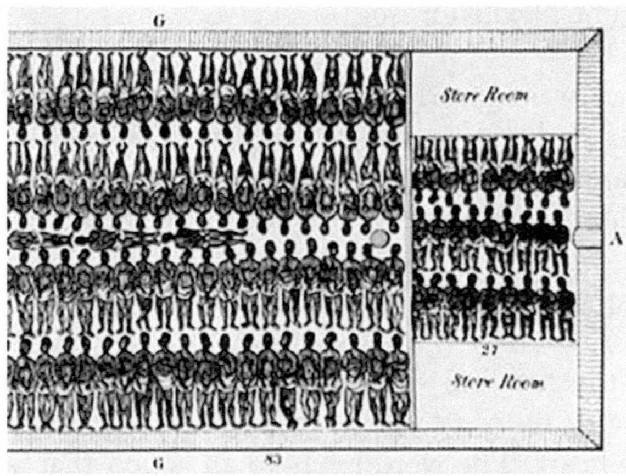


**CROSS SECTION OF THE HOLD**

The conditions aboard a slave ship didn't change until the British Parliament passed the Slave Trade Act of 1788. The law controlled the number of slaves on a ship. Also, a doctor had to be on each ship to keep medical records. The doctors received a bonus according to the number of slaves who survived. The new law, however, did not ban slavery. At the margins it simply tried to make the trade more civilized. There was simply too much profit in the business. It had a mercantile life of its own.

At this point we can cite the prosperity brought by the slave trade to the city of Liverpool, England. In the 1780's ships based in Liverpool carried more than 300,000 Africans into captivity. By 1795 Liverpool controlled over 60% of the British slave trade and 40% of the entire European slave trade. Thousands of Liverpool workers were needed to construct the slave ships and to equip them. There was a high demand for rope makers, dockworkers, carpenters, and sailors. Succinctly, the slave trade brought a degree of prosperity to the city and the country. In 1792 Britain had a banner year. Over 200 ships carried slaves from Africa to the Americas. That averaged out to four ships per week. From 1791 to 1807 British ships carried 52% of all enslaved people forcibly removed from Africa. In the period of 1791 to 1800 some 388,719 Africans were shipped to the New World.

It is difficult for us to fully appreciate the horrors of the Middle Passage. This leads me to a confession. I had family members who did not survive the Nazi plague of concentration camps and the attempt by a modern nation to use assembly-line techniques to destroy the Jews of Europe. The holocaust of the 1930's and '40's shows that atrocities are not limited to the past, and like a terrible plague can reappear. That demands of us constant vigilance.

The atrocities did not end when the slave ships pulled into American ports. The slaves had to be prepared for the auction block. What did that mean? They had to appear healthy "in order to raise the price they would fetch." Their skin was rubbed with oil to make them appear healthier than they were. Those who had been punished with whipping (flogging) had their scars disguised by covering the scars with tar. Older slaves had their hair cut to hide signs of grey hair.

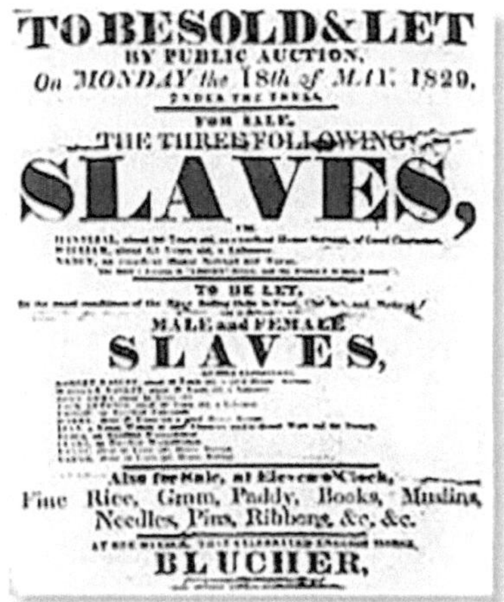


**ADVERTISING THE AUCTION**

Two methods were employed in selling the slaves. The first method was the *auction block*. An auctioneer sold enslaved people in lots (a group) or individually. Slaves were sold to the highest bidder. The second method was called scramble. The slaves were kept together in an enclosure. Potential owners paid a fixed sum. The enclosure was then opened. The buyers rushed in and grabbed the slaves they wanted. This meant that families, if they had survived the Middle Passage, were in many cases broken up. Children were torn from their parents. Husbands and wives were sold to different buyers. One can only imagine how terrifying this must have been. Those slaves who were not taken were called *refuse*. They were sold to anyone who would take them, usually at a cheap price. These slaves were poorly treated since they were seen as having little value in the marketplace. Recalcitrant slaves who resisted were sent to *seasoning camps* where up to 50% of them died before accepting their fate.

## Lecture Notes – The Zong Massacre

The *Zong* was a British enslaver that carried too many slaves. Some 442 slaves were stuffed aboard the ship. It was bound for Jamaica. This was twice the number the ship was designed to carry. On November 29, 1781 the crew participated in the mass killing of more than 130 slaves. What was the background to this atrocity?

On behalf of a syndicate of Liverpool merchants the ship was purchased in early March 1781. One member of the syndicate was William Gregson. He eventually had an interest in 50 slave ship trips between 1714 and 1780. Those ships carried an estimated 58,000 Africans to slavery in the United States. He lived handsomely on the profits from these endeavors. He became the mayor of Liverpool.

The *Zong* sailed from Accra August 18, 1781. Again, it had aboard more than twice the usual number of slaves it could safely transport. The typical slave ship in the 1870's carried about 193 slaves. The ship took on drinking water at Sao Tome before beginning its voyage across the Atlantic Ocean on September 6, 1781. According the ship's log, it reached Tobago in the Caribbean but didn't stop to replenish its water supplies.

They 442 slaves were part of the original purchase price. The ship was not insured until after it started its voyage. Insurance? What am I talking about? Another syndicate in Liverpool underwrote the ship and its slaves for up to 8,000 pounds. That was about half the slave's potential market value. Once more, you can see that the slaves were regarded as cargo. The remaining risk was, as was the custom of the time, borne by the ship's owners.

It was standard practice for "slavers to insure their cargo of slaves. If the *Zong* sank in a storm an insurance claim could be made and honored for the loss of the cargo. The deaths had to "arise from perils of the seas." The death of slaves due to disease or insurrection was not covered.

**THE ZONG**

Because of bad weather and navigational miscues, the voyage to the port of Black River, Jamaica was extended. Food provisions were running low. The same was true for available water. On November 27th the crew sighted Jamaica, still 31 miles distant. Unfortunately, the Jamaica was mistaken for the French colony of Saint-Domingo on the Island of Hispanola. The regrettable mistake was eventually identified when the *Zong* was 300 miles leeward of the island. The ship turned back. Because of malnutrition, overcrowding, accidents, and disease, at least 62 Africans had already died. It is believed that the ship only had four days of drinking water available for 10 to 13 more sailing days.

The captain, acting on behalf of the owners, realized that (1) if the slaves died on land, the insurers would not have to pay anything; there would be no redress for the syndicate. If, however, (2) the slaves died of "natural death" at sea," there would be no insurance payoff. But, if (3) slaves were thrown overboard in order to save the rest of the "cargo" or the ship, then a claim could be made. Since the ship's coverage was 30-pounds per person this seemed like the obvious action. A decision was made. On December 1, 1781 42 black males were thrown off the ship. Another 36 were killed over the next few days. Apparently in defiance of the crew 10 slaves chose to commit suicide by jumping into the water. In total the record indicates that 142 slaves died before reaching port.

The crew claimed the slaves were killed because the ship did not have enough water to keep all the slaves alive. This claim, as it turns out, was disputed when it was learned there was 420 imperial gallons of water on the ship when it finally docked in Jamaica on December 22nd. There was later testimony that it rained heavily after the first slaves were drowned, sufficient to last for at least 10 days.

**DROWNING SLAVES**

Once the *Zong* reached port the owners made a claim to their insurers for the slave loss. Essentially, they were seeking recompense for murder on the high seas. The insurers refused to pay. In the British court case that followed the court ruled that the murder of enslaved people was legal. The insurers were ordered to pay for the lost slaves. However, in a subsequent appeal hearing the court ruled against the ship owners because of new evidence indicating the captain and the crew were at fault for what happened. As might be expected the syndicate owners and the ship's crew were not indicted for murder.

The massacre did lead to some reforms. The neophyte abolitionist movement in England was stimulated. In 1788 the Parliament passed the Slave Trade Act. It was the first law regulating the slave trade. It limited the number of enslaved people per ship. It prohibited insurance companies from reimbursing ship owners if the slaves had been murdered. Years later --- in 1807 --- Parliament passed the Slave Trade Act, which abolished British participation in the African slave trade. The Act, however, did not outlaw slavery. A monument to the murdered Zong slaves can be found at Black River, Jamaica today.

# Chapter 6

# REBELLION

<u>February - A Short Time Later</u>

Dr. Lopez stopped reading. She had to. At that moment she was of two minds. On the one hand, she was affronted and disturbed by what she had read. Once more she felt anger rising in her. How could human beings purposely drown slaves in order to file an insurance claim? But then again, how could so-called civilized British citizens engage in this awful business? On the other hand, she was concerned for Dr. Goldman's students. How would they handle this terrible incident? And related to that question, what would the parents think if they read the lecture notes? The questions howled in the night. There was no immediate answer. She considered waking her husband to discuss the matter, but then thought better of it. Let him rest, she decided. It's Saturday. Already knowing what she was going to do, she propped herself up on her comfortable couch after first pouring herself another strong cup of Columbia's finest. She continued reading.

~

<u>Lecture Notes – The Treatment of Slaves</u>

Whether on the slave ships, at the auction block, or on the plantation, the slave owners attempted to maintain strict discipline and unconditioned submission. This was accomplished by instilling fear into the slaves. That emotion was engendered by beatings, whippings, and hanging. Every possible cruel action was used to keep the "slave in line," including branding and the mutilation. Any sign of disobedience or perceived infraction led to the owner reasserting himself as the master. Always, the effort was to keep the slave fearful, dependent, and hopeless through the constant threat of violence. One instrument of that threat was the bullwhip. It was a braided whip attached to a handle, approximately 16-inches in length. The reason the bullwhip hurt so much was that the tip of the whip moved very fast, causing the skin to tear.

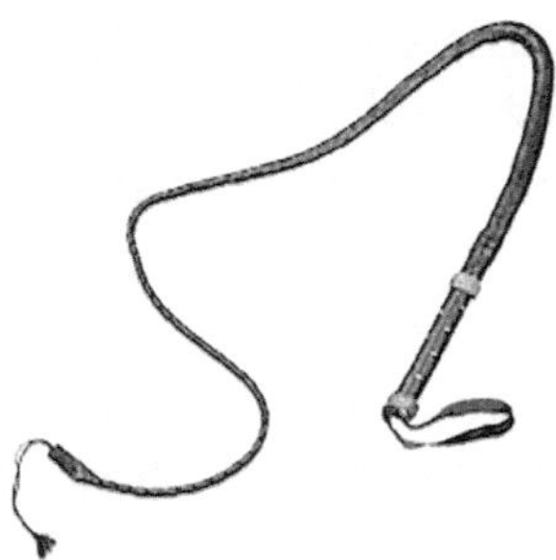

By law no slave could be educated. Slaves must be kept ignorant to preserve the slave system. For those owning slaves there was always the potential for a slave rebellion led by a slave who could read and write. Therefore, laws were passed in the South making it illegal to educate a slave.

Black female slaves were also the victims of rape. There was no real defense against this action, which was widespread and well known. The appearance of light-colored babies was evidence enough of what was going on. Mixed race children were treated only marginally better by their owners, if at all. The term mulatto defined this blending of the races. By 1850 there were approximately 250,000 mixed race slaves. By 1860 the number had increased to 411,00 according to census records out of a total slave population of 3.900,000 slaves. It would not surprise you to know that a double standard existed. If a black male was accused of rape he could be castrated or killed in order to maintain "racial purity." However, by law in the Deep South white men could legally rape black slaves. The slave owner was always the master.

Isabelle Gibbons was a slave who toiled at the University of Virginia. She left an account of the violence perpetrated on blacks by many masters:

*Can we forget the crack of the whip, the cowhide, whipping-post, the auction block, the iron collar, the Negro-trader tearing the young child from its mother's breast? Have we forgotten that by those horrible cruelties, hundreds of our race have been killed? No, we have not, nor ever will.*

There is a human trait (or perhaps a disposition) to deny those slices of our history that we find too repugnant, too violent. These "slices" assault our sensitivities. The desire to strike them from our consciousness is understandable. Who wants to look at a photograph of the radioactive mushroom cloud rising over Hiroshima? Who wants to peer into the ovens found in the Nazi death camps? Who wants to remember the dead, both blue and gray, strewn across the cornfields at Gettysburg? That is, of course, our dilemma. Only by assaulting our sensitivities can we eradicate that which we find unacceptable.

This photograph of a beaten slave was taken in 1863. He was a Louisiana slave and was known by the name of Gordon. The abolitionist movement in the North used this photograph to mobilize their crusade to outlaw slavery. If a picture can express a thousand words certainly this one did.

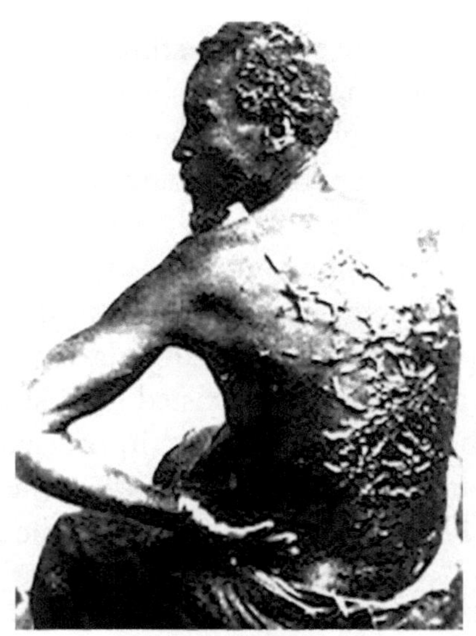

**GORDON**

## Lecture Notes – Passions Unhinged

Class it is appropriate to pause for a moment. The few paragraphs and perhaps far too many words already shared can only hint at the forced expulsion of blacks from the African Continent. Obviously, words cannot fully convey the absolute horror of being hunted down like an animal, and then imprisoned before being sold into bondage. Words cannot fully portray the desperation and hopelessness of the "Middle Passage" before reaching the auction block, there to see children torn from their mothers as family members were sold piecemeal. We must try, however, to understand the statistics and reported atrocities on a human scale of suffering. Our common humanity demands this. As you are just beginning to understand, the plantation system in the South required humans to toil in the hot sun to work the land of cotton and tobacco. New England ships from the North and auctioneers in the South perpetuated the Triangular Slave Trade and for a time the evil of slavery reigned supreme. But the odious enterprise could not last. By 1850 the warning signs were present. As one historian stated"

*The greatest danger to American survival at midcentury was a sectional conflict between the North and South over slavery. To many Americans, human bondage seemed incompatible with the founding ideals of the Republic. If all men were created equal and endowed by the creator with certain inalienable rights including liberty and the pursuit of happiness, what could justify the enslavement of several millions of these men and women?*

Slavery would end some thought, either by peaceful means, or by force of arms. No middle path by 1858 seemed possible. On the subject of the "peculiar institution, the *Charleston Mercury* stated in that year the possibility of a civil war.

*The North and South… are not only two Peoples, but they are rival, hostile Peoples.*

Thomas Jefferson examined the situation from another perspective. In a letter to a friend he wrote on April 22, 1820:

*We have the wolf (slavery) by he ear, and we can neither hold him, nor safely let him go. Justice is one scale, and self-preservation is in the other.*

Robert E. Lee, the future general of the Confederate armies provided another insight to the question of slavery to justify the institution:

*The blacks are immeasurably better off here than in Africa, morally, physically, and socially. The painful discipline they are undergoing is necessary for their further instruction as a race, and will prepare them, I hope, for better things. How long their servitude may be necessary is known and ordered by a merciful Providence.*

In 1837 John C. Calhoun declared in a booming voice a justification for slavery all too common in the Southern states. Slavery, he said was a positive good, not an evil. He argued:

*In every civilized society one portion of he community must live on the labor of another; learning, science, and the arts are built upon leisure; the African slave, kindly treated by his master and mistress and looked after in his old age, is better off than the free laborers of Europe.*

In a book entitled *The Universal Law of Slavery* George Fitzhugh defined the notion of white superiority to justify slavery. He stated:

*Slavery provides everything necessary for life and that the slave is unable to survive in a free world because he is lazy, and cannot compete with the intelligent European white race. The Negro slaves of the South are he happiest and in some sense, the freest people in the world. Without the South the slave would become an insufferable burden to society. Society has a right to prevent this, and can only do subjecting him (slaves) to domestic slavery.*

It is fair to say, I think, that elements of all these views are the brick and mortar that has been, and continues to be the foundation of institutional racism. Dismantling this situation was at the heart of the Reconstruction Era, and continues to be in our contemporary society. As would be expected there were passionate partisan positions in the post-Civil War period. Those passions continue today as we, as a society, continue to sort things out.

The extension of slavery into new territories taken from Mexico in 1848 was always an issue. Would the new territories eventually enter the Union free or slave. New pro-slave states meant greater representation in Congress, and to a degree greater control of the federal government. That political control went hand in hand with maintaining slavery. Representative David Wilmot (R, PA) rose in opposition to the expansion of slavery in 1848, stating:

*That as an express and fundamental condition of the acquisition of any territory from the Republic of Mexico… neither slavery nor involuntary servitude shall ever exist in any part of said territory.*

**DAVID WILMOT**

In many respect the emerging struggle between slave and non-slave states was in actuality a contest between free labor and slavery. The poet, editor, and writer, William Cullen Bryant stated the case as such:

*If slavery goes into the new territories the free labor of all the states will not. But if slavery is kept out the free labor of the states will go there and in a few years the country will teem with an active and energetic population.*

By the presidential election of 1860 the impending crisis could no longer be put off. Presidential hopeful Abraham Lincoln understood this.

*There can be no moral right in the enslaving of one man by another. When they (Southerners) tell us they are no more responsible for the origin of slavery, than we, I acknowledge the fact. When it is said that the institution exists and that it is very difficult to get rid of it, I acknowledge that fact also. I surely will not blame them for not doing what I should not know how to do myself. If all earthly power were given me, I should not know what to do, as to the existing institution.*

The future president went to note the challenge facing freeing the slaves:

*What then, free them and keep them among us as underlings? Is it quite certain that this betters their condition? What next? Free them, and make them politically and socially our equals? We well know that those of the great mass of white people will not… A universal feeling, whether well or ill founded, cannot be safely disregarded.*

In a few words Lincoln enunciated are the challenges we are still trying to resolve today. He also noted:

*When the white man governs himself that is self-government, but when he governs himself and also governs another man that is despotism. The Negro is a man. There can be no moral right in connection with on man's making a slave of another."*

**ABRAHAM LINCOLN**

Moral right. The words linger and challenge. When the vestige of segregation attitudes and discriminatory practices continue today, our social morality is disturbed. When the great grandchildren of slaves distrust the police, our social morality is unhinged. When black Americans were (or still are) systematically excluded from any avenue, our social morality is called into question. These issues we will deal with during the semester. However we define government and regardless of how we feel about our representatives, government is the vehicle by which we adjudicate our problems. The textbook doesn't do this. You do so by being informed and involved in tackling these problems. And, yes, by voting… That is the ultimate instrument by which to make your views known. So, when you can, register. If you get an A in this class and don't vote, we've both failed. If you get a C and vote, we're both winners. Bring your "proof of voting" certificate and I'll change your grade if you didn't get an A. Honestly, I will. Test me.

On another front… The topic of slavery, as advertised, may prove difficult for you. As I stated earlier it is also a challenge for me. That's okay. It is distressing what humans do to their fellow brothers. Understand you should not feel guilty about what took place long before you were born. You, however, as a citizen today have some responsibility in resolving the social justice issues of our day. The responsibility weighs heavily on those who wish to protect our Republic and maintain our democratic, constitutional form of government. Being such a citizen is not easy. The involvement is continuous, partially because of recurring elections, but also because history continues to flow, carrying us along, and demanding that we either sink or swim in the protection of our liberties.

## Lecture Notes – Resistance

Occasionally, one hears this question: why didn't the slaves fight back against the enslavers in Africa, or aboard the slave ships, and even later on the plantations? Why didn't they rise up and strangle their oppressors, especially when they far outnumbered their tormentors? These are the questions we will now deal with to conclude this week's work.

Perhaps we can answer these questions with a question? What did the following groups have in common? The gladiators of ancient Rome… The Cubans following Dr. Castro…The Russians in 1917… The Americans at Valley Forge… The Polish Jews in the Warsaw Ghetto in 1944 … The French manning the ramparts in 1789…. And black Africans in America … Indigenous natives at the Little Big Horn…

What did they have in common? First, a crucial number of oppressed people decided they had enough. They were willing to fight and die rather than continue to submit. Second, it was not possible to negotiate with the oppressor. No peaceful resolution was possible. Alexander Stephens of Georgia and later the Confederacy Vice-President stated on the eve of the American Civil War:

*The cornerstone of the new government, which would be based upon the great truth that the Negro is not equal to the white man; that slavery subordination to the superior race is his natural and normal condition.*

It was impossible with Stephens. The issue was literally black and white for him. It was an either or proposition… Take it or leave it… His views suggested a benign image of slaves happily going about their duties in an orderly agrarian paradise. It suggests childlike slaves who needed the protection of their owners. The imagery indicates beneficent masters who cared for their slaves. But all this cannot erase one overriding fact: the slaves were property without legal rights held by whites. Their fate was always in the hands of others. One suspects that the white nationalists of today have accepted this version of Southern propaganda predating the Civil War.

Third, histories written after the fact did not always portray the courage and resourcefulness of those rebelling. Slavery scholars have unearthed and documented the many ways African slaves rebelled: running away from the plantation; suicides at sea to escape the chains; mutinies and actual rebellions in heavily populated slave areas in the South. In doing all this, the black slaves did so in the face of a system of sustained brutality that included constant threats of torture, rape, and murder. We've all heard stories of the Underground Railroad that provided a risky escape to the North and a modicum of freedom. But there were other stories, too of those caught and what happened to them: torture, burning, dismemberment, and death.

**ALEXANDER STEPHENS**

The situation was not immediately resolved by emancipation and the outcome of the Civil War. Emerging in the South after 1876 was a system of enforced labor sanctified by law and upheld by the courts. Blacks were arrested for any number of reasons which led to convict leasing, a system that provided cheap labor to replace the lost slave labor. Blacks found without a job were identified as vagrants. On that basis they could be incarcerated at a rate 10 times that of the general population. Even after convict leasing was abolished, new laws and public policies in the South permitted the jailing of an astronomical number of blacks. This was especially true during the Jim Crow decades lasting until the 1960's. As one historian wrote:

*The criminal justice system was strategically employed to force African-Americans back into a system of extreme repression and control, a tactic that would continue to prove successful for generations.*

Some would argue we, as a society, are still dealing with aspects of this issue. Witness the *Black Lives Matter* crusade. Many connect police brutality with the whip once wielded by the white overseer. That is a matter you'll have to consider in time as a citizen-voter.

What follows is information about the most famous slave rebellion. There's a word or two in your US History text. Almost all US Government textbooks do not delve deeply into what happened in 1831. I will redress that deficiency now.

<u>Lecture Notes – Nat Turner</u>

In the early morning hours of August 12, 1831, a family slave, trusted and liked, climbed through the window of his master's home. He then opened a door to permit six of his companions to enter. They were armed with axes. Once inside they killed the Joseph Travis family. This began the most famous slave rebellion in American history. The man who led this rebellion was "a religious visionary" named Nat Turner.

A reward notice posted in 1831 described Nat Turner as follows:

*He is about 5 feet 6 or 8 inches high, and weighs between 150 and 160 pounds. He is light-colored in complexion, but is not a mulatto. He has broad shoulders and a large flat nose, large eyes, broad flat feet. He walks brisk and active. He has hair on the top of the head and is very thin. He has no beard, except on the upper lip and the top of the chin. He has a scar on one of his temples, and also one on the back of his neck. He has a large knot on one of the bones of his right arm, near the wrist, produced by a blow.*

**NAT TURNER**

Who was the man described as such? The most immediate answer is this. He was the leader of a slave rebellion of enslaved Virginians that took place in Southampton, Virginia in August 1831. The rebel slaves killed between 55 and 65 people. At least 51 of those killed were whites, including women and children. The rebellion only lasted a few days. It was suppressed at the Belmont Plantation on the morning of August 23rd. Nat Turner escaped and survived in hiding for more than two months before he was finally captured.

Turner was born on October 2, 1800. He died on November 11, 1831. The name "Nat" was given to Turner by his owner, one Benjamin Turner. In 1810 Samuel Turner inherited his father's slaves, including Nat. Very little is known about Nat Turner's family. It is thought his father escaped from slavery when Nat was a young boy.

Turner was taught how to read and write as a boy by his parents. Apparently, he was noted for having "natural intelligence and quickness of apprehension, surpassed by few." It is known that he was deeply religious. He was often seen fasting and praying. Information of the day indicates he was often "immersed" in reading stories from the Bible. Turner, it seems, was given to visions, which he interpreted as messages from God. In 1821 he escaped from bondage. As the story goes, he became delirious from hunger and had a second vision "to return to the service of his earthly master." This he did. In 1824 he was sold to Thomas Moore. While working for Moore in the fields Turner had another vision. Turner believed that "the Savior was about to lay down the yoke he had borne for the sins of men, and that the great day of judgment was at hand." Almost a decade would pass before that day arrived. In that interval Turner conducted services and preached the Bible to other slaves. He was dubbed "the Prophet."

In the spring of 1828 Turner was now convinced he "was ordained for some great purpose in the hands of the Almighty." While working he heard a "loud noise in the heavens." According to Turner a "Spirit instantly appeared to him." The Spirit said the Serpent was loosened, and Christ had laid down the yoke he had borne for the sins of men, and that he should take it on and fight against the Serpent. Obviously, the Serpent was slavery and rebellion was necessary to end it.

In 1830 Turner again had a new owner. This time it was Joseph Travis, who Turner described as a "kind master." A year later on February 12, 1831 Turner witnessed a solar eclipse. He was convinced it was a sign for which he was waiting. There is some testimony that Turner thought a black hand was covering the sun. Beginning then he began preparations for an uprising against the slave owners in Southampton County. Initially Turner shared his plans with four fellow slaves, Henry, Sam, Hark, and Nelson. On August 12th there was an atmospheric disturbance that made the sun over Virginia appear bluish-green. Turner interpreted this as another sign. Scientists believe the discoloration was due to an eruption on Ferdinandea Island off the coast of Sicily. A volcanic plume entered the atmosphere leading to Turner's last vision. This was a divine sign to start the rebellion.

About 70 fellow slaves joined with Turner. They, of course, did not have muskets or any sort of firearms. They only had knives, hatchets, axes, and whatever blunt things they could find. Once the rebellion began the slaves did not discriminate by age, or sex. Turner, it appears, told his followers to kill all white people, though he made exceptions for very impoverished people who were only a little better off than the slaves. Turner stated he only killed one person, Margaret Whitehead. He killed her with a fence post. In doing all this the slaves went from house to house, freeing others. According to the records, Turner believed that only violence would "serve to awaken the attitudes of whites to the reality of the inherent brutality in slave-holding." He wanted, as he said, "to spread terror and alarm" among whites.

Almost immediately the white population responded to the rebellion. The local militia and three companies of artillery were assisted by detachments from two naval vessels anchored in Norfolk, the *USS Natchez* and the *USS War*ren. In addition, militias from other counties in Virginia and North Carolina were sent to Southampton. In total the militias executed 56 black slaves and killed at least 100 others. Because of wild rumors that "armies of blacks were seen on the roads," the response to the uprising became even more violent as whites feared for their lives. Whites attacked blacks without cause.

This continued for two weeks long after the rebellion had collapsed. Those suspected of participating in the rebellion were beheaded and "their severed heads were mounted on poles at crossroads as a grisly form of intimidation."

On October 30th, Benjamin Phipps discovered Nat Turner hiding out. He was quickly taken into custody. He was tried on November 5, 1831. The charge was "conspiring to rebel and making insurrection." He was convicted and sentenced to death. When asked if he regretted what he had done, he responded, "Was Christ not crucified?" Turner was hanged on November 11, 1831 in Jerusalem, Virginia. His body was then dissected and flayed. His skin was used to make purses as souvenirs. The story of all this was written by Thomas Ruffin Gray, who was Turner's attorney. The book was entitled *The Confessions of Nat Turner*. Details in the book were from Gray's research before Turner was captured and through conversations he had with the accused. The book is the primary historical document regarding Nat Turner. Some scholars have questioned the validity of Gray's portrayal of Turner.

The legal response to Nat Turner's Rebellion was swift. The following year the Virginia General Assembly passed legislation "making it unlawful to teach reading and writing to either enslaved or free blacks." It also restricted all blacks from holding religious services without the presence of a licensed white minister. These were the seeds planted that later gave the South a harvest of Black Codes and later Jim Crow laws, and lastly, the segregationist and discriminatory attitudes that ruled southern states through the 1960's. For some two words describe all of this: American apartheid. Again, for many we are still unwinding this heritage with the promise of social justice.

Before his election Lincoln summed up the moral question on which the Civil War would be fought and the later efforts to improve the lot of former slaves during the Reconstruction Era.

*I have always hated slavery, I think as much as an Abolitionist. As I would not be a slave, so I would not be a master.*

<u>Reminders</u>

"Read chapters 7 and 8 for our next meeting and come prepared to discuss what you have heard today. As always, share with your parents, if you are so disposed, any and all of the content I provided you in these lectures."

~

Dr. Lopez once more put down the lecture notes. She realized her hands were balled into fists and that her muscles were tight and drawn as if preparing for a fight. It was at that moment her husband appeared, asking, "Well, by the stack of papers in front of you, you've been at it again." As he had said earlier, "Care to share?

"Yes, but only after a brisk run through the park, which I need in order to exorcise the demons scattered to the wind by…"

"That teacher, Goldman again?

"And then I want a long cold shower to wash away the horrors I've just learned about."

"And that, if I read you right, you will then require a sumptuous breakfast at the local International Pancake House, is that not so?"

"Damn right! A tall stack, three scrambled eggs, three sausages, a large glass of orange juice followed by two steaming cups of coffee."

"He really got to you?"

CHAPTER 7

---

# THE WOLVES CIRCLE

<u>Early March</u>

The old guy was at home, puttering around in his backyard. He had on an ancient pair of Levis, almost as old as the 1849 California gold rush itself. Patched and repaired over the years, they were his favorite weekend togs. Together with a colorful, checkered shirt of an undisclosed age and a pair of tennis shoes that had, of course, seen better day, he was dressed for his gardening chores. He never wore a hat. When in the garden he always followed the same ritual. First, he addressed the potted geranium plants, cutting off old leaves, stirring the soil, extracting unwelcomed weeds, and then adding a bit of fertilizer before watering. The tomato plants in large pots were next. Here he entered into a weekly conversation that fortunately only his wife overheard.

*"Alright guys. It's me."*
*"Are you going to be cross with us again?"*
*"I wasn't cross. I was adamant."*
*"You threatened to pull us out by our roots!"*
*"A momentary indiscretion and you know why."*
*"You promised tomatoes to the neighbors again."*
*"I did."*
*"And we're not producing?"*
*"That's about it."*
*"Well, now what happens?"*
*"You're on reprieve."*
*" For how long?"*

Before the Old Guy could answer, his wife interjected, "We need to talk. Stop threatening the cherry tomatoes, and sit down with me."

The Old Guy put down his weeding tools and sat down next to his wife. By the tone of her voice he knew better than to object. Lynn was wearing her usual gardening outfit: baggy cotton trousers, an extra large shirt, and an apron with many pockets into which she stuffed a trowel, and other items. Because of the hot valley sun, she always wore an old straw hat acquired years ago in Mexico.

"Here, drink your apple juice."

He did.

"How are you feeling today?"
"About the same."
"You took your medications?"
"Yes."
"I'll check the chart."
"Lynn, I'm not fibbing."

She disregarded his response.

"When is your next appointment?"
"Monday."
"No, it's Wednesday afternoon."
"Right."
"Now how are you really feelings?"
"Tired."

They had been together for over 30 years. Naturally, they knew each other's habits, including withholding things at times. That being the case, Lynn said, "You've clammed up for weeks now. It's time to share. Have I made myself clear?"
"Yes."
"So what happened when you met the Superintendent?"

∽

The old guy had met with the Superintendent two weeks earlier. They met in his expansive and very tidy office, indicating a man who liked things in place and predictable. As Superintendent of the Los Angeles School District, Dr. Benjamin Wetzel liked an orderly ship with all hands rowing, so to speak, in unison. That, he felt, was the best way to deal with changes in the weather and an occasional rough wave.

"Dr. Goldman, I've asked for a private meeting. Thanks for being prompt."

"Dr. Wetzel, how long have we known each other?"

"Almost forty years. You joined the District one year before I did."

"We taught in the same schools for a few years?"

"We did. Then I went into administration."

"That being the case, how about just Ben and Harold?"

The Superintendent smiled. He then spoke on his intercom requesting his secretary to permit no interruptions short of an emergency.

"Okay, Harold."

"What's the deal, Ben?

"The MAG mothers were here last week."

"Same complaints?"

"They want you out! That's the jist of it."

"No due process?"

"Out and now. You really got to them when they read your lecture notes on slavery. The words and the pictures upset them."

""What did you tell them?"

"Harold, I told them I'd look into the situation."

"Stalling, Ben."

"For only so long."

"You're an old history teacher. Did you read the lecture notes?

"Of course."

"Clean historicity?"

"As always, yes."

"But MAG didn't buy that, Ben?"

"They could care less about the validity of what you wrote. They're mad; this is personal with them. You're the poster boy for their grievances and anger. They've taken partisanship off the deep end."

"They mean to make me a scapegoat?"
"You appear to be the incarnation of all they despise."
"What do you want me to do?"

The Superintendent didn't answer immediately. He folded his hands before leaning back in his chair. He closed his eyes, momentarily. Abruptly he awoke from some distant locale in his mind. He looked directly at the old guy and spoke in a voice suggesting resignation and sadness.

"Harold you've been around. You know what I want."
"You want the problem to go away?"
"Exactly."
"But?"
"It's not that easy."
"Because?"
"Two members of the Congressional Black Caucus paid me a visit a few days ago. Both represent Congressional Districts in Los Angeles County."
"Ben, what did they want?"
"They knew about MAG's crusade to destroy you. They weren't delighted by that; in fact, they're up in arms about it."
"That's it?"
"They oppose firing you if, of course, I could find grounds for doing so. They also don't want you replaced. Lastly, they don't want the District to censor your lectures. As one of them said:

*You've got a teacher who is finally telling our story, the real story, not a cleaned up version to satisfy the sensitivities of white folks. This is important to us, particularly in this time of Black Live Matter. Muzzling or firing him would upset the black community and most probably lead to a media firestorm that couldn't be contained; all hell would break loose. The media would be front and center; the Internet would be alive with accusations and recriminations. Radio and television station would cover the story. Without doubt there would be demonstrations in the streets and at the schools, as well as the District Offices. We assume you, as Superintendent, would like to avoid that."*

They seem adamant."

"Harold, this whole business could swamp the District. Race would play a major role in what could be a bitter encounter. Certainly, the Asian and Hispanic communities wouldn't sit on the sidelines."

"Ben, MAG is aware of this?"

"I have been candid with them."

"And?"

"They don't seem to care. It's almost as if they want chaos in the District. Hard as it is to believe, they seem to want the instructional program brought to a screeching halt."

"What did you tell the Black Caucus?"

"As with MAG, I told them I'd look into the situation."

"They bought that?"

"For now, but not happily."

"So why am I here?"

"Your interview with FOX News upset the applecart."

"You saw it?"

"I can't believe what you said."

~

The Fox Interview

"You agreed to this interview, Dr. Goldman?"

"I did."

"You know FOX has a conservative bent?"

"Your reputation is well known."

The old guy was meeting with John Kelly, the undisputed king of FOX Radio. The *Kelly Show* was on at 8 to 11 p.m., daily through the week. King was an interesting guy. As far back as he could remember, his family always voted for the most conservative Republicans on the ballot. Three Republicans in particular were their heroes: Senator Joseph McCarthy in the 50's, Richard Nixon in the 70's, and Donald Trump in the new century. King inherited the family tradition, and beyond question he was the golden boy of C-PAC, the most far right partisans in the Republican Party. He had supported Trump's bid for the White House early on when other Republicans had challenged his qualifications. Once in office he supported Trump's policies, especially at the border, as well as America's relationship with NATO and President Putin of Russia. As expected, he defended President Trump through two impeachment efforts along with Sean Hannity, Laura Ingraham, and Tucker Carlson, the darlings of FOX. Unlike the others, Kelly had actually been a beat reporter for the *LA Times* and the *San Francisco Examiner*. He did have a healthy respect for the facts, almost equal to his desire to twist those facts to suit his point-of-view. That provided him with a hardcore listening audience, an abundance of advertisers, and a healthy paycheck, always six figures or more. Again, as expected, his interviews were always nuanced to favor Republicans. Not to put too fine a point on it, but any liberal who came on the show was raw meat for Kelly.

"Okay, then. Are you a Washington liberal, Dr. Goldman?"

"I'm a California independent."

"You vote mainly Democratic?"

"I vote for those who support the policies I believe should be in place."

"Left-wing policies."

"If supporting Medicare and Social Security is left-wing, yes."

"You're an open border advocate?"

"I'm for a realistic border policy."

"You probably want a route to citizenship for the Dreamers?"

"Don't you?"

John Kelly liked to ask the questions, not the other way around.

"What about defunding the police?"

"No I'm for reforming some police practices based on the judgment of police chiefs and mayors. I would expect you would be for that, too."

"Gun laws?

"I support the Second Amendment. If regulated and controlled, people should be able to own a pistol, but not a machine gun."

"You would take guns away from law-a-biding citizens?"

"Our constitutional rights are not absolutes. Adults can own guns, not children."

"Abortion on demand?"

"I accept Roe v. Wade as law."

"The military budget?"

"As appropriate as determined by the Joint Chiefs, along with the Congress."

"What about making sure all voters were legally registered?"

"Of course. However, I would look carefully at state laws that make it more difficult for non-white groups to vote."

"Let's move on."

"Mr. Kelly, you asked me a question. I'm not through answering it so please don't shut me off. It would give your radio audience the false impression that you're censoring me, wouldn't it?"

John Kelly was growing hot under the color. This old guy was a pain in the backside.

"Okay, continue, but remember we have only so much time."

"I'm for the John Lewis Act to protect all voters from discriminatory gerrymandering and partisan legislative attempts to limit access to the polls. Our country has had enough of Jim Crow laws."

John Kelly had heard enough. He realized this old guy was tough to corral. It was time to lasso him.

"You spoke with one of your students, Philip Reilly."

"Yes. He's senior in one of my classes. He's a fine young man, very bright and inquisitive."

"You spoke to him privately?"

"Yes."

"You're in the habit of doing this?

"If a student requests a moment, yes."

The rope was twirling in the air. Now, if only the old guy would allow it to snag him.

"You discussed fanaticism in politics, do you not?"

"That came up."

"How?"

"Philip had overheard his parents describing mask wearing during the epidemic as fanatical, along with enforced vaccinations. I pointed out that there was some degree of individual choice involved here and in many cases so-called edicts were only CDC recommendations based on the best known data."

"You called Trump a fanatic?"

"I did not. Philip wanted to know more about fanaticism."

"You indulged him and attacked Trump?"

"No, we discussed the characteristics of authoritarianism."

"I have copy of what you said. Philip taped your conversation. I read what you've said differently."

"You are entitled to your opinion, but that doesn't make you right. Perhaps just misguided."

John Kelly didn't like to be challenged. He was in control of the microphone. He would use that power to skin this old guy, head to toe.

"You said that people are afraid to cross Trump? Right?"

"Wrong, I said that authoritarians use *fear* to keep people in line."

"You said that Trump wants unchallenged *loyalty* from others."

"No. I said despots only accept complete loyalty."

"You said that Trump feels he must always be *right*."

"Again, off base. I said that authority figures brook no contrarian opinion."

"You said Trump believes in *censorship*?"

"You keep saying I said Trump believes in this or that. I didn't say anything about Trump. I did say that authoritarian leaders detest a free media. They burn books found objectionable. And, if that is not enough, they burn the authors, and eventually the readers. Censorship is in their DNA.

"You implied this is what Trump would do."

"I didn't imply anything. I simply stated the lessons of history. You're doing the implying."

John Kelly had enough. He would go for the jugular.

"You said Trump was at fault for the invasion of the Capitol, did you not. Dr. Goldman?"

"When Philip raised that question, I said…"

"That Trump caused the riot!"

"I said…"

"That Trump was willing to use violence to take over the government!"

"You told Philip that President Trump instigated the assault on the Capitol!"

"I…"

"You convinced that young man that our leader refused to leave office peacefully. You told this youth that the President should be indicted for criminal activities!"

"I did none of those things. I told Philip to review the material put out by the Congressional Committees, and to review as much information as possible, both pro and con. I told him to make up his own mind. That's what I told Philip so stop answering your own questions for me. I've had enough of your partisan bullying."

John Kelly almost burst a vein with that reply. No one told him what to do, not since he was a kid, and certainly not on his talk show. Raising his voice he said, "You took advantage of a poor, innocent boy, badgering him with far left, socialist leaning propaganda. What kind of teacher are you? Do you really hate America that much? Have you no shame?"

The old guy heard the words. They hurt. He knew that no matter what he said, many listeners would disbelieve him. He was out on a limb and John Kelly was trying to saw it off. Learned arguments and examples from history would not do with this crowd. He was already tried and convicted. Still, he had to respond. Somewhere in his home his wife was listening. Most probably MAG were turned in with bated breath. Members of the black caucus, he knew, were also attentive. The Board of Education was probably all ears. His superintendent buddy was, he figured, glued to the radio.

"Mr. Kelly, I would like one minute to respond, one uninterrupted minute. Is that okay with you?"

Joes Kelly said, "One minute," as he thought to himself under his breath. Go hang yourself buddy.

"Mr. Kelly, I gave Philip an unambiguous response to his questions. I tried to be clear and concise. I respected his interest and intellect. It's the same thing I've done with all my students over the years. I believe in constitutional government and a democratic system of electing our leaders. I am opposed to authoritarians in any form that rewrite history, and all too often use issues of race, and gender, and religion to seek votes. I believe that, those who believe, as I, must push back against those who would, either out of ignorance or the sheer desire for power, endanger our governance based on the rule of law. That is what I believe. Make of it what you will."

~

"Harold, don't say this publically, but I was really proud of what you said on the *Kelly Show*. However, as the Superintendent I must decide what to do. Any thoughts?"

"The semester is a third over. Buy me some time. You know I'm retiring at the end of the year. In a few months I'll be out of everyone's hair."

"The old bureaucratic stall?"

"Whatever."

"I can only do so much."

"Which I already appreciate."

~

The old guy was back in his backyard. He was sipping a second glass of apple juice.

"Harold, that was some conversation with the Superintendent."

"Wasn't it?"

"And with that wacko, John Kelly."

"Both the left and the right have their wackos, dear wife."

"I prefer mine on the left.

"Troublemaker."

"What happens now, dear husband?"

"I enjoy my weekend and Monday I go back to teach fortified with the lunches you make for me. Everything else is out of my control. You know that."

"Do you have the strength to see this through?"

"I can only try."

"Then we'll see everything through together."

"Then how about…"

Lynn got up and placed her hands on the Old Guy's face before gently kissing him on each cheek.

"Now go talk to your tomatoes. They're lonely. There will be time enough to deal with the wolves."

# CHAPTER 8

# RECONSTRUCTION AND VOTING

<u>March - The Next Class Meeting</u>

It had taken the old guy a few minutes to calm down his class. It wasn't that they were rowdy or disobedient. Rather, they wanted to talk endlessly about the FOX News interview. Always cognizant of the need to go "with the force," he did. Being pragmatic was simply another way to survive in the universe.

"Okay, just a few more questions. Walter, I see your hand waving strenuously."

"My dad though you were off base."

"On everything?"

"Pretty much."

"And you?"

"I'm still trying to figure a few things out."

"Excellent advice for all of us. Florence?"

"My folks got into a couple of arguments?"

"You refereed?"

"I stayed out of the way."

"Again, good advice. I do the same when my children argued. Willie, you want to say something?"

Willie was a husky varsity football player, sort of on the quiet side, but with eyes that took in everything. He was also black.

"My folks supported you, 100%. They disliked the way Kelly disrespected you. They especially appreciated the fact that you didn't shy away from the race issue."

"And what did you think, Willie?"

Willie paused, looked around the classroom, and then said in a voice clamoring for attention, "I sometimes wish the adults would just knock it off. They need to stop trying to make puppets out of us. We can think for ourselves. We don't need to be parental knockoffs!"

Unscripted the students stood up and applauded Willie. Before the old guy could say anything, Maria spoke up loudly. "I'm from an Hispanic family. I'm tired of the way politicians use fear to manipulate us, to turn us against each other in order to get our votes. I'm tired of hearing people say they've "lost their freedoms. What liberties have they lost? I haven't lost any. I can still worship as a Catholic. My family can live anywhere they can afford the rent. I have a scholarship to Long Beach State."
"I agree with Maria."
"Ann?"

Ann was a Chinese-America, quiet spoken, and very intelligent. Her ambition is to be a pediatrician.

"My family migrated from mainland China years ago. They lived in Hong Kong for a time before moving to France. From there they moved on to Canada and then to California. Why all these moves? I tell you. They wanted to reach the United States and our relatives. They wanted to enjoy the freedoms America offer. They wanted the economic opportunities so available here. They wanted their children to have a good life. Too many Americans don't know how good they have it. All these grievances… They're spoiled and selfish, these people brandishing guns and wanting to overthrow our government. And one more thing, I'm sick and tired of Asian bashing."

Once more the students applauded. It was time for the old guy to respond.

"Everything I've heard makes me proud of you and holds promise for our country. Partisanship simply for the sake of partisanship gets in the way of solving our problems. It's necessary for us to agree on things, but it is also necessary to accept differences of opinion. At some point, however, we must find an elusive compromise if we're to deal with out problems. Mr. Kelly has his views. I have mine. Neither one of us has a monopoly on wisdom. That said, we must return to our more traditional instruction. I trust you will accept this summary of our ad-hoc discussion.

The old guy's students now applauded him. Philip Reilly led them.

~

## Lecture – The Challenges of Reconstruction Policy

"As we noted earlier in the semester, the Reconstruction Era was generally accepted as 1865 (the end of the Civil War) to 1877 (the Hayes-Tilden election). During those years, two White House occupants, Presidents Abraham Lincoln and Andrew Johnson attempted to implement what many called a moderate and lenient plan by which the succeeding Southern States would rejoin the Union. Opposing those views were the so-call Radical Republicans. They wanted the former Confederate States treated harshly as traitors and as a defeated nation. The conflict between these almost polar opposite views would lead to a constitutional crisis and impeachment proceedings against a president.

Historians still debate the successes and failures of the period. There is common agreement, however, that the following was significant and should count as a success.

1. The Union remained intact.
2. There were only limited reprisals against the South.
3. The slaves were emancipated.
4. To a degree civil rights were extended to blacks.
5. Property ownership was possible for blacks.
6. The former Confederate States rejoined the Union.
7. An effort was made to assist former slaves in their transition to freedom.

In addition to all this three major Reconstruction Era Amendments to the Constitution were passed. Though we've alluded to them before it doesn't hurt to revisit them. The Thirteenth Amendment, as you know, abolished slavery once and forever in the United States. The Fourteenth Amendment, first proposed in 1866 and passed in 1869, guaranteed citizenship to all persons born or naturalized in the United States. The Fifteenth Amendment was passed in February 1870. In no uncertain terms it decreed that the right to vote could not be denied on the basis of "race, color, previous condition of servitude." That is, the former slave was entitled to vote.

Edmund G. Ross. I remind you, stated the problem clearly in relationship to what the three Amendments codified.

*The struggle being ended by the exhaustion of the insurgents, two conspicuous problems demanding immediate solution were developed. The status of the new ex-slaves, or freemen --- and the methods to be adopted for the rehabilitation of the revolted States, including the status of the state themselves.*

In the flowery yet legalistic langue of his day Ross pointed out the puzzling situation facing Washington.

*The sword had declared that they (Confederate States) had no constitutional power to withdraw from the Union, and the result demonstrated that they had not the physical power--- and therefore that they were in the anomalous condition of States of though not States technically in the Union --- and hence properly subject to the jurisdiction of the General Government, and bound by its judgment in any measures to be instituted by it for their future restoration to their former condition of co-equal States.*

That was it. The federal government would decide the when and how the Union would be restored. The Amendments noted would provide the constitutional brick and mortar by which this would be done. The challenge was straightforward, but not the potential policies. Again, Ross struck a compelling note, one he (and we) alluded to earlier.

*As history had recorded no similar conditions, and therefore no demand for the solution of such a problem, there were no examples or historic lights for the guidance of those upon whom the task had fallen.*

Ross noted the immensity of the challenge before the government in 1865 that many suggest continues today.

*Never had the nation or party thrust upon it a more delicate duty or graver responsibility. It was that of leading a conquered people to build a new civilization wholly different from the one in ruins. It was first to reconcile two races totally different from each other, so far as possible to move in harmony in supplanting servile by free labor, and the slave by a free American citizen. The transition was sudden, and the elements antagonistic in race, culture, self-governing power—indeed, in all the qualities which characterize a free people.*

"Let's stop for a moment and pose a question. How do you, as Ross stated, reconcile two races totally different from each other?" Any takers? Louis?"

"I'm not sure what Ross was getting at. I guess slave life was different from those who were free."

"Well, one group was educated. The other wasn't."

"Do you want to expand on that point, Evelyn?

"The freed slaves weren't prepared for emancipation other than as field hands."

"They bled just like whites."

"Willie?"

"In every way whites and blacks are the same. Only their backgrounds cause differences."

"Given an opportunity, those differences might be lessened."

"Good point, Ralph."

"Transitions are always hard."

"Meaning what, Philip?"

"Well… Leaving high school and going to college… That's a big change in our lives."

"My dad was grandfather was drafted for Vietnam. That was a big change for him."

"And pretty abrupt too, Steven."

"What about when the Soviet Union collapsed. That was sure a change."

"Zack, you bet it was."

The students were posing pretty good examples. It was time to move them on.

"In terms of Reconstruction, let's take a look at the most difficult problem facing the federal government then and now: voting.

"Voting is the key to any democratic form of government. The first decision that had to be made was whether 'to allow just some or all former Confederates to vote.' The second issue concerned the former slaves. As citizens would they have the vote? President Lincoln was open to permitting all former Confederate soldiers to vote. The Radical Republicans in his party were not so considerate. They didn't want ex-rebels coming back to power. That was Gospel with them. Thaddeus Stevens, perhaps the most radical of the Radical Republicans wanted to disenfranchise all Confederates for five years. That didn't happen. In the end, however, thousands of former soldiers lost their voting rights during the Reconstruction Era. Suffrage would be restored after the 1876 presidential election.

"Black voting rights were complex. The issue was this: would 4,000,000 freedmen citizens have the right to vote? An additional question emerged: how would black suffrage impact representation in the House of Representatives? That is, how would apportionment be affected? Recall that each state's number of representatives is based on population. This is determined by a census held every ten years. Large numbers of citizens equaled greater representation. Thus, California, because of its 37,000,000 people today has more House members than Wyoming. The current ratio is about 1 member per 650,000 people with all states guaranteed at least one representative.

"Prior to the Civil War the population of slaves was counted as *three-fifths* of a corresponding number of free white citizens. If, however, all freedmen were counted as full citizens, the South would gain additional seats in the House, deluding to some extent Northern political power. On the other hand, if blacks were denied the vote, only white people would represent them. White Southerners were opposed to blacks voting, as were many in the North, though perhaps for different reasons.

"President Lincoln proposed a compromise. He would allow blacks to vote if they served in the Union armies. This would reward them for their service. He also proposed giving "the very intelligent" the vote. This thinking was in line with then Governor Andrew Johnson, who said 1864:

*The better class of them will go to work and sustain themselves, and that class ought to be allowed to vote, on the ground that a loyal Negro is more worthy than a disloyal white man.*

"The question of literacy also raised its controversial head. Would literacy tests be applied equally to be whites and blacks? Would in fact illiterate whites be disenfranchised? Before 1880 there was little public education in the South. The white illiteracy rate was about 25% Kentucky, Alabama, and Georgia compared to the national rate of 9%. The black rate was 70% in the South.

"The Radical Republicans, fearful that whites would deny the vote to blacks in the South, reached the following conclusions. First, "substantial protection" for the freedman came only with the vote. Second, blacks could not gain political office without black suffrage. Third, domestic peace demanded the vote. To this end blacks voted for the first time in 1867. During the Reconstruction Era over 1,500 blacks held political office in the South. The record indicates that most served honorably and effectively. After 1868 the process of eliminating black suffrage accelerated, thereby leading to a decline in black office holders. This occurred even though the Fifteenth Amendment provided for the right to vote."

The old guy stopped to catch his breath and to steady himself for what would come next.

"Dr. Goldman, my mother is from Georgia, Atlanta to be exact. She was really upset with the state's recent election law changes, as were her friends. I'm not sure why? They kept saying, "Just like the old days." And, "They never stop." My uncle said, "You make a little progress and they want to take it away. Damn Jim Crow." What's going on?"

"Joshua, I'll try to answer your question."

Joshua was a tall, stringy Black kid on the varsity basketball team. A few local colleges had shown interest in him. Though innately bright, his grades had suffered due to traumas in the family. Only recently had he got his act together.

"Black history is replete with efforts, some legal, others extra-legal, to keep blacks from voting. Literacy tests were one example. Poll taxes were another method. Lack of property ownership was also used to deny blacks the vote. Loss of a job was a constant threat for those who voted, or voted the wrong way. Violent intimidation was too often used. This included beatings and murders. The whole ghastly business was summed up, as your uncle said, by two words: Jim Crow. Discrimination, segregation, and disenfranchise were the keys to this odious system."

"But exactly, what is going on in Georgia?"

The old guy heard the question, debated putting it off, and then made his decision. He would walk again on the knife's edge.

~

<u>Georgia</u>

"The state legislature has recently passed a series of provisions that many claim amounts to "voter suppression" falling heavily on people of color;' that is, the state's large black population. The provisions passed by a mainly party-line vote to restrict voting access include:

- Imposing new rigid voter identification requirements.
- Increasing restrictions on absentee balloting.

- Limiting drop-off boxes
- Reducing the number of polling stations.
- Restricting who can vote with a provisional ballot.
- Making it a misdemeanor to offer food or water to those waiting in line.
- Giving the state legislature greater power over elections.
- Imposing new oversight over county election boards.

"There are at least two ways of looking at these changes. Alan Powell is a Republican in the Georgia legislature. He is from northeastern Georgia. He defended the proposed legislation as follows:

*The Georgia election system was never made to be able to handle the volume of votes that it handled. What we've done is this bill in front of you is to clean up the workings, the mechanics of our election system.*

"Those opposed to the changes claim there were 'no credible reports of any fraud or irregularities that would have affected the results in the 20-20 election. Indeed, all investigations and judicial challenges to the 2020 election results have shown this to be the case. They argue that these changes are not only voter suppression, but are in fact racist and attempt to turn back the clock to the good old Jim Crow days. Erica Thomas, who is in the state legislature, stated her opposition by quoting a civil rights icon, John Lewis:

*Why do we rally, why do we protest voter suppression? It is because our ancestors are looking down right now on this House floor, praying and believing that their fight, was not in vain… History is watching.*

"I've heard of the John Lewis Act. Didn't Congress attempt to pass a law about elections in his name?"
"Very good, Charles. Nice to see that you're watching the news."
"It was on my Apple."

The old guy had to laugh. Times had changed. He was used to getting his news from his radio and on PBS via Channel 25. Getting your news off your cell phone, or an Apple watch was beyond him.

He read two newspapers each day. He looked at his watch to tell the time. No question about it, he was beginning to feel like a dinosaur.

"What's it all about, Dr. Goldman?"

Again, the Old Guy would have preferred the relative safety of the past, not the raging controversies of the present. The teacher DNA in him, of course, prohibited that.

"On August 23, 2021, the US House of Representatives passed the John Lewis Voting Rights Act, 219-212 on almost a strictly party basis. On November 3, 2021, the Senate voted. The bill failed. It didn't get the 60 votes necessary. As to the meat of the proposed legislation… According to its supporters, it would restore and strengthen the 1965 Voting Rights Act. The key point was a requirement that certain states *pre-clear* changes to their voting laws with the Justice Department. What did that mean? If a state legislature wanted to require a stricter voter I.D., eliminate same day voting registration, or shorten the early voting period these changes needed approval by the federal government if they restricted *people of color* from voting. In other words the legislature needed to stop voter suppression if it could be shown that this was actually taking place. That determination would be decided by the Justice Department. Of course, voter suppression had to be proved."

"Meaning, keeping blacks from voting."

"That's the way some see it, Willie."

"That's the way I see it."

**JOHN LEWIS**

It was time to end class. The Old Guy passed out the lecture notes for the next two meetings, Lincoln's 10% Plan and the Freedman's Bureau. He also admonished his students to double and triple check what he had said today. He also held up a small button, saying, "Earn this and treasure it."

# CHAPTER 9

# THE MAN BEHIND RECONSTRUCTION

<u>March - A Few Days Later – Lecture Notes</u>

Today we're going to deal with President Lincoln's effort to reunite the country once the Confederacy was defeated. As you already know this was always going to be a monumental task. How difficult is a question often asked? A century later the French author, Albert Camus, provided a possible answer. In his philosophical essay *The Myth of Sisyphus* Camus refers to Sisyphus, someone who defied the Gods. As a punishment he would have to push a rock up a mountain for all eternity. Once the rock reached the summit it would roll down again, causing Sisyphus to start over. Camus describes Sisyphus as an absurd hero who is condemned to a meaningless, endless task. Concerning Lincoln what can we derived from this story?

First, the President was not involved in an absurd undertaking. The rock he was trying to lift was the reunification of the nation. The top of the mountain was, of course, a Union looking forward with slavery in the back mirror. The boulder repetitively rolling backwards was symbolic of the many challenges the President faced to accomplish this task. No matter what he did there were vocal critics. Still, against all odds he had to persevere as he had in the prosecution of the war. There was no other choice. It was in this struggle that he could give meaning to the American experiment in democracy. Ahead was a bright future. That's what animated the President.

## PUSHING THE BOULDER

We tend to think of Lincoln in mythic terms, or merely see him as a marble statue in Washington. In truth he was an extraordinary person, who was gifted with a rational mind and skilled in the political arts. He was at the same time open to the frailties of any man. He could be angered. He could be petty. He could be selfish. In that he was no different than any of us. He has his fears; he has his hopes. He could be stubborn; he could be accommodating. He could argue with his wife and have tense moments with his eldest son, Robert. He could tell a humorous story, feel sadness, and descend into moments of depression. As President Lincoln he had to reach beyond all that. He was responsible for a nation. As Commander-and-Chief during the Civil War his every decision was destined to kill thousands of young men. He had to live with that. As with George Washington, flaws and all, Lincoln was the indispensible president the voters in 1860 chose to lead the nation.

Lincoln's own writings provide us, however, with an understanding of his reconstruction policies; that is, what he wanted to accomplish. About democratic government he said in 1854:"

*The legitimate object of government, is to do for a community of people, whatever they need to have done, but can not do, at all, or can not, so well do, for themselves --- in their separate and individual capacities...*

About reunification he said in 1864:

*The restoration of the Rebel States to the Union must rest upon the principle of civil and political equality of both races; and it must be sealed by general amnesty.*

In defining the peace he sought he said in 1860:

*Let us at all times remember that all American citizens are brothers of a common country, and should dwell together in the bonds of fraternal feeling.*

The President never lost sight of challenges before him. In 1862 he shared a warning with Northerners and to those in the South who chose to understand his words:

*The dogmas of the quiet past are inadequate to the stormy present. The occasion is piled high with difficulty, and we must rise---with the occasion. As our case is new, so we must think anew, and act anew. We must disenthrall ourselves, and then we shall save our country.*

As you read and reread what Lincoln said consider the import of his words long ago, and most importantly, how they can be applied today. What, for example, can our divided nation take from what he said? Given our racial issues of today is there hope in his use of language? No matter what we have done must we think *anew* today? In dealing with national reunification in the past are there lessons to help us reunite our polarized society?

Of all of Lincoln's qualities that influenced his reconstruction policies, one stands out: *empathy*. It was the driving force behind his actions. If this is a new word for you check it out in the dictionary. It is the action of understanding how another person feels; that is, being sensitive to the thoughts and experiences of another. In short, empathy involves putting yourself in another person's shoes. This is not always easily done. One has to work at it. Lincoln, by all accounts, had this innate capacity. He felt for the plight of the slave and slave owner alike, each bound to the other by an odious economic system.

As commander and chief, he knew, as already said, that every decision he made would lead to the death of thousands. Over 360,000 Union soldiers died. The South lost 238,000 plus soldiers. Added together 618,000 died. Beyond that, it is estimated that 50,000 civilians died. All this weighed heavily on the President. Each death was like a son lost. Empathy is important; it is also painful. What follows clearly shows this.

**AN EMPATHETIC PRESIDENT**

## The Bixby Letter

On October 1, 1864, William Schouler sent a messenger to the home of Lydia Parker Bixby, a poor widow living in Boston. Schouler was the Adjutant General of Massachusetts. The messenger was to determine the names and military units of Mrs. Bixby's five sons. That information was later delivered to the President by Edwin Stanton, who was the Secretary of War. At the time it was thought that all five sons had died for the Union. Perhaps with the assistance of his private secretary, Lincoln wrote a letter condolence to Mrs. Bixby. Next to the Gettysburg Address, the letter is considered one of Lincoln's finest literary efforts. As you read it (and I do so aloud) in its entirety consider all the young men and women, then and now, who have died in the service of our country. Also recall, they didn't die as Republicans or Democrats. They didn't die as residents of Red or Blue States. They bled and died as Americans. If you can understand this you're being empathetic.

*Executive Mansion,*
*Washington, Nov. 21, 1864*

*Dear Madam,*

*I have been shown in the files of the War Department a statement of the Adjutant General of Massachusetts that you are the mother of five sons who have died gloriously on the field of battle.*

*I feel how weak and fruitless must be any words of mine, which should attempt to beguile you from the grief of a loss so overwhelming. But I cannot refrain from tendering to you the consolation that may be found in the thanks of the Republic they died to save.*

*I pray that our Heavenly Father may assuage the anguish of your bereavement, and leave you only the cherished memory of the love and lost, and the solemn pride that must by yours to have laid so costly a sacrifice upon the altar of Freedom.*

*Yours, very sincerely and respectfully,*
*A. Lincoln*

~

The old guy stopped reading. Those closest to him noted silent tears caressing his cheek. Gloria, a quiet soul could not refrain from asking, "Dr. Goldman, your tears?"

The old guy wiped away the tears with a well-worn handkerchief, saying, "You'll have to excuse me. It is difficult for me to read the Bixby Letter without recalling the names of my former students who died in Vietnam and in the Gulf Wars. I trust you'll understand."

"You still remember them?"
"As if they were still seated before me. Gloria."

Silence encompassed the classroom as the old guy composed himself. The tears stilled. The anguish on his face retreated into the past. Ever so slowly he returned to the task at hand.

~

By now the name Edmund G. Ross is familiar to you, if not his writing style. He described the President as such:

*He was a just man, and a sincere, broad-brained, patriot and far-seeing statesman; he instinctively rejected the many drastic schemes, which filled a large portion of the public press of the North and afterwards characterized many of the suggestions of Congressional action.*

Going on Ross said:

*With him the prime purpose of the war was the preservation of the political, territorial and economic integrity of the Republic --- a word, to restore the Union, without needless humiliation to the defeated party, or he imposition of unnecessarily rigorous terms which could but result in future friction --- without slavery --- and yet with sufficient safeguards against future disloyal association of the sections; and that purpose had been approved by an overwhelming majority of the people in his re-election in 1864.*

The premature death of the President by a bullet in his brain brought these words from Senator Ross:

*He had become the best loved, and the most masterful of living man in the control of the future. In his death the Union lost its most sagacious and best-trusted leader, and the South its ablest, truest, and wisest friend.*

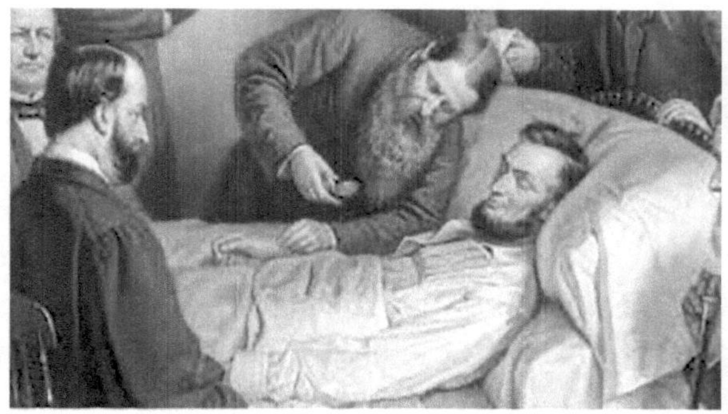

"One terrible moment at Fords Theater... One unmerciful bullet... The pages of history altered..."

# CHAPTER 10

# THE 10% PLAN

March - Lecture - A Moderate Plan

It is officially known as the Proclamation of Amnesty and Reconstruction. Unofficially, it known as the 10% Plan. It was issued by presidential proclamation on December 8, 1863. Already three years into the Civil War the Union Army had finally pushed the Confederate Army out of several areas of the South. Some of the state governments in these areas were willing to have their governments (and states) rebuilt. Lincoln's moderate plan established an orderly process by which this would be done. The President desired a speedy restoration of the Confederate States. The first model for this attempt would be the state of Louisiana.

The plan did the following:

- Amnesty was granted to rebels who took an oath of loyalty to the Union.
- Black freedmen (former slaves) would be paid $10 per month for working on the plantations.
- Only 10% of the state's electorate had to take the loyalty oath in order for the state to be readmitted into the US Congress.
- A general amnesty would be granted to all who would take an oath of loyalty to the United States and pledge to obey all federal laws pertaining to slavery.
- The state in question was required to abolish slavery in its new state constitution.
- Voters in the state could elect delegates to draft the new (or revised) constitution.

- All Southerners except for high-ranking Confederate army officers and government officials would be granted a full pardon.
- Southerners were guaranteed that they could keep their private property, but not their slaves.

The 10% Plan was the key to Lincoln's overall reconstruction effort. On the surface this plan seemed simple enough. By December 1864 Lincoln's plan was implemented in Louisiana. The state sent two senators and five representatives to Washington. However, Congress, now under the control of Radical Republicans, refused to seat them. This action was a total rejection of the President's efforts.

The Radicals were motivated by three main factors. The first was revenge. There was a desire to punish the South for causing the war and the terrible loss in lives and national wealth. They considered Lincoln's plan too lenient toward the South. Second, there was concern for the freedmen. Who would look after them in the aftermath of the conflict? Could the Southerners be trusted to treat the former slaves as a citizen, not as property? Third, they wanted to keep Republicans in power in the defeated Confederate States and well as in the North. Here domestic interests played a role. The Radicals supported high tariffs and a pro-business national banking system, as well as a liberal land policy for settlers in the West. They also supported federal aid for railroad development. If the South reinstated the Democratic Party in the South these programs might not be implemented. In a cynical sense this was one reason why Republicans voted for the Fifteenth Amendment. It was assumed grateful blacks would vote for their Republican saviors, not for the Southern Democratic Party that had supported slavery.

## A Harsh Plan

The Radicals wanted to transform Southern society, by law if possible, or by the military occupation of the defeated Confederate States. They wanted to end the power of the planter aristocracy that encouraged rebellion, and to redistribute land to poor whites and the freedmen. They also wanted to develop industry, including railroads. They civil liberties of the former slaves were important to them. They wanted those liberties protected. To do all this they supported the Wade-Davis Bill.

The Senate and House passed this legislation on July 2, 1864. Senator Benjamin Wade of Ohio, and Representative Henry Winter Davis of Maryland sponsored the bill. Essentially, the federal government had the power to guarantee a republican form of government. Readmission to the Union demanded that a majority of each ex-Confederate State to take the "Ironclad Oath." It was an attempt to remove ex-Confederates from political power. An individual had to swear that he had never "voluntarily borne arms against he United States," or had "voluntarily given no aid, countenance, counsel or encouragement" to persons in the rebellion. Furthermore, the individual had to attest he had not "exercised or attempted to exercise the functions of no office under the Confederacy." Southerners detested the "Oath." It was almost impossible for most people to take. It certainly was at odds with Lincoln's efforts. A brewing conflict was emerging as to which branch of the government would drive the nation's Reconstruction policies.

**BENJAMIN WADE**

## The Pocket Veto

Lincoln antagonized the Radicals by a slight-of-hand and all too legal maneuver. He took no action on the Wade-Davis bill. He didn't sign it, nor did he officially veto it. He just kept it in his pocket, so to speak. Therefore, the Wade-Davis Bill did not become law. He killed the bill by failing to act within a specified period following the adjournment of the Congress. Why the backhanded veto?

Lincoln believed that technically the South had never left the Union, since they were not constitutionally allowed to secede. From this perspective the Confederacy was still part of the Union. He didn't believe the war was fought against "treasonous States." Rather, it was fought against "rebellious individuals." For Lincoln the technicality opened a road to a lasting peace. Another aspect of the bill was troubling to the President. Under Wade-Davis former Confederate States had to ban slavery in their new constitutions. That was plainly unconstitutional since the slaves were still property, and because the Thirteenth Amendment had not yet been passed. His Emancipation Proclamation was limited, legalistically speaking, only to areas controlled by Union armies. Most importantly, Lincoln felt the bill would sabotage his own reconstruction plans.

The Radical response to the veto was bitter. They believed in two main themes. First, a hard reconstruction plan, as noted earlier, was needed. Second, Congress should be in charge of developing a plan, not the President. In other words, Lincoln should "obey and execute" the law as determined by the legislative branch. The resolution of this situation was resolved by bullet fired by John Wilkes Booth that killed the President, and by the Republican victory in the congressional elections of 1866. The death of Lincoln ushered in the vice-president, Andrew Johnson of Tennessee. It also brought the Radical Republicans fully to power with the ability to override a presidential veto. They would now be in charge of reconstruction.

**ANDREW JOHNSON**

## The Radicals in Power

The Military Reconstruction Acts passed by Congress on March 4, 1867 is better known by its abbreviated name: the Reconstruction of 1867. It did the following:

- The South was divided into five military districts and governed by military governors. Civilian control would resume after an acceptable state constitution was written and approved by Congress.
- Regardless of race all males could participate in the constitutional conventions that formed the new governments in each state. Only former Confederate leaders were excluded.
- All new state constitutions were required to provide for universal manhood suffrage (voting rights) without regard to race.
- States were required to ratify the Fourteenth Amendment that defined citizenship (thus making former slaves citizens) in order to be readmitted to the Union.

Northerners generally supported the legislation. They felt that Lincoln and later Johnson's policies had not led to healing or justice. Had Lincoln lived to fulfill his vision of reconstruction … Of course, that is a question that cannot be fully answered beyond speculation. Oh, what might have been takes us into a different realm of historical interpretation.

The most radical of Republicans agreed with Senator Charles Sumner view of presidential reconstruction under President Johnson, who seemed too sympathetic to the former Confederates.

*This is one of the last great battles with slavery. Driven from the legislative chambers, driven from the field of war, this monstrous power (slavery) has found refuge in the executive mansion (President Johnson), where, in utter disregard of the Constitution and laws, it seeks to exercise its ancient far-reaching sway. All this is very plain. Nobody can question it. Andrew Johnson is the impersonation of the tyrannical slave power. In him it lives again.*

**CHARLES SUMNER**

President Johnson had vetoed the Reconstruction act of 1867. But, as always, there were other factors. The Black Codes instituted in the South enraged Northerners. These were laws in the former Confederate States that called into question all the suffering and sacrifice of the war. The Black Codes would not and could not be tolerated. Johnson was perceived as too accepting of the Codes.

## The Black Codes

Following the Civil War, the Codes were an attempt in Southern States to codify political and social distinctions between free whites and free colored persons. Essentially, this was an organized endeavor to restrict the freedom of Blacks in order to maintain and perpetuate white dominance over the former slave.

The Black Codes restrictions included: (a) the right of freedmen to own property; (b) their right to conduct business; (c) their ability to buy or lease land; (d) their right to move freely in public areas; and (e) the right to bear arms. The net result of these laws was the inability of blacks to earn money through independent farming. Beyond these restrictions was the emergence of Jim Crow laws, which would define a system of social discrimination and segregationist practices leading a whole system of repressive rules. These included: (a) separate public schools for blacks and whites; (b) separate accommodations in restaurants and hotels; where you could live; (c) where you would sit in a bus or on a train; (d) and even what water fountain you could use, or which restroom was available to you.

**RACIAL PREJUDICE**

## Personal Stories

"A momentary departure… Three personal stories to make a point about race… Years ago, a good friend visited his family in Mississippi. Glenn was about ten years of age at the time. He was white and had been raised in California. One day, as he was walking with his relative in the downtown area, Glenn saw an elderly black man coming toward them. He moved aside to let the man pass. The man, however, moved to the curb before stepping into the street, thereby permitting Glenn and his relative to pass. Glenn didn't understand what had happened. The relative then explained the situation. The local custom was that blacks deferred to whites. It was as simple as that. Glenn absorbed that lesson and determined to oppose such practices if he ever had the chance.

"A second story… Years ago my wife and I were traveling in Northern California. It was about 1968. After stopping for a Big Mac we found a nice motel. Ahead of us in the lobby was a nicely dressed black couple. They were told that there were no rooms available. They left. We started to do the same. The manager stopped us, saying, "He had one room left." We declined his invitation and left. It was our way of rejecting racism.

"A last story… Back in the early 1950's when I was, believe it or not, a teenager, some of our neighbors visited our home. From what I could tell they were really upset. Apparently, the word was out. Two families wanted to purchase houses on the street. The problem was that one was black and the other was Asian. Our white neighbors were opposed to that. I'm not exactly sure what transpired, but in the end the neighbors left in a huff. My father had rejected their pleas to join them in pushing the real estate agents to only get white clients. In time I came to appreciate my family's small victory over racism.

"The point of all this ... Racial issues have thrived on the American continent since the first Europeans planted their national flags in the New World. The introduction of African slaves in the Americas all but guaranteed this. The Civil War was a partial adjudication of the situation through military action. The Jim Crow days that followed were racial to their core in the South and to a degree in the North. Unfortunately, the legacy of race still challenges us today, leaving us with unsatisfactory questions. Why do people discriminate? Why is bigotry so difficult to eradicate? How is it that race, gender, and religion still invoke in many the darker side of their personalities? As future voting citizens it will be your turn to grapple with these questions. Possibly you will do better than the older generation."

<u>Race and Employment</u>

One odious aspect of the Codes was the requirement of blacks to show written proof of employment. A violation of this requirement could lead to arrest on the basis of vagrancy. Such violations allowed local authorities to arrest people for minor infractions and then to commit them to "involuntary labor." This led to "convict leasing." This was a system in which state prisons "hired out convicts for labor" for public projects and private businesses, especially in agriculture where they worked for planters as free workers. The system created an incentive to arrest black men. The working conditions were miserable. Some called it "slavery by another name." For many Northerners it appeared the South was creating a form of "quasi-slavery" to negate the results of the war. And more to the point, the South was trying to maintain the old political order.

Words often fail us in describing painful topics. Photographs can provide more truthful images of social issues. Consider the photos that follow:

**CONVICT LEASING**

**THE CHAIN GANG**

The Black Codes did not emerge out of a void. As an example… On March 21, 1861 Alexander H. Stephens delivered his infamous *Cornerstone Address* in Atlanta, Georgia. We have alluded to this statement before. At that time he was the Vice President of the Confederacy. Recall what he stated:

*Our new government's foundations are laid, its cornerstone rests, upon the great truth that the Negro is not equal to the white man, that slavery --- subordination to the superior race --- is his natural and normal condition. This is our new government…*

With the emergency of the Black Codes many Northerners saw the hateful reincarnation of Stephens' vision. That was unacceptable. A brewing conflict between the Lincoln/Johnson plans for mild reconstruction and the harsher demands of the Radical Republicans in Congress was unavoidable. A looming constitutional crisis was at hand. Edmund G. Ross was not immune to this conflict, and to the emotions of the moment felt by those who had fought to end slavery. On December 20, 1866 he spoke before the US Senate and eloquently stated the case for the Union.

*We have with us the widowed and orphaned ones of this war. We have with us an army of maimed heroes who are condemned, but wrecks of their former selves, to walk the earth in sadness and sorrow all their after lives. We remember that it was by this great affliction that the country was saved---that they unflinchingly stood in the breach between the Republic and her foes, and we will be true to them.*

Ross was one of only a few members of Congress who had actually seen combat. He never forgot that experience or his comrades. In light of the violence occurring in the South toward the former slave, a harsh but equitable peace, he concluded, must be fastened on the former Confederacy. There was no other way. The sacrifice was too great.

**THE SOLDIER**

Again, Ross stated a soldier's view of why a harsher reconstruction policy was necessary:

*We who have stood should to should in the battle's red front, where the fires of carnage lighted the souls of brave comrades to death and immortality, will not now insult the cherished names of the dead, will not falsity the issues upon which we have fought and conquered in this war; will not now blacked the record of devotion to our country and to liberty…*

The lines were drawn. Brought to power by Lincoln's death, Andrew Johnson would either exceed to the Radical Republicans or be the first president in American history to be impeached. As the country turned in this direction an almost unknown reconstruction success story was lost in the din of rhetorical combat. It was called the Freedman's Bureau. It is our next topic.

# CHAPTER 11

# THE FREEDMEN'S BUREAU

<u>Lecture Notes – The Ruins of War</u>

How are the years 1865 and 1945 related? What could the cities of Richmond, Virginia and Berlin, Germany possibly have in common? Two photographs will tie these places and dates together

**RICHMOND, VIRGINIA 1865**

**BERLIN, GERMANY 1945**

In 1865 the Confederate capital was in ruins, destroyed by four years of terrible conflict leading to a Union victory. Eighty years later the capital of Nazi Germany was rubble, pounded into the earth by four years of bitter warfare leading to an Allied victory. What was said of one city was true of the other. War had devastated each country, leaving millions displaced. Farmland was dilapidated and massive amounts of capital destroyed. Industry was nearly non-existent. The social order was coming apart. The homeless numbered in the millions. A disturbed population lacked food, medicine, and shelter. Chaos reigned. Something had to be done. The defeated Confederacy and the destroyed Nazi Reich were not in a position to deal with the crises on their own. An outside entity was needed for the restoration of the South and a European country. Two programs would enter our historical lexicon to do this.

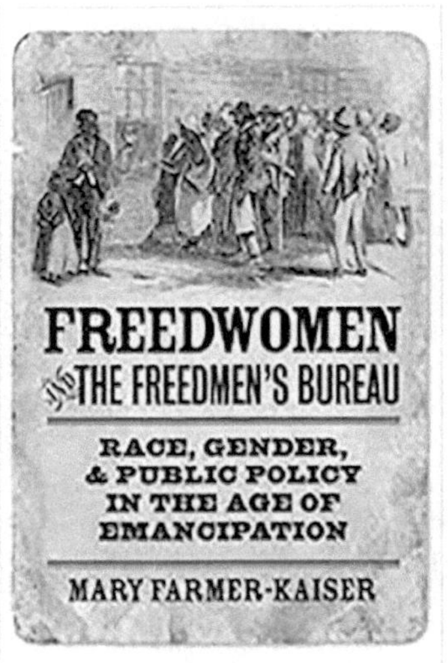

Before moving on… History teachers have a choice… They can either take a linear view, requiring the past to be taught before the present, or they link the past and present, seeking in the process to provide perspective and relevancy. That is what I now proposed to do. Let's begin with the Marshall Plan.

In June 1947 George Marshall spoke at Harvard University. As the General of the American armies in World War II and as Secretary of State, he commanded a respectful audience. He laid out the situation in one sentence. The devastated Western European nations needed American assistance. The specter of political revolution and the threat of communism spreading into France, Italy, and Germany were too great to be ignored. In the absence of European prosperity, the United States would find it difficult to export to Europe. The Marshall Plan could, if adopted, mitigate these challenges. A bi-partisan effort was needed. The Republican Congress worked with the President Harry S. Truman, a Democrat, to spend $13-billion dollars to restore prosperity in Western Europe. That would be about $115 billion in today's dollars. The plan was a success. Along with NATO, the North American Treaty Organization, the Marshall Plan was a bulwark against an expansionist Soviet Union.

## Congress Acts

In 1863 the American Freedmen's Inquiry Commission was establish to determine what measures would best contribute "to the protection and improvement of the recently emancipated freedmen of the United States, and to their self-defense and self-support." The Commission took almost a year to do this with the goal in mind to alleviate suffering and provide legal justice, education, and land redistribution. The sum of their recommendations was this:

*Offer the freedmen temporary aid and counsel until they become a little accustomed to their new sphere of life; secure to them, by law, their just rights of person and property, relieve them, by a far and equal administration of justice, from the depressing influence of disgraceful prejudice; above all, guard them against the virtual restoration of slavery in any form, and let them take care of themselves.*

What would be the result of such an effort? The Commission argued:

*If we do this, the future of the African race in this country will be conducive to its prosperity and association with its wellbeing. There will be nothing connected with it to excite regret to inspire apprehension.*

On March 3, 1865 the Bureau of Refugees, Freedmen, and Abandoned Lands became law. With the stroke of his signature Abraham Lincoln created the Freedmen's Bureau, which was placed under the Department of War for funding. General Otis Oliver Howard was given placed in charge of the enterprise.

**GENERAL HOWARD**

Howard was an interesting choice. He was known as "the Christian general" because he based his policy decisions on "his deep, evangelical piety." His war record was beyond dispute. He had lost his right arm when leading his men against Confederate forces at the Battle of Fair Oaks in June 1862. He was awarded the Congressional Medal of Honor for his courage in that battle. He also participated in two major battles, Chancellorsville and Gettysburg in 1863. Once appointed to head the Freedmen's Bureau he worked hard on behalf of the former slaves and poor whites. Lost in the clamor of the past were his efforts to promote higher education for freedmen. He was instrumental in establishing Howard University in Washington. He served as its president, 1867-1873. He aided in writing the charter of the university, and of Atlanta University, now known as Clark Atlanta University.

The Radical Republicans supported Howard. They invested immense legal and economic powers in his agency. Because of this, he ultimately clashed with President Johnson. The new president, who harbored Southern sympathies, called Howard a "fanatic." Along with other critics of reconstruction, mainly Southern democrats in Congress, he was criticized for running a "centralized dictatorship." To a degree that was the case. Howard described his immense powers as:

*Almost unlimited authority gave me scope and liberty of action… Legislative, judicial and executive powers were combined in my commission.*

Johnson described Howard as an "absolute monarch." He said:

*Being bound by no State law, and there being no other law to regulate the subject, he may make a criminal code of his own; and can make it as bloody as any in history. Everything is a crime, which he chooses to call so, and all persons are condemned who he pronounces to be guilty.*

Such statements by Johnson only encouraged the evolving rift with the Radical Republicans, and down a road to eventual impeachment proceedings.

## Accomplishments of the Bureau – Relief Services

A major function of the bureau was relief; that is, to feed people. Because poor crop yields, the abandonment of plantations, and abject unemployment, a staggering number of individuals needed food, whether white or Black. The Bureau responded by providing rations. A ration was defined as enough corn meal, flour, and sugar to feed a person for one week. During the first 15 months of operation the Bureau provided over 13 million rations, two-thirds of which went to blacks. The effort helped stave off starvation.

There was, however, a problem that still stalks welfare agencies today. The staggering amount of assistance led some to believe that it would cause idleness, and that recipients wouldn't want to work. In our time this accusation has also been made. People on welfare have been described as lazy, especially if they "people of color." "Welfare mom" entered our partisan vocabulary. The fact that a majority of Americans on welfare were white has not ended the charge. We also see this ugliness with our current Co-vid pandemic. Some viewed Federal assistance checks as keeping people out of the labor market, especially the fast-food industry and restaurants generally. Under intense pressure, Howard ended the ration program.

<u>Health Care</u>

The health situation for blacks was atrocious. Howard understood that. Almost no hospital or doctor could be relied upon to treat blacks. Few blacks had the financial ability to pay. All too often, pandemics of cholera and outbreaks of smallpox killed thousands of Blacks. Howard did what he could. During pandemics Bureau agents tried to relocate freed-persons to less contagion-ridden places. If that were not possible, agents imposed quarantines to prevent the spread of disease. A mandatory rule required weekly inspections of freedmen's homes to check for filth and overcrowding.

Hospital care was difficult to provide. The Bureau took over the operations of some hospitals. Army hospitals were also used. Dispensaries were established to provide basic services, somewhat similar to our Urgent Care Centers today, or the Emergency Ward. Drugs were provided free, or at a nominal price. It was the Medicare system of its time. Historians agree that an estimated half million suffering freedmen received care.

<u>Education</u>

As we have already noted, before the Civil War the sixteen slave states refused to educate blacks. It was a policy to whip, or imprison those who gave instruction to blacks or mulattos. This policy restricted the educational opportunities of slaves. Once emancipated, the former slave lacked the literacy skills necessary to protect themselves from discrimination and exploitation. This was especially true in a free labor system. The freedmen couldn't read contracts, the local newspaper, trade journals, or even the Bible.

General Howard realized that education was the key to everything. It would be the Bureau's most important undertaking. To that end, the Bureau was successful in establishing a vast network of schools. Over 1600 day schools were implemented. They would educate over 100,000 blacks. At its peak the Bureau was running 1,173 day and night schools and employing 2,799 teachers. In addition, 1,034 Sabbath schools were receiving Bureau assistance. Almost 5,000 teachers were involved in this program. Instruction was provided to 85,557 students.

**A BUREAU SCHOOL**

**EDUCATION IS THE KEY**

Who were the teachers? Many well-educated Northern women migrated southward to teach. They were motivated by religious impulses and their views on abolition. It should be noted, however, that half the teachers were southern whites and about one-third were blacks. All were spurred by humanitarian considerations, but not all white teachers accepted racial equality. As to the black students… One Bureau agent stated:

*The freedmen have the natural thirst for knowledge and aspire to power and influence… coupled with learning. They are excited by the special study of books.*

By any standard the Bureau accomplished a Herculean task. Overall, the Bureau spent $5 million to set up schools for blacks. It is little known that the Bureau published its own textbooks. The books emphasized a "bootstrap" philosophy. They encouraged freedmen to believe that "each person had the ability to work hard and to do better in life." This was a traditional Horatio Alger theme emphasizing overcoming adversity, leading a productive life, and enjoying social mobility. In the presence of KKK violence, the instigation of Jim Crow laws, and the notion of "white supremacy," such idealism was warranted but not always enjoyed by blacks.

**HORATIO ALGER**

Not to be forgotten is this. In our own time the Civilian Conservation Corp (the CCC) provided education to illiterate whites raised in the South. This New Deal program during the Great Depression had the same goal in mind: educate people. This impulse continued after World War II when Congress enacted the G.I. Bill. This permitted millions of young men to attend colleges and universities. What began with the Freedmen's Bureau continues with our currents efforts to legislate universal early childhood education patterned after the Head Start Program, and to make a college education more affordable.

**THE GI BILL FOR VETS**

## Legal Efforts

The Bureau had judicial authority to "secure equal justice from the state and local authorities" for blacks and white Unionists. In situations where freedmen could not adjudicate their complaints, the Bureau could and did establish courts. Where state courts functioned the Bureau could overturn decisions that were clearly discriminatory toward blacks. Agents could also exercise their authority in courts where blacks were not permitted to testify. The Bureau also provided other legal services. Agents helped legitimize slave marriages. They also presided over freedmen marriage ceremonies in areas where white officials obstructed black marriages. The Bureau filed claims on behalf of black soldiers for back pay and pensions. In sum, the Bureau tried to protect the black's legal rights.

## Labor Relations

This was always going to be a difficult challenge. Economic confusion existed in the South after slavery ended. How would planters find workers? Would freedmen want to work for former slave owners? What would they be paid? Into this morass stepped the Bureau in the role of an intermediary. Agents tried to help planters and freedmen draft contracts mutually agreeable to both parties. Over several hundred thousand contracts were drawn up. The Bureau attempted to get all parties to abide by the contracts.

The Bureau had an impossible task. The planter's complaints included: (a) they couldn't use corporal punishment as in the past; (b) there were limitations on their activities; and (c) the contracts were too restrictive and caused productivity to decline. The freedmen felt that (a) the contracts didn't allow them to move freely; and (b) and to compete for other jobs. How to assist the planters, while avoiding abuses of the workers was, as always, the challenging question. Historians are split as to which group was most favored. In time market forces would settle the issue; tenant farming emerged as the agricultural model in the post-war South. Former slaves would work for former slave owners. One owned the land; the other provided the labor. A mutually necessary but harsh arrangement evolved and continued into the next century.

## Land Redistribution

This challenge proved intractable. During the war a considerable amount of land was confiscated or abandoned by the Confederacy.

There were those in Congress who wanted to redistribute this land to the freemen. This would enable them to be economically self-sufficient. That was the hope and promise of "forty acres and a mule." Before this could happen President Johnson restored confiscated property back to many Confederates in addition to pardoning them. General Howard took on Johnson. He instructed his agents to conserve forty-acre tracts of land for the freedmen. The White House quickly rescinded Howard's orders. There would be no land redistribution. Howard's efforts, at least to a degree, might have provided an early attempt at reparations for the harm done to blacks by slavery. The Radical Republicans were not overjoyed by Johnson's actions.

## The Bureau and Women

This was another difficult area for Howard. How should black women be treated? Many black women refused to contract their labor. Black families wanted their women withdrawn from fieldwork. Agents for the Bureau tried to force freedwomen to work. They insisted that their husbands had signed contracts requiring the whole family to work as field labor in the cotton fields. They maintained that unemployed freedwomen would be treated as vagrants just as black men were. That would lead to fines, jail, or enforced work in the fields.  Some exceptions were permitted. Worthy women who were widows or abandoned and had large families to look after didn't have to do fieldwork. If your husband was gainfully employed, that was sometimes sufficient to avoid forced work. Unworthy women who were unruly or prostitutes were subject to the vagrancy laws. All together it wasn't a pretty picture.

## The End of the Bureau

By 1872 the political support for the Freedmen's Bureau had waned. An attempt to establish a permanent bureau of some sort for blacks was considered too radical to override a sure presidential veto. The country was moving on even as new Southern state governments hostile to the Bureau emerged. Ahead lay the Plessy v. Ferguson decision in 1890 to permit "separate but equal" school rooms and in public accommodations. Sixty years later the Supreme Court ended this practice in our public schools, at least on paper (Brown v. the Board of Education of Topeka, Kansas). The notion of "all deliberate speed" still challenges our society.

**1954**

The Freedmen's Bureau was an imperfect program existing in a chaotic situation in a hostile section of the country. By easing the transition from a slave economy and social culture, it was running headlong into 200 years of racial history in the South. That being the case it is remarkable that it did as well as it did. It put into practice an early version of a welfare state in its effort to bring the black community into the mainstream of American life under constitutional law. In no small measure it anticipated the Marshall Plan already noted.

Writing years later our friend Edmund G. Ross spoke to the issues faced by the Freedmen's Bureau, stating:

*What the country needed was a focused effort by the president and Congress to assist former slaves. The future of four million or so freed slaves cried out for strong and compassionate presidential leadership. The difference that such leadership would have made cannot be known, but what Lincoln would have done surely would have significance while Johnson did less than nothing, constantly opposing legislation offered on behalf of freedmen and offering no alternatives."*

Again, we are left with a troubling question. Had Lincoln lived would the Freedman's Bureau been more successful? The question entices.

# CHAPTER 12

# LUNCH AT BRENT'S

<u>April – Brent's Deli</u>

"I can't believe you took your class there."
"Can we get to that later? The young man is waiting for our order."

The old guy and Dr. Lopez were at Brent's Deli in Northridge, deep in the northwestern part of the San Fernando Valley. Brent's, operating since 1969, proclaimed it had the best Jewish deli food outside of New York City. Its specialties included crispy potato latkes, homemade crepe cheese blintzes, and sandwiches of every sort, piled high with quality sliced meats, including, of course, corned beef. If you wanted Kosher-style cuisine, great side dishes, and crisp pickles, this was the place to go.

"Your order?" the young man asked Dr. Lopez.
"A Reuben sandwich and ice tea."
"Sir?"
"Matzo ball soup and a diet root beer."

Because of the pandemic they were sitting in an outdoor area, separated from the closely packed tables inside the Deli. The outside eating area was nothing more than the parking lot that Brent's had preempted. With the sun warming the day and only the slightest of breezes, it was a nice makeshift venue.

"We've ordered, Dr. Goldman. Now back to my question. Why take your students to those two places?"

"A slight interruption before I answer, please."

"Stalling!"

"Perhaps, but I need to know why you invited me to Brent's for a late lunch?"

"Our half-day schedule provided the time and I wanted to discuss things with you outside of my office."

"Unusual for a plebian to consort that way with the proletariat."

"You can be so insufferable, Dr. Goldman."

"You've laid that claim on me before."

"Because it fits."

To anyone watching the two of them it looked like a father having lunch with his daughter. The young woman was dressed fashionably, wearing a black pants suit, trimmed by her blouse's white collar. Shining black high heels complete her stylish look. As to the senor citizen his brown, corduroy jacket was a perfect match for his rumpled off-brown pants, and his tan Dr. Scholl's shoes. Just a little family get together or so it seemed.

"I think you're stalling now, Dr. Lopez/"

"My reasons are personal."

"Then I won't use my Perry Mason line of questioning."

"Perry Mason?"

"Before your time. A 50's attorney in black and white on our thirteen inch Admiral television set."

"Admiral?"

Before the old guy could deal with that one, the youthful waiter reappeared with their meals and cool drinks, asking, "Will there be anything else?" They nodded no and he departed with a smile, reminding them as he did that key lime pie was available for dessert.

"Dr. Goldman?"

"Permit me one last evasion. Does your husband know you're meeting with me?"

"Yes."

"He approves?"

"He wants me to get you out of my system."

"Well, soon enough, it will be all over. I'll no longer be an irritant. Tell him that?"

"And your wife, Dr. Goldman. She is aware of our meeting?"

"Absolutely. She reminded me to be on my best behavior, no hanky-panky, and to take my medications."

"Good advice. Now…"

"I took the class to the Westwood Military Cemetery in Los Angeles to prove a point."

"And to the Self-Realization Fellowship Center in Pacific Palisades?"

"To give them time to reflect on what they learned."

"And the later stop at Burger King?"

"My bribe for the first two stops."

"My phone has been ringing off the hook."

"Supportive parents?"

"Only a few."

"I can see where this is going, Dr. Lopez."

"Your trip caught me off guard. I wasn't ready for a community backlash."

"For that I apologize, but I did follow all school regulations concerning field trips. Parents were informed. A district bus was used. All students had permission to go. Everything was on the up and up."

"Many parents say they didn't give permission."

"It would appear then that we have some creative students."

"Then we are back to my question. Why did you take them there?"

"I was a victim of circumstances."

On that response Dr. Lopez swallowed hard on her Reuben before saying, "Do tell."

~

"We were dealing with my last three lectures, which I submitted to you as per our unofficial agreement. We talked about Lincoln and the notion of empathy, something lost in our current highly polarized political environment. We reviewed Lincoln's mild reconstruction plan and that of the Radical Republicans. We included the President's successor, Andrew Johnson in our discussion. In addition, we spent considerable time reviewing the Freedmen's Bureau and the impact it had on the former slaves."

"You also shared some personal stories?"

"Three in fact and all extemporaneous."

"All dealing with race?"

"You already know the answer to your question."

"The word reached me and many parents."

"Partially leading to this meeting?"

"Yes. Now as to the field trip?"

"I gave into my worst instincts."

~

"One of my students… I think it was Ralph. He mentioned the movie, *Saving Private Ryan*, and asked if that film was like the Bixby Letter? I said yes, pointing out that Steven Spielberg's film even mentioned Lincoln's letter. In the film General George Marshall wants to save the last surviving fictional brother of four. The three others have already died in action. As you can see, Ralph had made the connection."

**SAVING PRIVATE RYAN**

"Then?"

"I mentioned the Sullivan Brothers."

"I..."

"Five Irish Americans were serving together on the *USS Juneau*. They were all killed on November 13, 1942 during Guadalcanal Campaign against Imperial Japan. When they joined the Navy it was with one stipulation. They wanted to serve together. Though the Navy had a policy to separate siblings, it was not strictly enforced. They were all assigned to the same light cruiser. The *I-26*, a Japanese submarine, ended their lives with one torpedo. Joe, Frank, and Matt were killed instantly. Al drowned the next day. George survived for four days. My students understood the connections to a film and Mrs. Bixby."

**THE SULLIVANS**

"Such a loss."

Dr. Lopez and the old guy continued with their lunch knowing that there was still more to be said.

~

"From some perspectives, this is where things got out of hand. Another student referred to the brother's as Irish-Americans. I responded by saying, 'No.' Emphatically, I said they were not Irish-Americans." Joshua, speaking loudly, said he was a "Black-American."

Again, I rejected that terminology. Ann said she was a Chinese-American. Evelyn piped in. She called herself a Hispanic-American. Steven proclaimed himself an Italian-American. On and on it went… I dismissed all statements. Finally, one student asked me if I was a Jewish-American. I rejected that."

"You had a purpose to all this?"

"Not one I planned in my lectures. It was sort of off the wall."

"Meaning?"

"I turned the tables on my students. I said I was an American who happened to be Jewish, just as many of them were Americans who were Catholics, or Americans who were Italian, Chinese, or black. This led to challenges by the students. That's when I dipped into hot water. I said the notion of hyphenated-Americans was getting our country into trouble. It was causing divisions in our society, pitting groups against each other, shading us with blue and red political pigmentation, and diminishing the notion of whatever it is to be American. Of course, the class fought me on all this, which I considered a good thing. They were thinking on their own, not just buying my spiel." They kept demanding proof, evidence to support my claims. So I summoned the past to help me."

"You improvised?"

"Whatever. I mentioned D-Day, June 6, 1944. I asked the class if the German defenders at Normandy distinguished between Irish or Italian Americans storming the beaches, or did they just see the enemy, American soldiers all.

**D-DAY**

"I asked them if the Japanese kamikaze pilots considered hyphenation as they barreled out of the sky to crash into American ships off Okinawa in May of 1945, leading to the death of over 5,000 sailors? Of course, I might as well have been talking about the ancient Roman Empire.

"I needed to provide examples closer to home. I needed to be relevant."

~

"I told the class about the Boston Marathon bombing that occurred on April 15, 2013. This domestic terrorist attack took place during the annual Boston Marathon. Two brothers planted two homemade pressure cooker bombs. They detonated at 2:49 p.m. near the finish line of the race. Three people were killed and hundreds were injured, and seventeen people lost limbs. A terrorist group called A-Qaeda inspired the two brothers. Only one of my students knew anything about the atrocity. Naturally, I pointed out that the terrorists didn't care if you were a Catholic, Jew, Moslem, or Protestant. Nor they care if the victims were black, white, Asia, indigenous America, or any other combination of color or ethnicity. They were all Americans and, therefore, the enemy."

"I was beginning to make a small dent in the ill-advised notion of hyphenated Americans. I continued to summon evidence."

"As you saw it?"

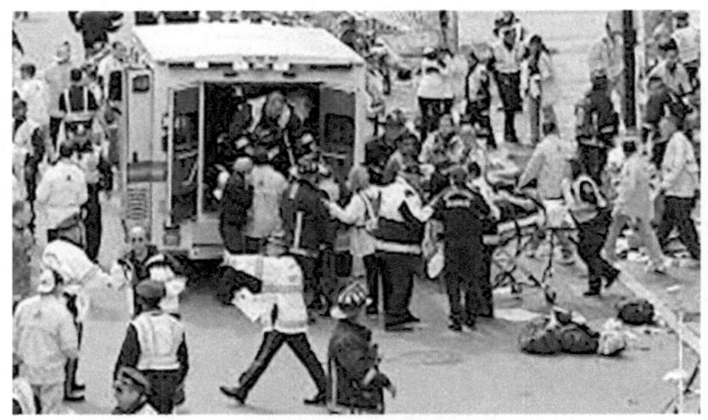

**BOSTON MARATHON ATTACK**

"I laid bare my prejudices. I told the students about the Oklahoma City bombing on Wednesday, April 19, 1995. Two white nationalists blew up a federal building in the city. They were anti-government extremists with right-wing terrorist sympathies. The explosions occurred at 9:02 a.m. At least 168 people were killed. More than 680 people were injured. Over 300 other buildings were damaged within a 16-block radius. Again, the killers made no distinctions based on hyphenated categories.

**OKLAHOMA BOMBING**

The old guy needed to change the subject, at least for the moment. Two more examples were yet to be discussed.

"How's the Reuben?"
"As always, great. Your soup?"

"Very Jewish and made by a host of Hispanic cooks in the backroom, cultural differences notwithstanding."

"You know the parents were quite upset with your use of the term 'white nationalists."

"Well, according to the FBI, they weren't Asian nationalists. They were as white as snow, but not as pure."

"Calling them anti-government extremists didn't help."

"I'm only quoted the Bureau. What do the parents want for their tax dollar?"

"Your head."

"Such compassionate people."

"You've continued to strike nerves."

"That I cannot deny, especially with my last two examples."

~

"This time the students knew what I was talking about. I recounted the attack on September 9, 2001. They knew about the attacks on the Twin Towers in New York City by two terrorist groups. The first took over American Airlines Flight 11. It crashed into the World Trade Center at 8:46 a.m. Seventeen minutes later United Airlines Flight 175 hit the South Tower. A third commercial plan crashed into the Pentagon in Arlington, Virginia. The fourth and final attack failed thanks to passengers who tried to stop the al-Qaeda terrorists. Its target was the Capitol Building or the White House. Instead, it buried itself in a field in Pennsylvania. The loss was enormous. There were 2,977 fatalities and over 25,000 injuries. Some 3240 firefighters and law enforcement officers were killed. There was at least $120 billion dollars in property damage. It was and remains the single 'most deadly terrorist attack in human history.'"

"Once more the terrorists had no qualms about killing indiscriminately. Regardless of your race, ethnicity, religion, or gender, the killers were interested in artificial distinctions. They just killed."

"Many parents, Dr. Goldman, still saw race as somehow a hidden agenda in all that you said."

"Well, perhaps they're right. You do know about the list?"

"The one you gave to your students, which the parents got a hold of, yes. That was like pouring kerosene on a fire."

"For which the parents blame me for being an arsonist?"

"Without question. Now, let's get back to the list."

"I passed out a list of attacks against black churches. By my count there have been over 70 documented cases of bombings, mass murder, hate crimes, and white supremacists-inspired examples of domestic terrorism related to Black churches and schools. Our other examples targeted all Americans. This list documents violence against one particular racial group, almost always by another easily identified group. There's no getting away from it. Whites have been destroying black churches since 1822, when the Emanuel African Methodist Episcopal Church in Charleston, South Carolina was burned to the ground. The students found this hard to believe, even as I do. But the record is clear. Violence against black churches by some is as American as apple pie."

"You had to say that?"

"You would have preferred cherry pie?"

"You're being insolent."

"You're right. I apologize."

"The parents say you're on the guilt-baiting bit again."

"There I disagree. I just want my students to know about the depraved people who committed these crimes. I want them to recognize such people today who in a more sophisticated way are equally as violent with their poisonous rhetoric to divide us into warring camps, people who seem to want and invite a racial war, people who want chaos based on their extremist conspiratorial theories. By identifying them in the past we can recognize them in the present and fight back against them. If the parents can't handle that, that's their problem."

"Perhaps, but it is also my problem when they come thundering into my office."

"Well, it appears I've put you into the middle of no man's land."

"You certainly did when you told the students about 'Bombingham.'"

"Given the city's violence against blacks, the name was aptly deserved.

~

"In the 1950's and 1960's Birmingham, Alabama was considered the most segregated city in the United States. It also had the reputation as a 'tense and violent racially divided city.' It had no black firefighters or police officers. The disenfranchisement of most blacks was complete. Very few blacks were registered to vote. Even the most timid efforts for racial integration were met to violent resistance. And worst of all, the bombings of black homes and institutions were an increasingly regular occurrence. According to the city records, there were at least 21 separate explosions on black properties, including churches in the eight years prior to 1963. Why is that year important?"

"You're about to tell me."

On Sunday, September 15, 1963, four members of the local Ku Klux Klan planted 19 sticks of dynamite on the east side of the 16th Street Baptist Church. The dynamite was attached to a timer hidden beneath the church's steps. Once exploded, the homemade bomb injured as many as 22 people. Four girls were killed. It wasn't until 1977 that the four white men involved were prosecuted.

**REMEMBER AN ATROCITY**

"So tell me, Dr. Lopez, did this horrendous act also upset some parents?"

"The guilt thing again, I'm afraid."

"Well, what would they have done? Should we burn every newspaper that covered the story? Should we ban the books written about the outrage? Should the FBI's records be cleansed because of some disgruntled white parents? Do we really want such people dictating and censoring what is taught in the schools? These parents, Dr. Lopez, are not a war with facts; they are at war with history itself, leaving us with no choice. We must call them out. They are bigots."

"Leaving you with no choice, Dr. Goldman?"

The waiter interrupted their conversation. He brought them two helpings of key lime pie, along with an ice tea refill for Dr. Lopez and another diet root beer for the old guy. The interruption was warranted and needed.

"It's too bad Moses didn't know about key lime pie, Dr. Lopez. There would have been less emphasis on matzo. Come to think of it, if the Prophet from the Mount had turned southward, the flock could have settled where the oil was located. The land of milk and honey sounds great, but such territory doesn't run a car or turn on the lights."

"You are an interesting kind of Jew, Dr. Goldman."

"According to the orthodox in Israel I'm not even a Jew given my liberal proclivities. That's sad because I held up my part of the bargain, circumcision and bar mitzvah. What more do they want? Unthinking, blind obedience to the past? When my wife is not watching I like bagels, cream cheese, and chopped liver. I also like Jewish rye bread. I can even deal with Jewish women, though, I must admit, I married a nice gal from the local Unitarian Church."

"An interesting and funny Jew."

"And you, Dr. Lopez? What kind of Catholic are you?"

"Just put it this way… Those old men in Rome would probably run me out of town."

"You're an emancipated woman?"

"In more than one way. I'm pro-choice and that's for your ears only. I hate the scandals drowning the church in a sea of red ink. Those holy men who molested boys are an embarrassment to all Catholics."

"Well, it would seem we're both on the same side of things."

"As always, you're charming, but I can't let you off the hook. Tell me about the field trip."

# CHAPTER 13

# THE FIELD TRIP

<u>April - Still at Brent's</u>

"After considerable discussion about hyphenated Americans I placed a wager before the class. We would go to the VA Cemetery in West Los Angles. There we would walk around an hour or so. If any student found a marker indicating a political party, I would buy Burger King specials for everyone. If anyone found a marker referring to a red or blue state as such, the same deal. If someone found a hyphenated name referring to race or ethnic, I was buying. So off went in the school bus after a little negotiation."

"Negotiation?"

"The youthful, hungry boys demanded double cheese burgers and extra large French fries if they hit pay dirt. Giving into the inevitable, I acquiesced."

"Smart."

"At the cemetery the students strolled through the forest of gravestones. Eventually, we gathered together where, as fate would have it, a young solder was being buried. He had been killed in the Middle East.

Though the situation was unrehearsed and certainly unpredictable, the students gathered around the few family members in attendance. We tried to be as unobtrusive as possible. The Army chaplain read from the scriptures. The VFW representative placed a folded American flag in the hands of the bereaving young widow as a two-year child looked on. Then "taps" was played. The notes floated in the morning breeze announcing the finality of the moment. The ceremony ended. The family members departed. Only my class remained as the cemetery workers shoveled dirt into the grave. I found myself thinking of the students I taught who died in the Vietnam Conflict and the Gulf Wars, and of my own father and brother, veterans of World II, who were buried in at a VA cemetery in Northern California. I could only wonder what my students were thinking and feeling.

"Dr. Goldman…"
"Yes, Philip?"
"We understand."

~

The old guy turned to Dr. Lopez to ask her something… It was then that he saw the tears.

"Dr. Lopez…"
"You must excuse me… "

The old guy waited. Then…

"My favorite uncle is buried in this cemetery. He was buried here fifteen years ago. Somehow I had forgotten that."
Our minds are a strange and wonderful gift. They shield and share as if of their own volition. I hope I haven't caused pain."
"You have, but to know love is ultimately to know pain, my dear Dr. Goldman."

They picked at the remains of the key lime pie. Finally, Dr. Lopez said, "Tell me about your last stop."

~

"Our bus joined the typical LA car crush and we headed down the serpentine road that is Sunset Boulevard. For miles the bus maneuvered through the winding road and passed the plush homes of the very affluent. About a mile from their destination the bus paused high on a bluff after passing through the town of Pacific Palisades. In the distance one could see the rolling waves of the Pacific Ocean careening towards the shores. It was a sight to behold.

The bus then continued down the last two miles of curving concrete before shuddering to a stop at the Self-Realization Fellowship."
"You've been planning this trip for a long time, I think."
"Through a lifetime of teaching."
"You prepared the students for the visit?"
"Of course. I explained that the Fellowship Center was founded and dedicated on August 20, 1950. Paramahansa Yogananda was the driving force behind an ecumenical place of prayer, meditation, and faith. It was his forceful leadership that encouraged the development of the ten acres, which were dedicated to all in the search of peace, or what some might refer to as enlightenment. At the dedication Yogananda said:

*We must recognize the unity of mankind, remembering that we are all made in the image of God. There must be world brotherhood if we are able to practice the true art of living. This Shrine has been created for all religions, that all may feel the unity of a common faith.*

"The Fellowship Center, as the students soon found out, had lush gardens and a variety of flora and fauna. A large spring-fed lake was formed by the natural hillsides. The lake is alive with swans, ducks, koi, turtles, and lotus flowers. Around the lake was a weaving trail with frequent stops for meditation. At the entrance to the Center is the Court of Religions, where all the great religions were together, not in opposition but in unity.

**COURT OF RELIGIONS**

"Of course, the students recognized the cross for Christianity and the Star of David for Judaism. As to the Wheel of Law for Buddhism, that was new to them as was the Om symbol for Hinduism. They did know the crescent moon and star for Islam."

"Here I had the students stop and reflect on what was before them."

"Many of the parents considered that an assault on their religion, that you were attacking their beliefs."

"You know better and they should."

"It was an issue I could not debate with them."

"That I understand, truly I do. I walked with the students. We came to the famous windmill, which is used as a chapel. There we meditated inside for a few minutes."

**THE WINDMILL**

"Some of the parents didn't like that."

"Well, given their proclivity for anxiety, they should try it. Meditation works better than the anti-depressant pills they should be taking."

"You would tell them that?"

"Of course, but only on my last day on the job."

"But not before?"

"Like most people I can only be pushed so far, Dr. Lopez. Under the right circumstances all bets are off."

"Perhaps we can avoid that. What came next?"

"We came to Mahatma Gandhi World Peace Memorial. It is an outdoor shrine. At the shrine there is an authentic 1,000-year old Chinese stone sarcophagus. It holds a portion of the ashes of the great leader who led the subcontinent to independence and helped create the modern state of India. It is visible from all parts of the grounds. There is a golden lotus archway to the shrine. It is trimmed with blue tile and topped with gold lotus blossoms. Here the students gathered for a group picture.

**A PLACE OF PEACE**

Here I also shared with the class my favorite Gandhi quote:

*Power is of two kinds. One is obtained by the fear of punishment and the other by acts of love. Power based on love is a thousand times more effective and permanent then the one derived from fear of punishment.*

**GANDHI**

"We spent a total of two hours at the Fellowship Center. It was time well spent. If you speak with the students I think you'll find they agree."

"I have and they do."

The old guy smiled. Affirmation was a wonderful tonic. At that moment, married or not, he could have given his boss a sincere hug and a well-deserved kiss. He fought back the impulse, saying, "I'm surprised you haven't asked me about our last stop."

"Now that you mention it."

"We descended like a flock of ravenous vultures on the local Burger King, which was only a quarter of a mile from the ocean. It was ideally placed for the students I was chaperoning. The Burger King folks didn't know what to make of us. About twenty minutes later, burger bags in hand, we parked the bus on the south side Coast Highway. My motley crew of mainly seniors exited the bus and headed for the beach. Alone with the bus driver we watched youth on the move, each thinking how nice it is to have that kind of energy. We then attacked our cheeseburgers and French fries, drowning all with chocolate milk shakes."

"I'm jealous."

"I'll make it up to you. When we next meet on the sly I'll treat at the first Burger King we find. Okay?"

"Okay."

"Dr. Lopez could only grin. She found this little light flirtation quite enjoyable. She barely resisted the urge to give the old guy a slight kiss on the cheek.

"I'm afraid its time for us to depart, Dr. Goldman."

"Yes, it would seem so. But I was just thinking…"

"About?"

"If all the world believed as Yoganada those four little girls would be alive today."

"And all the post-Civil War violence might be erased from history."

"So true… What will you do now, Dr. Lopez?"

"I'll go home and prepare to meet with the Superintendent next week. You can guess, I think, what will be the focus of our attention."

"Alas, yes."

"To assuage the parents the Superintendent wants your students tested by a third party before final grades are given. That would be in addition to your final. Can you accept that?"

"As long as it covers the required course material, yes. No questions from left field."

"Agreed."

"And what will you do, Dr. Goldman with your weekend?"

"I'll pick up a loaf of rye bread on the way out and review my notes for next week. It's time to take on Andrew Johnson."

# CHAPTER 14

# TIDYING THINGS UP

<u>April - A Few Days Later</u>

The old guy was pulling a few loose ends together. Teachers have been known to do that. It helps to keep both students and their teachers focused. It's the "3-R's," but not the ones you're thinking of: reading, writing, and arithmetic. The hidden "3 R's" in a teacher's toolbox, includes review, rewrite, and refocus. And that's what the old guy was doing now… As he was about to do so the door opened and Dr. Florence Williams entered the room, nodded to him, and quietly took a seat in the back of the room. She was dressed in a gloomy black dress that seemed altogether appropriate since the long arm of the District was again reaching out to ensnare him. Of that he had no doubts.

"Class, I suggest you review the syllabus. Don't let anything catch you by surprise. As to your essay that is half the final, don't forget to start early, write a first draft, and then rewrite. You'll be pleasantly surprised by how good your essay will be by doing this. It sure beats typing away in the wee hours the night before the assignment is due. And remember… This is expository writing. You know what that's means: thesis, support, and conclusion. Tell the reader what you're going to do. Then do it and finally remind the reader what you did.

"Dr. Goldman, the focus is still on race?"

"Any aspect of the subject, yes, Marie."

"Based on the lectures and text?"

"As some of your sources, of course."

"With footnotes?"

"And double-spaced typing, as you recall, for my old eyes."

"Can we turn in our first draft for review prior to the due date?"

"If you wish, Louis."

That out of the way the old guy handed back what in college they call a mid-term. In this case 100 multiple choice questions on all work done to this point.

"I delighted to announce that the average score was 94. You guys and ladies did a great job. Apparently, superb instruction and serious students has led to this happy moment.

All this the old guy said with a light smile.

"Dr. Goldman?"
"Yes, Louis?"
"My folks think we should be following the text more than we do."
"Well, the text is only one resource. As long as we cover the District requirements and you're prepared for the graduation exit exam, there's really no problem."
"They think you dismiss the text because you have an ulterior motive in mind, especially with our focus on race."
"That again… Well, I must admit there's some truth to their view. We have focused on race. I cannot think of any more important issue for our society. As to the text, a moment, please."

The Old Guy reached back to a bookcase. From it he took five items, which he placed on his desk for all to see: a cookbook, a dictionary, an atlas, a repair book, and the class text. Turning to the class, he said: "Okay, what do all of these things have in common?"

Confusion reigned. No one responded. Then, Susan timidly said, "They are all resources of some sort."
"Right. Now what else."
"They tell you how to do things?"
"Right, Phillip. Now, what don't they do?

There was no reply as the old guy had hoped. That provided him with an opportunity to get his point across. He had done this many times before. He had it down to an art form.

"Take the atlas as an example. It shows locations, mileage, and often sights to see as you travel. What it doesn't show is the enjoyment of travel on the open road. The dictionary is full of words and their meanings, but unless you string them together in coherent way, they're meaningless. Pull them together and you have poetry, possibly an on-the-edge murder mystery, or as Mr. Lincoln did, the Gettysburg Address. The cookbook has all the recipes, including the ingredients, and measurements, and how long to do what. But until you put it all together, there's no cherry pie in the oven. The same is true of the repair books. All the directions are there, but once more, until you try your hand the dishwasher continues to burp and stutter, as if an off key band was trapped inside. Okay, what's left?"

"Our text, Dr. Goldman."

"That's right, Evelyn. So?"

"Just words on a page."

"Exactly, young lady, just words."

"Your lectures pull it all together?"

"Hopefully, Marcus. The text tells you how a president might be impeached. That's it. That's like telling you that a kiss is nice. The concept is great, but where's the action? That's what I try to do; I try to provide the action."

"Race is the action?"

"Unfortunately, yes, Ben."

"My folks still think you're overdoing it?"

The old guys reached into his desk and pulled out copies of the most recent *USA Today* newspaper.

"Do they? I would submit that, if anything, I'm underplaying the issue. Permit me to defend myself. Each day, Monday through Friday, *USA Today* devotes a full page to the states, sharing some special news for each one.

"For example:

*Louisiana – Baton Rouge: The Louisiana State Police have hired an outside consultant to conduct a top-to-bottom review of the scandal-plagued agency, a potentially years-long process intended to help restore public trust following a string of high profile beatings of Black motorists.*

*Mississippi – Jackson: Relatives of Emmett Till joined with supporters Friday at the state Capitol in asking authorities to reverse their decision to close an investigation of the Black teenager's 1955 lynching and instead prosecute a white woman at the center of the case from the start.*

*West Virginia – Charleston: The Legislature's Republican supermajority failed to pass a controversial bill restricting how race is taught in public schools.*

*North Carolina – Pittsboro: A superintendent has apologized for a mock "slave auction" in which white middle school students pretended to sell their Black classmates.*

*Mississippi – Jackson: Governor Tate Reeves signed a bill Monday to limit how race can be discussed in classrooms. It became a law immediately.*

*Maryland – Easton: A statue that was thought to be the last Confederate monument on public property in the state was removed Monday.*

*Alabama – Montgomery: A legislative committee took seconds Tuesday to advance a bill banning "divisive concepts" in classroom lessons and in state diversity training.*

*Minnesota – Minneapolis: May Jacob Frey on Monday announced a new policy for search warrants following the police shooting of a Black man, with officers required to knock and wait a certain length of time before entering a residence.*

*Tennessee – Memphis: Marvis LaVerne Kneeland Jones, an educator and activist who was one of eight Black students who integrated Memphis State University in 1959, has died at age 81.*

*Idaho – Boise: The state House has approved a resolution that characterizes The New York Times'1619 Project' as a divisive reeducation campaign about slavery that causes shame, while promoting ex-President Donald Trump's 17176 Commission, which historians have rejected as political propaganda.*

*Louisiana – Houma: A white high school student was charged with a hate crime after throwing cotton balls at a Black student and whipping him with his belt, authorities said.*

The old guy stopped providing examples. He simply pointed out that each day the *USA Today* had a few abbreviated race-related stories. The students quickly got the point. Questions concerning race seemed to be in the paper everyday. The old guy decided to change the topic.

"Before we get into the lecture notes I've given you --- Andrew Johnson, the man behind the name --- a word about the field trip. Based on your review of the outing, it was a good experience for all. I would ask you to remember that behind each marker at the VA Cemetery in West LA there was a lively young man with his future ahead of him. When questions of war arise keep that in mind. There is no such thing as a cheap war for the men and women who sacrificed for our country. As to the Self-realization Fellowship Center in Pacific Palisades, I hope you will return on your own. It is a place of peace and meditation, where we can reflect on our lives and, hopefully, gain some perspective on things."

"You didn't mention the burger joint."

"That's true, Joe."

"We have a deal for you."

"Does it concern a hamburger?"

"If we all pass the class, Dr. Goldman, how about a redo?"

"Pass with flying colors and no "C's."

"We're up to it."

"You're the class spokesperson?"

"Duly appointed."

"Done."

The old guy could only smile. As he had learned years ago, whatever it takes in the classroom is the way to go short of an outright monetary bribe. A burger and French fries was not objectionable. He also wondered if Dr. Williams enjoyed a cheeseburger? That thought passed and he turned to the class, saying," It's time to talk about Andrew Johnson, but again before that take out the copy of the Lincoln's speech I asked you to read. His speech will assist us in understanding much of what followed his untimely death, and the challenges faced by his successor, Andrew Johnson."

∼

Lincoln's Second Inaugural Address

"You've read the President's speech. Any thoughts?"

The class was unusually quiet. No hands went up. No one punctuated the silence. Then…

"Dr. Goldman, the speech had such sadness. I don't understand that. The secessionists were losing the war and slavery was coming to an end. I would have thought the President would be celebrating."

"Rita, you're right about military victory and the near emancipation of the slaves. March 4, 1865 was a good day for the Union."

"Then why the gloomy rhetoric?"

"Perhaps the word perspective is a better descriptive term. The President was trying to balance the need to conclude the war, while he was already considering how to reunite the Union."

"Wasn't he being too easy on the Confederates? His speech seems to indicate that."

"Martin, that is, of course, a matter of interpretation. Some historians see the speech as an attempt to avoid a harsh treatment of the defeated rebels. Recall, he reminded the listeners that both sides had been wrong in imaging what "lay ahead of them when the war began four years earlier." He pointed this out, saying:

*Both parties deprecated war, but one of them would make war rather than let the nation survive, and the other would accept war rather than let it perish. And the war came.*

He added:

*Neither party expected for the war the magnitude or the duration, which it has already attained. Each looked for an easier triumph and a result less fundamental and astounding.*

"Both sides thought the war would be quick and victorious, is that right?"

"Walter, there are countless examples of nations falling into this fatal trap. Our recent wars in Vietnam and the Middle East are reminders of how easy it is to get into a war, and how hard it is to end one."

"The war thrust on the Union was really about slavery, wasn't it?

"Lincoln's own words leads to that conclusion, Thomas. Again, recall what he said:

*One-eighth of the whole population were colored slaves, not distributed generally over the Union, but localized in the southern part of it. These slaves constituted a peculiar and powerful interest. All knew that this interest was somehow the cause of the war. To strengthen, perpetuate, and extend this interest was the object for which the insurgents would rend the Union even by war.*

"I noticed that the President brought God into his speech. I thought there was a separation of religion and government. Am I incorrect?"

"Not in the least, Joshua. In my opinion the President didn't cross this line. What he did what to touch on the question of Divine Providence in human affairs? That led him to a challenging inquiry. What, he wondered, was God's will in allowing this terrible war to come about. He attempted to deal with this question with allusions form the *Bible*. He pointed out:

*Both read the same Bible and prayed to the same God, and each invoked His aid against the other."*

"Like in World War I, isn't that so, Dr. Goldman?"

"Sadly, correct, Florence. Men of God prayed for salvation and then charged headlong across 'no man's land' in an attempt to destroy the foe. The French and Germans did this until millions were killed. In World War II all sides again did this. There is a degree of absurdity here as the President pointed out:

*The prayers of both could not be answered. That of neither has been answered fully. The Almighty has His own purposes.*

"Of course, neither side could resist the temptation claim God's support. The Confederacy staked its claim, stating *Deo vindice* as its motto. Freely translated: *God will vindicate us.* The North adopted Julia Ward Howe's *Battle Hymn of the Republic.*

*Mine eyes have seen the glory of the coming of the Lord*
*He is trampling out the vintage where the grapes of wrath are stored*
*He have loosed the fateful lightening of His terrible swift sword*
*His truth is marching on*

"Lincoln was a religious man?"

"Ann, he knew his *Bible* and much like another slain President almost a hundred years later, Lincoln sought some understanding of the Divine Will, while recognizing the need for human involvement in overcoming the troubles of his time. I am speaking, of course, of John F. Kennedy. Somehow, each thought, the nation's life or end was a reflection of some grand plan not fully in our understanding. That plan, I think, Lincoln alluded to towards the end of this speech."

*Fondly do we hope, fervently do we pray, that this might scourge f war may speedily pass away. Yet, if God wills that it continue until all the wealth pied by the bondsman's two hundred and fifty year of unrequited toil shall be sunk, and until every drop of blood drawn with the lash shall be aid by another drawn with the sword, as was said three thousand years ago, so still it must said "the judgments of the Lord are true and righteous altogether.*

"His words were like poetry."

"Maria, very much like the Prime Minister of Britain, Winston Churchill, in the 1940's, Lincoln summoned the English language to help Northerners understand the crisis before them, as well as the opportunities to rid the nation of a sinful past."

"People don' talk that way today."

"True enough, Willie. All too often they don't even talk to each other. They talk past each other, trying to score points, as if to win an argument, as if their home team must win regardless of consequences. Lincoln spoke directly to the humanity of the conflict and to the need for healing. That brings us to the last paragraph of the inaugural, which in many ways was a prerequisite for what he hoped to accomplish in peacetime."

"May I read it?"

"Phillip?"

"It really got to me."

*With malice toward none, with charity for all, with firmness in the right as God gives us to see the right, let us strive on to finish the work we are in, to bind up the nation's wounds, to care for him who shall have borne the battle and for his widow and his orphan, to do all which may achieve and cherish a just and lasting peace among ourselves and with all nations.*

As if on cue the school bell announced the end of class. As the students left, he reminded them to read the lecture notes about Andrew Johnson. A moment later he was left with Dr. Williams.

"That instruction was most interesting, Dr. Goldman."

"And enlightening, I trust?"

"For us, yes. For your students, I hope so. For the parents, I'm not sure. Some may see bringing the Almighty into the classroom as offensive. Turning the lectern into a pulpit might strike some as too much."

"Dr. Williams, if that is the case, those upset parents will, I believe, have to take up the issue with God."

"They will, I'm afraid, take it up with the Board."

"If that's the case they might as well bring the National Park Service into this fracas."

"Because?"

"Along with the Gettysburg Address, the Second Inaugural Address is inscribed in the Lincoln Memorial. Perhaps that should come up before the Board, too? After getting rid of me do they wish to demolish the Memorial? To do one without the other would seem a fruitless waste of time. And, as long as we're sliding down this slippery slope, perhaps the *Bible* should be thrown into rubble. After all, Lincoln repeatedly quotes from the scriptures to bolster his vision."

"You would say this before the Board?"

"If tested, yes."

# THE MAN WHO WOULD BE IMPEACHED

<u>April – Lecture Notes - The Take by Historians</u>

Almost all Americans know what took place on April 14, 1865 at Ford's Theatre. The Civil War was at an end. President Lincoln attended a play entitled *Our American Cousin*. There he was shot and mortally wounded by a Confederate sympathizer, John Wilkes Booth. The assassination was part of a conspiracy to kill the President, Andrew Johnson, the Vice-President, and the Secretary of State, William Seward, during the same night. Seward was wounded but survived. Andrew Johnson was spared because his assassin, one Gorge Atzerodt, got drunk and didn't attempt to kill the VP, who was boarding at the Kirkwood House. There he learned of the President's dire situation. Seward immediately rushed to the President's deathbed. Upon seeing the President, he said, "They shall suffer for this." At 7:22 am the President died. Secretary Stanton then voiced the immortal words: "Now He Belongs to the Ages. "The next day, around 10:30 am, Andrew Johnson took the oath of office. He was now the head of the government. Salmon P. Chase, who was the Chief Justice of the Supreme Court, presided. Most of Lincoln's cabinet was present.

After being sworn in the parlor of his hotel, Johnson said:

*I feel incompetent to perform duties so important and responsible as those, which has been so unexpectedly thrown upon me. The course, which I have taken in the past in connection with the rebellion, must be regarded as a guaranty of the future...*

**BOOTH**

Continuing he said:

*The best energies of my life have been spent in endeavoring o establish and perpetuate the principles of free government, and I believe that the Government in passing through its present perils will settle down upon principles consonant with popular rights more permanent and enduring than heretofore. I have long labored to ameliorate and elevate the condition of the great mass of the American people. Toil and an honest advocacy of the great principles of free government have been my lot. Duties have mind; consequences are God's. This has been the foundation of my political creed, and I feel that in the end the Government will triumph and that these great principles will be permanently established.*

The loss of the President was later aptly immortalized by Walt Whitman in his poem, *'O Captain! My Captain!'*

*Oh Captain! My Captain! Our fearful trip is done,*
*The ship has weather'd every rack, the prize we sought is won,*
*The port is near, the bells I hear, the people all exulting,*
*While fellow eyes the steady keel, the vessel grim and daring,*
*But O Heart! Heart! Heart!*
*O the bleeding drops of red,*
*Where on the deck my Captain lies,*
*Fallen cold and dead.*

Lincoln's body, after lying in state at the Capitol, was placed on a train draped in black for the trip to Springfield, Illinois. Millions lined the route of the 1,700-mile journey. In their sorrow they mirrored Whitman's elegy to the slain president.

**WALT WHITMAN**

According to many historians, few presidents faced a greater challenge than did the incoming president. As if hit by lightning he was faced with reuniting the nation and also determining what would happen to the emancipated slave population in the first years of Reconstruction. Eighty years later President Harry S. Truman faced the enormous challenge of ending World War II and then assisting war-torn Europe and a devastated Japan in the first days of the Cold War. Each president found himself at a pivotal point in history and both would endure controversies.

According to Edmund G. Ross:

*Mr. Johnson was practically unknown to the great mass of the people of the North until he succeeded to the Presidency. He was in no sense regarded as or assumed to be the leader of the dominant party; while those who on Mr. Lincoln's death became leaders of the dominant party in opposition to Mr. Johnson's administration and policies, were widely known and of long public experience, and had the correspondingly the confidence of their party.*

Johnson, as president, had his supporters and detractors. The historians who favor him argue this: Congressional Reconstruction under the influence of the Radical Republicans was a generally bad idea in that it was a mistake to grant blacks equal civil and political rights so soon after emancipation. They viewed Johnson as a champion of the Constitution, who tried to bring true reconciliation between the North and South. From their vantage point Johnson never deserved impeachment.

Others have reached a different verdict. Johnson is seen as opposed to the Freedmen's Bureau, the Fourteenth and Fifteenth Amendments, the Civil Rights Act of 1866, all of which tried to assist the former slave. They condemn Johnson as an inept racist who deserved to be pilloried by the Senate, or by cartoonists who harshly depicted him.

The harshest historians view Johnson as:

*The worst possible person to have served as President at the end of the American Civil War... Because of his gross incompetence in federal office and his incredible miscalculation of the extent of public support for his polices, Johnson is judged as a great failure in making a satisfying and just peace.*

Between the extremes of these views are those in the middle. These historians see a mix of possibilities. They do, however, agree that historical cards were stacked against the new president. Why was this? First, he was a Southerner and a Democrat heading a government controlled by Northerners and the Republican Party. The contention is that, unlike Lincoln, he had little understanding or sympathy for their views, or the emotional investment they had made in the four years of conflict.

"Second, unfairly or not, Johnson lacked the moral and political authority of the slain president, or of an elected president for that matter. A poor analogy might be the divorced mother who remarries. There's the biological father and the "new guy." Johnson was the new guy.

"Third, unlike Lincoln, Johnson had difficulty in compromising; that is, finding the middle ground. He lacked the "rail splitter's" tact, tied to forcefulness and an abundance of wisdom.

"Fourth, he never saw the "bigger picture." He never quite fathomed that a revolution was taking place. As had happened at Yorktown in 1783, the world was turned upside down. The Confederacy was gone. The slaves were free. Painfully or not, a new society was being born. Political power, once vested equally between the legislature and the executive, had shifted to Congress. Johnson had difficulty accepting these realities.

Ross spoke to the new president's moderate and conservative views on Reconstruction, pointing out --- from a soldier's perspective --- that:

*They found little favor with the mass of the veterans of the Union armies, who had but lately returned from he victorious fields of the South, their blood not yet cooled after the fury and heat of the strife.*

The question of race hovered over Johnson. Not unlike most Americans, he considered blacks inferior. And like most Northerners he accepted the Emancipation Proclamation and the Thirteenth Amendment. Lastly, as with most citizens, he felt full equality of the races was not in the cards. He had owned 14 slaves before becoming the Vice-President in 1864. He had had freed them a year earlier.

There is little evidence that outward racism influenced his policies. He perceived, many argue, "the enormous obstacles that lay in the way of equality for blacks. Given the social realities, as he saw them, the status of blacks in the South would eventually be dictated by whites. After the election of 1876 this proved to the case. As one historian stated:

*In Johnson's mind, the issue of what to do with the defeated Southern states was simple: impose conditions upon their return to full standing, such as the irrevocable abolition of slavery but do not impose black suffrage as a condition of readmission.*

So how should be judge Andrew Johnson? I suggest we withhold rendering a decision until we know more about the man and his times. Let's begin.

Lecture Notes – The Formative Years

Like many others of his time, Johnson was born in a log cabin in Raleigh, North Carolina. The date was December 29, 1808. A few months later Abraham Lincoln was born on February 12, 1809 in Hodgenville, Kentucky. Johnson parents were poor and essentially illiterate. The Johnson children never attended a formal school. At the age of 10 he, as was his brother, William, were apprenticed as tailors to James Selby. The brothers were contracted for a ten-year period as indentured servants. One of Selby's employees taught Johnson how to read as they worked. He also listened to others as he cut cloth and sewed. After five years the brothers abandoned Selby. They ran away. His employer then put a ten-dollar award on them. After reuniting with his parents the entire family headed to Tennessee where they found a new home in Greenville. It was there that Johnson met and married Eliza McCardle. She was the daughter of a local shoemaker. He was 18; she was 16. A Justice of the Peace married them. His name was Mordecal Lincoln. He was, as it turns out, the first cousin of Thomas Lincoln, who was the father of Abraham Lincoln. That, as they say, shows how small the world is at times. The young couple would be married for almost 50-years. Five children were born to them.

**ELIZA JOHNSON**

Johnson's wife encouraged his education. She improved his reading skills and taught him mathematics. He became a vivacious reader. She also worked on his social skills. Apparently, she had a head for improving his tailoring business, as well as assisting him in wise investments in real estate. His business prospered. He was apt to say, "My work never ripped or gave way." His later detractors might have added, "If only that had been true of his Reconstruction policy."

**JOHNSON'S TAILOR SHOP**

## Slave Ownership

In 1842 Andrew Johnson entered politics in a big way. He became a member of the Tennessee State Senate. During that year he also bought his first slave. According to a bill of sale, n November 29th he paid $541 for Sam. He was a young man, perhaps 14-years of age. A few months later the future president paid $500 for Dolly. She was Sam's half-sister. She was 19-years old. Some fourteen years later he paid $1015 for Henry, who was a 13-year old. Johnson eventually brought Henry to the White House after Lincoln's death. According to the records, all his purchases were "warranted to be sound, healthy, sensible, and a slave for life." The Johnson family ended up owning at least ten slaves.

**SAM IN HIS LATER YEARS**

**DOLLY CARING FOR A JOHNSON CHILD**

In time Sam married a woman named Margaret. They had nine children. Three were born into slavery. Dolly had three children. All were born into slavery. Sam proved to be a most useful slave. Johnson's private journals indicates that Sam was hired out to people around the town for odd jobs, such as "plastering a house, pulling corn, cutting oats with a scythe and cradle, and doing janitorial work." Johnson earned extra income for these services performed by Sam. There is evidence that Sam received some pay for his work. Years later he became a commissioner of the Freedmen's Bureau. How's that as a quirk of history?

On August 8, 1863 Johnson freed all of his slaves. They remained with him as servants. A year later, as the military governor of Tennessee, he freed all the slaves in the state. The emancipated slaves, it appears, gave him a watch. It was inscribed as such: "Untiring Energy in the Cause of Freedom."

<u>Moving Up</u>

In 1857 Johnson was elected to the US Senate. In one of his first speeches he "decried Northerners who would endanger the Union by seeking to outlaw slavery." In another speech he said, "all men are created equal from the Declaration of Independence but that did not apply to African-Americans." In perhaps his best speech in the Senate, one that was warmly received in the North, he said:

> *No; I intend to stand by it… and I invite very man who is a patriot to… rally around the altar of our common country… and swear by our God, and all that is sacred and hold, that the Constitution shall be saved, and the Union preserved.*

After Lincoln's election Johnson encouraged Southern senators to stay in the government. He had a belief "in an indissoluble Union." He didn't want senators to resign and for their states to secede from the Union. He pointed out to Jefferson Davis that if Democrats held their seats and control of the Senate, there was little Lincoln could do about slavery. The future president of the Confederacy declined the overture.

Johnson left Washington when his state took up the issue of secession. The state legislature organized a referendum on whether to have a constitutional convention to authorize secession. They effort failed. The question was then put before the public. A popular vote would decide the issue. Johnson campaigned against dissolving the Union. He did this despite threats on his life and actual assaults. Apparently, he would speak with a gun on the lectern before him. In the end Tennessee voted to leave the Union, June 1861. With his life in jeopardy he was forced to leave the state. In time the Confederates confiscated his land and slaves. They turned his home into a military hospital. In the end Johnson was the only member of a seceded state to remain in the Senate. In doing so he became the most prominent Southern Unionist, and that brought him to the attention of the new president.

In March 1862 Lincoln appointed Johnson the military governor of Tennessee. He was confirmed by the Senate and given the rank of brigadier general. He took to the job with zest. He demanded loyalty oaths from public officials. He shut down all newspapers owned by Confederate sympathizers. In a state divided by the war he organized the defense of Nashville from repeated attacks by General Nathan Bedford Forrest. Eventual defeat of the Confederates in the state occurred in 1863.

Once Lincoln issued the Emancipation Proclamation in January 1863, Johnson threw his political weight in support of the White House. Johnson had decided that slavery must end. He said:

*If the institution of slavery... seeks to overthrow it (the Government), then the Government has a clear right to destroy it.*

Though he was reluctant to enlist former slaves into the Union Army, he eventually succeeded in recruiting upward of 20,000 black soldiers to serve the Union. He had come a long way from feeling that blacks should only do menial tasks in order for whites to do the fighting.

## The Election of 1864

In this election the Democratic Party's candidate was one of Lincoln's former generals, George B. McClellan, a formidable rival running as a Democrat. The general was no pushover. He was for making peace with the Confederacy in order to bring the war to an end. This, of course, would have left the planter power structure in place, as well as slavery. Many Northerners, put off by the staggering Union loses and weary of an endless war, supported McClellan.

**THE GENERAL**

For pragmatic political reasons Lincoln decided to replace his running mate in the 1860 election, Vice-President Hannibal Hamlin of Maine. The President wanted a Southerner on the ticket in order to gain the support of Union Democrats who were opposed to the Confederacy. Lincoln said of his running mate, "Andy Johnson, I think, is a good man." Together Lincoln and Johnson ran under the banner of the National Union Party rather than that of the Republican Party per se. The election was a clear victory for this ticket. The popular vote was 2,213,635 to 1,805,237. The electoral vote was 212 to 21.

**THE LINCOLN-JOHNSON TICKET**

The cartoonists of the day illustrated the challenges facing Lincoln and Johnson. In the political cartoon below Lincoln leverages his strength to reunite the Union, even as Johnson, always the tailor, uses his sewing skills to do the same.

**LINCOLN AND JOHNSON AT WORK**

Andrew Johnson was now the Vice-President of the United States. One bullet would soon elevate him to the presidency. Again, according to Ross:

*In Lincoln's death the Union lost its most sagacious and best trusted leader, and, the South its ablest, truest, and wises friend.*

Now Andrew Johnson, born into poverty and illiteracy, who had persevered and reached the highest level of political success, found himself at a crisis point in our history. Ahead of him were challenges he could not fully appreciate.

# CHAPTER 16

# CONFRONTATION

<u>May - Lecture Notes – Johnson in Power</u>

The new president had three main goals in mind, once at the helm of the government. The first was the speedy restoration of the states on the grounds that they had never left the Union. Here he was following in Lincoln's footsteps. Reunion for Johnson, he thought, should be "easy and certain." His second goal was to break the power of the planter class, replacing them with small farmers and business people. In this he was not out of step with Lincoln. Few in the North wanted this elite class to regain power. A third goal was to win reelection in 1868. That meant defeating the more than potential candidacy of General Grant for the Republican Party nomination.

As to slavery… Here there was a half-step departure from Lincoln. Johnson felt that suffrage for blacks was a "delay and a distraction in reuniting the Union." Johnson did not want to "Africanize the South." He feared that the slaves might "vote as the planter class wanted them to." That view ran counter to the Radical Republican desire for black votes to keep them in power in the South. Either way, the black vote was a pawn in an intensely competitive world of politics.

Ross saw in Johnson a man trying desperately to emulate Lincoln's approach, though lacking in his predecessor's skills: For Lincoln and now Johnson:

*The primary purpose of the war was the preservation of the political, territorial and economic integrity of the Republic --- in a word to restore the Union, without needless humiliation to the defeated party, or the imposition of unnecessarily rigorous terms which could but result in future frictions --- without slavery --- and yet with sufficient safeguards against future disloyal association of the sections; and that purpose had been approved by an overwhelming majority of the people in the election in 1864.*

## Pardons

Almost immediately Johnson ran afoul of the Radical Republicans on this issue. A pardon is the "use of executive power that exempts the individual to whom it was given from punishment." The president's pardon power is based on Article II of the Constitution which states: "… he shall have power to grant reprieves and pardons for offenses against the United States, except in cases of impeachment."

The criticism was that he had pardoned too many Confederate leaders, or was too lenient in jail sentences. As an example, Jefferson Davis, the former Confederate president, served only two years at Fort Monroe. He was never tried for treason. Only Henry Wirz, the Camp Commander of Camp Sumter near Andersonville, Georgia was executed. The camp held Union prisoners-of-war. Thousands of Union soldiers died there. Wirz took the hit. Many felt that more Confederate leaders and officers should have been jailed, and in some cases faced a firing squad. Johnson, it seems, was trying to follow Lincoln's Proclamation of Amnesty and Reconstruction, showing strength and mercy, always a difficult thing to do in the aftermath of war.

*I, Abraham Lincoln, President of the United States, do proclaim, declare, and make known to all persons who have, directly or by implication, participated in the existing rebellion, except as hereinafter excepted, that a full pardon is hereby granted to them and each of them, with restoration of all rights of property, except as to slaves.*

## The Black Codes

Here again the new president swam upstream against public opinion in the North and with Radicals in the Senate. He was perceived as too accepting of the Black Codes, which were enacted by Southern states to restrict the former slaves, legally, economically, and, most importantly, at the ballot box. Under the Black Codes, as most historians saw it:

*The freedmen would have more rights than did free blacks before the war, but they would still have only second-class civil rights, no voting rights, and no citizenship. They could not own firearms, serve on a jury in a lawsuit involving whites, or move about without employment.*

Rather than more forcibly challenging the Black Codes, the President seemed to acquiesce. That left a void that even the moderate Senate Republicans were all too eager to fill. Senator Lyman Trumbull of Illinois took affront to the Black Codes. He proposed a Civil Rights Act to redress the problem. In presenting his case he said:

*A law that does not allow a colored person to go from one county to another, and one that does not allow him to hold property, to teach, to preach, are certainly laws in violation of the rights of a freeman... The purpose of this bill is to destroy all these discriminations.*

**BLACK CODES SUPPORTED
BY THE KKK AND THE WHITE LEAGUE**

The first Civil Rights Bill 1866 was passed by the Senate on February 2nd. On March 13th the House voted 111 to 38 for passage. The bill had two goals; first, Congress would define citizenship. Second, all citizens were equally protected by the law; it was unlawful to deprive any person of citizenship rights "on the basis of race, color, or prior condition of slavery or involuntary servitude." Unwisely, some thought, the President vetoed the bill. A two-thirds majority in each chamber overrode this veto. This allowed the bill to become law without a presidential signature. This marked the first time in American history that Congress overturned a veto.

Why the veto? The President argued that 11 of the 36 states were not represented in Congress. Thus, those 11 states, though they were not present for the debate on the bill, were still forced to accept it. That being the case it was an invasion of federal authority of the rights of the states and was, therefore, unconstitutional. If that were true the bill portrayed an immense stride toward the concentration of power in a centralized national government. That was another way of saying the power of state legislatures was being diminished. Perhaps Johnson's most compelling reason centered on what he considered to be the law's effort to fix "a perfect equality of the black and white races."

Senator Trumbull rejected the President's views. He said:

*It (the bill) provides for the equality of citizens of the United States in the enjoyment of "civil rights ad immunities." What do these terms mean? Do they mean that in all things civil, social, political, all citizens, without distinction of race or color, shall be equal? By no means can they be so construed.*

An aside ... Many people think that public schools must guarantee equal outcomes if full equality is to be achieved. That is a misunderstanding. Public schools can only provide equal opportunity, nothing more beyond allocating equal resources to all schools. Everyone has a right to an attorney, assuming he needs one. But there is no guarantee that one attorney will be as competent or savvy as another. Everyone should have an equal right to apply for a job but once in place skill and competency should determine promotion.

Naturally, that is theory. In practice that is not always the case. As the old saying goes, "Who you know maybe more important than what you know."

Continuing with Trumbull's argument:

*Do they mean (civil rights and immunities) that all citizens shall vote in the several States? No; for suffrage is a political right which has been left under the control of the several States, subject to the action of Congress only when it becomes necessary to enforce the guarantee of a republican form of government. Nor do they mean that all citizens shall sit on the juries, or that their children shall attend the same schools.*

**LYMAN TRUMBULL**

Another aside…The world has changed since Trumbull justified the Civil Rights Bill. As was to be expected, each generation has debated the issues raised by the bill. Those debates continue today, witness the heated discussions about affirmative action programs, voter restrictions, equal treatment by law enforcement, and the need to redress economic inequalities in our society. That being the case, the Civil Rights Bill of 1866 was a starting point, not the finish line.

## Doubling Down

Though sympathetic to the "black problem," the President still vetoed the Freedmen's Bill in 1866. He opposed federal assistance, of which you are aware, arguing that whites had never received such aid. An outraged Senate overrode his veto on February 20, 1866.

The Fourteenth Amendment was perhaps the Johnson's last chance to reach an agreement with the Senate Radicals. Again, he did not. Though a president plays no part in the ratification of an amendment, Johnson, by his opposition, stirred already troubled waters. Had he been more supportive, the movement toward later impeachment might have been mitigated. Written by Trumbull and others, the amendment was sent to the state legislatures for ratification on June 13, 1866. It was finally ratified on July 9, 1868.

What did the amendment provide? Except for native-Americans on reservations, citizenship was extended to every person born in the United States. It penalized states that did not give the vote to freedmen. Federal civil rights could be protected in federal courts. Also included was the provision to pay off the federal debt, but forbade any repayment of Confederate debt. The amendment also disqualified many former Confederates from office. In summary, the amendment put into the US Constitution the key provisions of the Civil Rights Act: "no state could deprive any person of life, liberty, or property without due process of law."

## The Question

Recalling Johnson's goals… There would be no fast and easy reunification of the nation directed by the president. That task fell to the Congress. The power of the planter class was reduced but not eliminated, and certainly the white establishment regained power, especially after Union troops left the South. Last, Johnson's hope an election victory in 1868 were dashed by his impending impeachment.

Of course, if Lincoln had not died, would he have been more successful than Johnson? Unequivocally, the answer is yes. As one historian stated:

*It is likely that he lived, Lincoln would have followed a policy similar to Johnson's, the he would have clashed with the congressional Radicals, that he would have produced a better result for the freedmen than occurred, and that his political skills would have helped him avoid Johnson's mistakes.*

# CHAPTER 17

# ERUPTION

<u>May - A Few Days Later – The Parking Lot</u>

The Old Guy was driving to school. Unlike the past few days he was feeling better. Thanks to an abundance of *Mylanta* his indigestion seemed under control. Again, thanks to a little white pill his high blood pressure stabilized something short of exploding an artery. The troubling headaches still assaulted him, but his high-powered painkillers were doing their job. Getting old, he reminded himself, was not for sissies.

As he approached his ubiquitous parking lot, he noticed a throng of people marching in front of the school. Scattered in front of them were LA's finest, hopefully to "protect and serve." Nearby were panel trucks emblazoned with numbers and letters: Channel 2 – NBC, Channel 4 – CBS, and Channel 7 – ABC. Of course, the print media vans were also there: *LA Times, USA Today*, and the *Daily News*.

The Old Guy slowed his VW van. He had no desire to run over a demonstrator, at least not yet. As he did, he heard shouts: "There he is." "That's his van." "Get him." Quickly the Old Guy figured out who the "he" was. As he pulled into his parking place, more voices were heard: "Pull him out of the car." "Don't let him get into the building." "Any hanging tree around here?"

The Old Guy was beginning to think he had stumbled into a remake of the *Ox Bow Incident*. He considered putting the VW into reverse and scampering for safety. Surrounded as he was that was no longer possible.

*"What's happening?"*
*"Pomp, I'm not sure."*
*"Those people look really mean?"*
*"They do seem upset."*
*"With you?"*
*"Could be."*
*"They won't hurt me, will they?"*
*"Not if I can help it, old buddy."*

Heart in hand the old guy existed the VW. Immediately, he heard a torrent of abuse.

"Stop with the race stuff, you bastard." "Get out of the classroom, you knucklehead." "Take your venom elsewhere, like to the sewers where you came from."

Two shouts in particular caught his attention. "My kid doesn't have any racial problems and I don't want him talking about them." Had he had a therapist on call, the old guy would have discussed that comment with him. Then there was: "Get back into the classroom and stop talking about race, you Communist." That demand left the old guy somewhat perplexed.

He also noticed the various physical demonstrations of unhappiness; that is, the number of people pointing the middle finger at him. For a moment he wondered if there was any relationship between the length of that finger and the vehemence behind it. He also noticed clenched fists, and again he wondered if fist size could be coordinated with anger. He quickly dispensed with those questions, leaving them for some future Sherlock Holmes to figure out.

Then and very unexpectedly, the crowd parted and quieted. Stepping in front of him was Mrs. Sharon Reilly, the leader of MAG. You remember, the Mothers Against Guilt. Her lips parted, even as spittle descended down the side of her right check. In a high-pitched voice she said, "We've got you now!"

Unsure as to how to respond, the old guy noticed the television cameras recording all. The first of two epiphanies struck him.

"You seem really upset, Mrs. Reilly. If you're concerned about your son's last grade, I'd be glad to discuss it with you."

A glowering face and more spittle was his answer.

"Perhaps we could talk about things in private?"
"Not today you creep."

Surrounded as he was on all sides, it was time to charge. The old guy decided to tease and taunt Mrs. Reilly hoping she would be tempted to really lose her cool with the cameras rolling.

"Mrs. Reilly, you really need to see a psychologist for your anger management which at the moment is non-existent. If you would prefer I can recommend someone if you would like?"

That did it. Brandishing her placard she moved in for the kill, even as the crowd tightened the circle around the old guy. However, before she could land a lethal blow, an elderly, very thin Medicare recipient with bluish-colored hair slammed the old guy across his forehead with her wooden sign. Immediately, a trickle of blood and more was seen. Stunned by the hit, the old guy could only think out loud, "And I had to take my blood thinner today." That's when the second epiphany occurred. The old guy reached up as to stem the flow of blood. Instead he wiped it across his face giving the impression, of course, that he had barely survived a riot at a soccer game in Mexico, or a post-World War II nylon sale at Macys. As expected, the media broadcasted all to the world.

<u>The Nurse's Office - Later</u>

The school nurse as caring for the old guy, once two police officers rescued him from the parking lot mob. They were alone for a moment in her office.

"So, you've been fighting with the children again."

"Their parents."

"Coming up in the world, are you?"

"How's the cut?"

"You'll live."

"You're all heart. Still, I'm glad you were here today."

"You would have dealt with it. Remember, I know your secret."

~

A few years earlier a younger old guy had broken up a fight between two football players during lunch. One had been hit in the face, leading to a nose spouting blood. That kid the old guy took to the Nurse's office. Unfortunately, the nurse was out of school on purchasing supplies. The old guy had to do the repairs himself. Upon returning she viewed his handiwork.

"Not bad. In fact, very good… Where did you get your training?"

"The Boy Scouts."

"Where else?"

"If I tell you, it's our secret?"

"Okay."

"In '57 I turned eighteen. Uncle Sam sent me a draft notice. I had read *All Quiet on the Western Front* and *The Red Badge of Courage*. I knew the Army wasn't for me. It wasn't that I was a coward. I just wasn't a hero. I needed to find a spot between those poles. I enlisted in the Navy. I already had pacifist leanings. I didn't want to kill anyone. Anyway, I signed up for medic school. A year later the Navy kicked me out. They found a serious irregular heartbeat. I got an honorable, medical discharge. That's the story."

~

The door to the Nurse's Office burst open to reveal Dr. Lopez and a school police officer.

"Are you okay?"

"Surviving."

"I'm sending you home."

"No. I have my classes."

"We'll cover for you."

"Not for the class, you won't."

"You are so pig-headed."

"Please, Dr. Lopez. If I don't show up, MAG will have won."

"No!"

"Please!"

"On one condition… An officer stands outside of the room."

"Okay. Now, what's happening outside?"

"The crowd is disbursing, but promising to return tomorrow and every day until the District sends you to Siberia."

"And the Superintendent?"

"I've never seen him so upset, so angry, Dr. Goldman."

"At me?"

"For once, no. To quote him, 'No group of parents is going to lynch one of my teachers."

"Even me?"

"Especially you."

At that moment the door again opened, this time revealing the old guy's wife.

"Harold, I saw you on the television. Tell me you're okay."

"I'm okay, Lynn."

"Turning to the school nurse, she asked, "Is he fibbing?"

"Not today."

"Lynn, you remember my boss, Dr. Lopez?"

"Of course."

After a moment…

"Harold, are you sure you want to stay. You remember what the doctor said about getting upset?"

"I can't let that class down. You understand?"

It was then that Lynn had her epiphany. She thought: you old rascal. You can't fool me. You're going to use this business to make points with the students about race. You're going to use your bloody face as a teachable moment. I bet you and Pomp planned this little conspiracy the moment you saw the crowd. I wouldn't put it past you.

"Lynn, tell the kids their father is alive and kicking and that I love them."
"You have your pills?"
"All three."
"Make sure you take them."

The old guy's wife left after giving him a peck on the cheek. He and Dr. Lopez headed to his classroom, escorted by the officer. Once he was in his room she left. As she walked back to her office, she was troubled by one word: pills. Was Dr. Goldman really in good health? She had seen the way his wife looked at him. There was real concern there.

∼

Back in his room the old guy taught his classes, answering questions about what happened as best he could. He was candid and as objective as he could be. Once that was over he said. "It time to get back to impeaching a president."

∼

Of course, he couldn't predict what would happen the next day. MAG was there, placards and all, but so were counter-demonstrators with their own signs and chants. Beyond disputing rhetoric one thing was clear. Almost all of Mag was composed of white people, whereas the other group was a reflection of a diverse society --- people of every race and ethnicity. Sides had been chosen it what was going to prove a protracted and bitter conflict. The worlds of "cancel history" and "cultural wars" had landed in the old guy's backyard.

# CHAPTER 18

# WASHINGTON BOILS OVER

<u>May – On a Roll</u>

The old guy was pontificating. Occasionally, he couldn't resist the temptation to preach even if it was annoying to others. Though he tried not to be pompous that was not always how the victims of his words saw it. Why he did it he wasn't quite sure. He once compared this need to Yellowstone's Old Faithful. Every now and then he needed to spout. This was one of those days.

"Synchronicity, ever heard of it?"

Nothing. The class was as still as a graveyard at midnight. The old guy had anticipated that.

"Okay, how about Carl G. Jung?"

If silence could deepen it did. Blank looks gazed at him. The old guy might as well be speaking German or a Swiss dialect, which in a way he was.

"You want to know what's going on?"

Twenty- five students let out a communal plea. "Yes!"

"Okay, Jung was an analytical psychologist and a buddy of Sigmund Freud a very long time ago. Surely, you've heard of him. They were delving into the unconscious, exploring our dreams and the causes of our conscious behavior. Along the way Jung realized that people (in therapy} described events that appeared related in a meaningful way, yet seemed without any causal connection. In other words, there was a coincidence between events in our minds and the outside world, which at first glance seemed to have unknown connections. This concept he called synchronicity. Of course, you're asking, 'What does this have to do with Andrew Johnson?' That's a good question, so I'd better answer it.

**CARL JUNG**

"Let's take three events: first, a single bullet from Wilkes' gun alters history. Second, before that event, Lincoln wants to get reelected in 1864. He needs a Unionist Democrat. He finds one in Andrew Johnson. Third, the Congress, weary of feuding with Lincoln's successor over Reconstruction Policy, decides to go for the constitutional jugular; that is, impeachment. Taken individually, each event seems unrelated to the others. Seen from a distance, however, a connection is discerned; the events are not casually unrelated.

"Are these random acts alone, or are they connected by difficult to see historical dynamics; that is, do human events equate to a plan that we only recognize after the fact? Lincoln alluded to this when he spoke of the Almighty in his Second Augural Address. Of course, others might dismiss the metaphysical to focus on our need to see earthly patterns. Somehow this must be connected to that in order to get this. Unsure about this view, are you? Well, look at three dots. What do you see? Three dots… But if you connect them, you might observe a straight line, or a triangle. So let's do that. Let's connect three dots. We'll begin with the most recent one."

## The Tenure of Office Act

"The Senate, dominated by the Radical Republicans passed this act on March 2, 1867. It would be declared unconstitutional in 1887 by the US Supreme Court. The period between would include a constitutional crisis about which will soon be our focus. Specifically, the Act restricted the power of the president to remove certain officeholders from their positions when the Senate was not in session. In the 1860's the Senate sat a relatively small portion of the year compared to today. If a president removed an official, the Senate could reinstate the individual once it was back in session. Essentially, the Senate wanted to approve appointments and dismissals. As stated in the Act:

*The law denied the president the power to remove any executive official who had been appointed by the president with the advice and consent of the Senate, unless the Senate approved the removal during the next full session of the Congress.*

"President Johnson vetoed the act. His veto was overridden. What was behind all this? Simply put, a feud. In post-war Washington, there were contending theories concerning Reconstruction. One theory, which President Johnson adopted, argued:

*The states of the United States are indestructible by the acts of their own people and state sovereignty cannot be forfeited to the national government. Under this, the only task for the Federal Government was to suppress the insurrection, replace its leaders, and provide an opportunity for free government to re-emerge. Rehabilitation of the state was a job for the state itself.*

"The second theory, proclaimed and by the Radical Republicans, argued:

*The Civil War was a struggle between two governments, and that the southern territory was conquered land, without internal borders, much less places with a right to statehood. Under this theory, the Federal Government might rule this territory as it pleased, admitting places as states under whatever rules it might prescribe.*

"That the two theories were in opposition to each other was all too obvious. Something had to give. One or the other would prevail. There was no longer an acceptable middle ground.

"On the surface the Tenure of Office Act was passed in order to exert Congressional power. Beneath the surface was an equally compelling reason, which was to remove President Johnson from office by getting him to violate the Act. In other words, provoke the President in being complicit in his own undoing."

"This sounds like entrapment, Dr. Goldman."

"Ralph, in a way it was?"

"And the President fell for it?"

"As they say, Mario, lock, stock, and barrel."

"Didn't he see what was happening?"

"Claudia, of course he did."

"But…"

"He was constrained by his own beliefs, the first theory we've discussed. In the final analysis, whether he couldn't or wouldn't extricate himself from this view of Reconstruction, it didn't matter. History records that he remained adamant."

"He was stubborn?"

"Or principled, John."

"Johnson knew what the Radicals would do once he was impeached?"

"No question about that, Sal. Harsh Reconstruction policies would continue in the South."

It was time to get into the heart of the matter. The students were primed.

"The Act (or bait) was passed to protect Edwin Stanton. As Secretary of War, he was a holdover from Lincoln's Administration, and a favorite of the Radical Republicans. It was well known that Stanton was a hardliner. Stanton administered the military zones in the South, and wanted to do so until the former Confederate States established bi-racial governments and ratified the Fourteenth Amendment. In theory the Department of War was under President Johnson. Under Stanton it was acting almost as an independent organization enforcing the wishes of the Radicals. By 1867 Johnson had enough. He wanted Stanton out. The Radicals wanted him in office as 'their trusty outpost in the camp of the enemy.'"

"Senator Edmund Ross had reservations about the Act. He summarized his views, stating:"

*Its specific purpose was to prevent the removable of the Secretary of War, Mr. Stanton, with the manifest if not avowed intent, as the sequel shows, to make that Secretary not only independent of his chief, but also to make him the immediate instrument of Congress in whatever disposition of the Army, or of military affairs generally relating to the government of the Southern States, the majority of Congress might dictate. In a word, the Congress, in that Act, virtually assumed or attempted to assume, that control of the Army, which the Constitution rests on the President.*

"What was Ross saying in the flowery language of his day? Simply put, regardless of its intent and many justifications, the Congress was possibly overreaching in its grasp for power."

"In August 1867 the President sent Secretary Stanton an unequivocal note: 'Sir, public consideration of a high character constrains me to say that your resignation as Secretary of War will be accepted." Stanton responded in kind. 'The public considerations of a high character constrain me not to resign.'"

**EDWIN STANTON**

Since Congress was out of session, the President responded by suspending Stanton and replacing him with a true war hero, Ulysses S. Grant." The general held the job for a short time before bowing out. This was a politically expedient thing to do since he was already a frontrunner for the 1866 Republican Party nomination. Why stand on the railroad tracks with two trains barreling toward each other?"

"This is like a sit-com."

"Phillip, you're right."

"So what happened next?"

"Maria, so impatient."

There is a moment when a teacher is in Seventh Heaven, whatever that is supposed to mean. The old guy was there. Tests and assignment were forgotten. His students had swallowed the hook. Now if only the old guy could land them.

"In January of 1868 the Senate, now back in session, took up the issue of Secretary Stanton's suspension. The Senate voted 35 to 6 not to concur. A few days later Stanton walked (or marched) back to his old office in the War Building. That said, how would the President respond? He had two choices: he could do nothing and let the whole thing blow over, or he could challenge the Act in terms of its constitutionality. Since Lincoln had chosen Stanton, the President didn't believe he was violating the Act. Stated another way, he believed that each president had a right to select his own Cabinet members. For Johnson the Act only applied to newly confirmed officers, not to those from a previous administration. On that basis he decided to defy the Senate. After Grant departed, he named Major General Lorenzo Thomas the new Secretary of War. Upon hearing this Stanton informed his allies on Capital Hill. He was told by telegram to 'Stick.' He would not vacate the office. He literally barricaded himself in his office. He even had General Thomas arrested."

"It's difficult to follow all this, Dr. Goldman."

"You're right, Joshua."

"What happened next?"

"I'm sure you can guess, Monica. The Radical Republicans were outraged that Johnson would challenge their Congressional authority in regard to the Tenure of Office Act and to post-war reconstruction.

From their view they had tolerated the President's obstructionism long enough. The appointment of Lorenzo Thomas made impeachment proceedings inevitable. Representative William D. Kelley sentiments were not uncommon at that time. On February 22, 1868 he declared."

*Sir, the bloody and untilled fields of the ten unreconstructed states, the unsheeted ghosts of the two thousand murdered Negroes in Texas, cry, if the dead ever evoke vengeance, for the punishment of Andrew Johnson.*

"Two days later the House voted to impeach President Johnson 126 to 47. Seventeen members chose not to vote. The House adopted formal Articles of Impeachment five days later. The road was now open to a trial in the Senate."

"It's hard for me to figure out who was right? He seems like the President Johnson was being railroaded."

"Some thought so, Sandra."

"But he did block the Congressional programs, didn't he?"

"That's correct, Charles."

"Wasn't this just an argument over policy, or maybe just big egos?"

"Sandra, perhaps both were involved."

"We'll get into the trial?"

"Of course, but first we need to meet our old friend Ross. After all, as you already, it was his vote that saved President Johnson. Keep in mind what Ross said many years later when he wrote about the effort to impeach the President.

*The Tenure of Office Act constituted the ostensible basis of his impeachment in 1868. It has been passed for he purpose of restricting the power of the President over Executive appointments. That Act, therefore, becomes a very important and conspicuous incident in the impeachment affair, as its alleged violation constituted the only material accusation set out in various forms, in the entire list of charges.*

Our next lecture will be by zoom, I'm sorry to say. It will, however, help us to understand what made this Kansan tick.

# CHAPTER 19

# ROSS OF KANSAS

May – A Zooming Lecture

What follows is a brief outline of Edmund G. Ross' life prior to his famous (or infamous) vote to save President Johnson from impeachment. We begin, as we must, with his early years.

Ross was born in in Ashland, Ohio, on December 7, 1826. He was the third of fourteen children born to Sylvester Ross Sr. and Cynthia (Rice) Ross. Talk about a large family. He received a good education for he time. At the age of 11 he was apprenticed as a printer in Huron, Ohio, There he worked for the *Commercial Advertiser*. This was the beginning of a lifetime relationship with ink, the press, and the newspaper business. In 1841 he moved to Sandusky, Ohio to work for the *Sandusky Mirror*, which was owned by his brother, Sylvester. During the next twenty years Ross was employed as a journeyman printer and typesetter. He traveled roads throughout Ohio and several close by states to accept temporary work. In 1852 he moved to Milwaukee, Wisconsin where he worked for two newspapers, the *Milwaukee Daily Sentinel* and the *Milwaukee Free Democrat*. While in the city he participated in aiding Joshua Glover, an early example of his strong willingness to defend his abolitionist beliefs by taking action.

Who was Joshua Glover? He was a fugitive slave from St. Louis, Missouri. He sought safety in Racine, Wisconsin in 1854. A Mr. Garland, Glover's slave owner, attempted to enforce the Fugitive Slave Act to recover his property. Glover was captured and placed in a Milwaukee jail. On March 18, 1854 a mob broke into the jail to rescue Glover. Ross, as you probably guessed, helped free Glover. The runaway slave was taken secretively back to Racine. From there he traveled to Canada by boat. He spent most of the rest of his life in Ontario.

**JOSHUA GLOVER**

Ross married Fannie Lathrop in Sandusky, Ohio. The year was 1848. He was twenty-two. She was a year younger. They would raise a family of seven children and be together for almost 50-years. He met his bride-to-be in the local Congregational Church, where he sang in the church choir. Church, family, and singing would animate their long lives. Without question they shared a common distaste for slavery. That said they were drawn to the abolitionist movement. Fanny would be an inspirational force in his life, especially when the finally decided to move to Kansas in 1856. That trip meant taking three young children over 700-miles through dangerous territory to a territory split down the middle with pro and anti-slavery settlers. A mini-civil war was about to break out in "Bloody Kansas/"

For abolitionists the struggle for a free Kansas was a holy war. Ross and his family were not the only ones headed to the disputed territory. People crossed the country from as faraway as New England. They were willing to face the hardships of travel and a difficult pioneer life in support of their beliefs. As for the Ross family... Along with 100 wagons they crossed into Kansas after a difficult 83-days trip that included numerous river crossings and terrible weather. As you can imagine packing for this trip meant sacrificing prized possessions that

**FANNY ROSS**

were too large or heavy. Fanny had to sell off pieces of furniture. Ross, on the hand, would not do so with his books. Heavy as they were he brought the works of Shakespeare and Milton, plus his medical journals into Kansas. He also took with him a heavily bound portfolio of his best work. It was filled with samples of "stock certificates, letterheads, invoice forms, and posters, some of which were printed in colors.

In addition to taking care of the children and cooking evening and morning meals, Fanny Ross had other necessary responsibilities. She was the treasurer of common funds used for purchases of meat, milk, and other needed items from local merchants. In the evening she would gather with others on any available knoll to sing in her "high soprano voice." Apparently, she was enthralled with John Greenleaf Whittier's Hymn --- *The Song of the Kansas Emigrants.*

*We cross the prairie as of old*
*The fathers crossed the sea;*
*To make the West, as they the East,*
*The Homestead of the free...*
*We go to rear a wall of men*
*On Freedom's southern line,*
*And plant beside the cotton tree*
*The rugged northern pine...*
*Upbearing like the ark of old,*

*The Bible is our van,*
*We go to test the truth of God*
*Against the fraud of man...*

**JOHN G. WHITTIER**

Once settled in Topeka, Kansas, Ross became a leader in the "Free Kansas Movement." He was also in the newspaper business again. He was the publisher of the *Topeka Tribune* (1856-1858) and the founder of the *Kansas State Record* in 1859. In addition, he joined the Board of Directors of the Atchison, Topeka, and Sana Fe Railway, where he was an enthusiastic supporter and promoter. During this period he was elected a delegate to the Kansas constitutional convention (1859-1861) that dealt with the difficult question of slavery.

At the time Ross was highly praised as such by a Leavenworth newspaper:

*He is one of the former Editors of that sterling sheet --- The Kansas Tribune. He worthily represents the craft, though from subduing the Border Ruffians by aid of type and pen, (and sometimes with a shooting stick,) he has taken to subduing the soil and making that responsive to the Freeman's industry.*

With the coming of the Civil War, Ross put aside his ink pen and type to be a soldier. He joined the Union Army as a private in 1862. He was soon commissioned as a captain in command of Company E, 11th Kansas Volunteer Cavalry Regiment. This group took part in at least seven major engagements. In time he was promoted to major. He was, as were others, mustered out after the surrender of the Confederacy in 1865. There is no question that Ross distinguished himself as a leader of men in battle. Ross' bravery and leadership were well known to all who served with him.

Post-War Politician

Ross returned to Kansas after the war. He had three main goals that always seemed to motivate his life: first, to be with his family; second, to operate a printing business; and third, to publish his own newspaper, which he was soon doing as the editor of he *Kansas Tribune* (1865-1866). Once more he was echoing his views: On January 4, 1866 Ross' editorial on Reconstruction clearly stated his hopes for the country.

> *The only hope of a thorough reconstruction of those states, is to couple amnesty with suffrage --- put the Negro in a political position which he has merited by his loyalty and services, in which he can protect himself if the government will not protect him.*

Troubled by the plight of the former slave in the South, he editorialized:

> *Future generations would ask, What manner of men were those who in their hour of extremity called to their assistance this race of people, and, when their country was saved, lacked the courage and generosity to grant them the rights their blood paid for?*

Speaking before the US Senate he pointed out the all to obvious for him:

> *Slavery is not dead, however, until all its supports are removed. It will never die until the Negro is placed in a position of political*

*equality… Without the ballot he is the slave of public prejudice and public caprice.*

The Governor of Kansas appointed Ross to the US Senate in 1866 following the suicide of the incumbent, James H. Lane. By now Ross was a Republican in good standing. The state legislature later elected him to complete Lane's term. Ross would serve from July 19, 1866 to March 3, 1871. Because of his vote to save President Johnson, Ross was not reelected to office.

## A Comment

Again and again you have, I hoped, noticed the connection between the black and the vote, whether in the 1860's or today. Without the vote you are not a full citizen. Then and now unnecessarily restrictive voting requirement that seem to disproportionately to fall on people of color have by their very nature a racist tone to them. All claims to protect the security of our elections and to guarantee an honest election outcome are a sham to maintain white political control. We must be clear on that point. That was true in Ross' time. It is true in our own. By any accepted measurement and analysis, for example, the recent presidential election in 2020 was the most secure election in our history. Those who challenge that are more than sour losers. They're not upset so much that they lost as that they lost because people of color tipped the scales.

## A Commentary

By now, I trust, you see the power of primary sources. What Ross said comes across better in his own words, certainly more than my mimicking them, or reading what historians say they meant. The power of primary resources permits you to think through things on your own. Of course, the more you delve into a topic the more things you must think through. That's the challenge of a serious student or citizen. Folks who only listen to what they want to hear are fortunate. They don't have to think. Folks who won't listen to other points of view can be easily manipulated, though they would argue differently. Folks who equate truth with tribalism, my guy (or gal) right or wrong, are a danger to our democratic system since they frown on compromise and eschew respect for the other view.

But beware this social/political disease infects both the left and the right at the extremes, leaving only the center to moderate our differences. At the extremes there is no room for deliberation and thoughtful consideration of the issues. Everything is about winning political power and then shoehorning your views on others. Though they call themselves patriots, they are the antithesis of what our Republic is all about. You can take that to the bank. But, as always, check out everything I say. I have no monopoly on truth or wisdom.

<u>Reminders</u>

"Read the chapter on the impeachment process, and review the sets of lecture notes on Johnson's trial. Also, most of you are looking forward to the senior prom and graduation. Don't forget to slip in your research papers. Stay well."

# CHAPTER 20

# THE VISIT

<u>Late May – Northridge, California</u>

The weather over the San Fernando Valley was, to put it mildly, gloomy. Almost obliterating the sun, dark clouds paraded across the skies to the roar of celestial booms as thunder roared and lightning laced the sky. And then the rain began, torrential and unpredictable in this semi-arid landscape of residential homes and a multitude of apartment houses lining the busiest streets. The flood of water overwhelmed the drainage system and the reservoirs. Soon large pools of water make it difficult for those dependent on their cars to get from Point A to Point B. Certainly, as expected, vehicle collisions increased almost exponentially as the slick streets took their toll. The AAA tow trucks were in great demand, as was the LAPD to resolve disputes between irate motorists with damaged fenders. In short, it was probably a good day to stay in your home next to a warm fire and with a hot beverage in hand or in your office thinking about staying at home.

One driver, who would have preferred being in her office, was Dr. Lopez. The stormy weather seemed symbolic of her task today. That was for sure. There was, however, no choice. Things had come to a head.

Though she had plugged her destination into the navigation system, she was still having trouble finding the house. As she drove slowly down Prospect Street she scanned the curb numbers through the driving rain. Finally, both her eyes and the monotone voice in her navigation system concurred. She had reached her destination. She went through the ritual of turning off the engine, grabbing her purse and umbrella, putting on a storm hat, and then checking her watch: 12 Noon straight up. She was on time. She exited her car and, bending to the wind gusts, walked as quickly as the wet concrete sidewalk and driveway permitted. She didn't open her umbrella. To do so would have had her competing with Mary Poppins. She slouched her way to the front door and knocked. It opened on her first rap.

"Come in, Dr. Lopez. I can't have you wading in our front yard. What would Harold think?"

"Dr. Lopez entered. Quickly, she took off her heavy raincoat. She placed her umbrella by the front door, and then settled into a comfortable chair in the kitchen, as she was directed. The room radiated with warmth and delightful aromas. Even as she sat down a hot cup of tea was placed before her, along with a large grilled cheese sandwich.

"Comfort food on a wintery day, Dr. Lopez. Enjoy."
"Please, Mrs. Goldman, call me Eleanor and thanks for the comfort food. It's fun to be a kid now and then."
"My pleasure."
"If I may ask, what's cooking in the oven? Something smells so good."
"An apricot pie. My brother has a heavily laden tree and I have the recipe. Soon we'll have the baked bounty of his tree. And, please call me Lynn, okay?"
"Of course."
"Let's eat and talk. Surely you didn't cut class just to talk to an old lady?"
"As you say, Lynn, I'm truant. There was no other way."
"You wanted privacy, Eleanor?"
"Yes."
"Well, let me guess, Harold is in trouble again?"
"Big time."
"What's he done now?"

The words hung in the air. Mrs. Goldman was not surprised by the situation. Over four decades of marriage her husband seemed addicted to getting into trouble. She was, however, surprised that Dr. Lopez had asked to speak to her in private and in her home. No administrator had ever done that before.

"He's found a way to tick off MAG, a Heinz Variety of white nationalist groups, normative conservatives, the Board of Education, and even his friend, the Superintendent. Talk radio is abuzz with his indiscretions and the local papers are editorializing. He found a way to revive the demonstrations in front of the school. They had been on the decline."

"Harold did all that?"

"You read or heard his last lecture?"

"Not this time. I was busy quilting and listening to a British who-done-it. What did he say?"

"He criticized people who only listen to the news they want to hear. Both the left and the right took exception to that. He said people who do that are lucky; they don't have to think. Someone else does it for them."

"Harold said that?"

"There's more."

"Please."

"He said such people are into tribalism and that they are a danger to our democratic system. He all but said they weren't patriots."

"And all that brought you to my doorstep?"

"Yes. I like your husband. He's a fine teacher. I know that. I've tried to run interference for him, as have others. I'm afraid the situation is now out of hand. There's too much pressure on everyone to clean things up."

Mrs. Goldman didn't say a word. She got up and put on heavy mittens. She then went to the oven, opened it and pulled out the apricot pie. She placed it on a plastic trivet she had bought years ago in Thailand. She turned back to Dr. Lopez. She appeared to be mulling over something in her mind. Finally, she spoke.

"We'll let the pie cool. Later we'll feast. I've got some wicked vanilla ice cream in the freeze. Fortified with that we'll try to deal with Harold's sins. That's why you're here, isn't it?"

"I was hoping you could exert some influence on him. You know, get him to back off. Tone it down. Anything…"

The old guy's wife didn't answer immediately. Again, she appeared to be mulling things over. She gathered herself and spoke.

"I've lived with Harold for many years. I've got a pretty good handle on what makes him tick. Permit me to share a few things with you. First, you should know this; Harold has a crush on you. Don't be offended or blush. He'd never admit it, but I hear it in his voice. He so enjoyed having lunch with you at Brent's. You should hear the way he speaks of you. Quite simply, he sees you as the best principal he's ever worked for, and he's worked for many. There's deep respect for you. There's also affection and, if you will accept this, a sincere desire not to hurt you through his questionable actions. I mean that, and that's part of the problem he's having trouble resolving. He wants to be true to his principles, and at the same time not hurt the principal he cares about."

Seldom was Dr. Lopez at a loss for words. What Mrs. Goldman said challenged that. At last she said…

"I've come to care about him, too. "
"That's why you're here?"
"I don't know how to save him. He won't listen to me."
"Oh, he listens."
"Then?"
"He's trapped."
"Lynn, I don't understand."
"Let's have some pie and I'll tell you a story."

~

The Story

"Years ago when we were first dating I took him to see a play. I'm sure you've heard of it: *The Man of La Mancha.*"
"Of course, I've seen the movie with Peter O'Toole and Sophia Loren."

"And James Coco as the manservant, Sancho Panza."

"Such a fine actor."

"We saw the Broadway musical in Pasadena. We had wonderful tickets, fifth row and really up close. It was almost like being on stage. Harold had an aisle seat and then it happened…"

"What?"

"Don Quixote was singing *the Impossible Dream*. He was halfway through the lyrics when he sang:

*And I know if I'll only be true*
*To the glorious quest*
*That my heart will be peaceful and calm*
*When I'm laid to my rest.*

*And the world will be better for this*
*That one man, scorned and covered with scars*
*Still strove with his last ounce of courage*
*To reach the unreachable*
*The unreachable*
*The unreachable star…*

"Harold got so caught up in the moment… He rose from his seat. I'll sure he wanted to join the cast. He wanted to…

*To dream the impossible dream*
*To fight the unbeatable foe*
*To bear with unbearable sorrow*
*And to run where the brave dare not go…*

"I had to grab him by his coattails and haul him back into his seat. It took quite an effort. I've always wondered what would have happened if he had actually gone on stage. You know, he can't carry a tune if his life depended on it…"

"That's quite a story."

"Eleanor, that's who Harold is. No matter what he says, he's not a hard nosed realistic who sees the world in its starkest and darkest reality. Don't be fooled. He's a full-fledged idealist. He's appropriated Miguel de Cervantes' hero. He's been taking on windmills since he got his teaching credential and will continue to do so until the last school bell rings for him. He can't do other. When he speaks of social justice in the classroom… When he cries out against the bigotry of our times to his students…When he shouts to the high heavens racism is wrong, that's Don Quixote speaking. That's Harold, my husband."

*This is my quest*
*To follow the star*
*No matter how hopeless*
*No matter how far…*

~

The two women were eating the apricot pie with a large lump of vanilla ice cream on the side. They needed the nourishment. For her part Dr. Lopez had the feeling that another story had yet to be told.

"You must me your recipe. What wonderful crust."
"Before you leave, yes. Now, what are you going to do about Harold?"
"My masters want him out. I can't defy downtown."
"There's only a month to go. The semester is ending."
"Lynn, the pressure is intense."
"There's nothing that can be done?"
"One possibility, and I'm not sure about that."
"And that is?"
"If he could make a public statement, a bit of an apology, something that his critics might accept…"
"Something the Board might buy?"
"Yes. If you would speak to your husband…"
"I can. I will. It will not be easy. He can be a stubborn old cuss."
"Whatever you can do. It's important."
"It is, but not just for reasons you might think."
"I…"
"Eleanor, a confession is in order."

## The Confession

"My husband is dying. He has a cancer."

Two sentences and Dr. Lopez's world was thrown into turmoil. A thousand other things might have been said, but not this. An impossible question assaulted her.

"How long?"

"Three perhaps four months at the most."

"There's no hope."

"Chemo helps. The painkillers help. But, no, there's no hope."

"I noticed he was absent on Tuesday, almost every other week."

"Chemo. How he gets to school the next day, I'll never understand. He just prods along, one step after another."

"Your children know?"

"Yes."

"But not the school district?"

"Correct and we want to keep it that way."

"Lynn, what is it you want me to do?"

"Help him to finish the semester. That class and those kids mean so much to hm. He seems himself on the ramparts defending the Republic and the right of his students to think. He's fighting against censorship and all those who would dictate what a teacher will say in the classroom. He is defending freedom of choice and speech, as he understands it. He is battering against prejudice and discrimination, and all the social ills he hates. He sees himself as bloodied, but not beaten. He is in his own mind the iconic idealist in a war against evil."

"What can be done will be."

"That is all I can ask. But please, he must not know of this meeting and what you know. No one else must know, and certainly not his students. If possible, let Harold finish the school year on his own terms. That's so important to him."

"I understand."

The two women hugged before Mrs. Lopez retreated to her car. The storm was passing and sunlight filtered through the few lingering clouds. She got into her car, paused and then banged her hands against the dashboard. She found herself saying, "Dear Dr. Goldman, darn you for finding a way into my heart." She then drove back to the high school. There was unfinished work to be done. As she drove she heard the words of Don Quixote:

*And I'll always dream the impossible dream*
*Yes, and I'll reach the unreachable star...*

~

That night Lynn spoke to her husband. They talked a length.

"More nasty phone calls, Lynn?"
"Three."
"Threatening?"
"After describing you as the incarnation of sin, yes, Harold."
"Serious stuff?"
"It's hard to tell."
"How are you holding up, dear lady?"

The Old Guy's wife didn't answer his query. Instead, she shifted subjects. She suggested that he write some sort of public apology to drive the wolves away. Perhaps that would tone down the phone calls. As she expected, he resisted and then finally agreed once she pointed out the obvious. "If you care about Dr. Lopez take her out of harm's way."

~

Two days later a letter was read on talk radio. It also appeared in the local newspapers.

*To The Community,*

*I wish to apologize to the parents of my students and, of course, to my students, as well as to the community in general for anything I might have said that in some way made them feel ill at ease. That was not my intention, though in my zealousness I might have given that impression. As a history teacher it was my desire to make my classes relevant to the issues faced by our society today. One of those issues concerned racial relations. By necessity, I delved into the past to bring a degree of understanding and perspective to my students. Again, if any student or parent felt uncomfortable with this, I apologize. As to the concern about "guilt," I restate what I told my students. They are not guilty of past events in our history anymore than my grandchildren. That said I must now prepare my students for their finals and the District Exit Examination.*

*Sincerely,*
*Dr. Harold Goldman*

~

"Dr. Lopez, you read what he said?"
"Superintendent, I did."
"It was a lawyer's response."
"Hopefully, he bought some time, Sir?"

C H A P T E R 21

---

# IMPEACHMENT

<u>June – Monroe High School</u>

The old guy glanced around his classroom. What he saw was quite a spectacle, which was apart of an agreement reached with the District. Outside groups would be allowed to be present in the classroom. This was to mollify their concerns about what was going on with the old guy. in the classroom. As always, it now seemed, there would also be a District administrator in the classroom. In this case Dr. Lopez.

First, there were the five adult representatives of various activist groups: Mrs. Sylvia Jones stood in for MAG. Her credentials were in order. She was white, pro-Trump and anti-abortion on demand. A tall black man was present on behalf of FAR, Fathers Against Racism. He had voted for President Biden. A slender Asian woman, Miss Nancy Chou, represented AIR, Asians Involved in Racial Studies. An extremely handsome senior, Mr. Jose Lopez was present for HIP, Hispanics Involved in Politics. The PTA decided to sit this one out, preferring to sell cookies and drinks outside of the classroom. One should never miss a fundraiser was their motto. Two groups were not permitted to participate: Cowboys for Trump and Cowgirls for Biden.

All representatives had to meet certain decorum restrictions. Conservative dress and grooming was mandated. No buttons or placards indicating political views. No overt facial looks such as grimaces or laughter was permitted. No interference of any sort with the classroom instruction. All were reminded that the District TV camera would film everything. Violations would lead to immediate ejection.

Outside of the school enthusiastic demonstrators, relishing television time before the cameras, pranced around chanting and howling their lungs out. Most of what they said was intellectually difficult to understand, as well as tough on the ears. A careful observer of the marchers noticed numerous gestures to underscore partisan views. Naturally, there was a considerable police presence to maintain some semblance of order.

Inside the school police were stationed at every entrance, including three outside of the old guy's room. Anyone entering had to submit to a search. All briefcases and backpacks were opened and checked. This, of course, led to a question before class started.

"Dr. Goldman, did the police search your briefcase?"
"They did, Tim. You'll be delighted to know that my lunch passed inspection. The two apricots were not mini-bombs. The tuna sandwich was carefully examined. No explosive material was found. My thermo demanded scrutiny. It was determined that the chicken soup was just that."
"In other words you're not a terrorist?"
"At least my lunch isn't, Claudia."

In his downtown office the Superintendent, having heard the old guy's lunch menu voiced for the world to hear, smiled and quietly remarked to no one in particular, "Smart ass." In her seat in the back of the classroom, Dr. Lopez grinned internally, if that's possible, thinking, "You had to taunt, didn't you, you rascal?" As to his students most agreed that in retirement Dr. Goldman should take to his act to the Comedy Club in Los Angeles.

<u>Class Begins</u>

Things began innocently enough. Of course, looks can be deceiving, can't they?

"As you recall your essay is due next week. If you own a dog, please keep him away from your work. 'My German Shepard ate my essay' is no longer acceptable. Also, the double check you're up on the last reading assignments. As I'm prone to say, 'It behooves you to peruse the syllabus.' Right?"

Across the city there were many responses to the old guy's question. For example: "What the hell is a syllabus? It sounds like a social disease." Behoove… Is that a word?" Does peruse mean to use something again?" Of course, those who had attended UCLA had no problem with the terminology. They did wonder, however, if the students over a USC did. They shouldn't have worried. A slight majority did.

In her home the old guy's wife watched the biggest show in town with one of her sons. "Mom, can dad get through this?"
"Rob, he must."

Indictment of President Andrew Johnson

"Today we begin our investigation of the impeachment of President Andrew Johnson. According to our Constitution, 'the House of Representatives shall have the sole power of impeachment (Article I, section 2), and the Senate 'shall have the sole power to try all impeachments.' Article II, section 4 of the Constitution defines the grounds for impeachment and conviction of 'treason, bribery, or other high crimes and misdemeanors.' Essentially, the US Constitution states that even the highest official in the land is accountable to the people, subject to removal from office. The only penalty that can be imposed on someone who has been impeached is removal from office, or disqualification of being in a future position of office.

"It is important to note that violations of the Constitution made 'unintentionally, in good faith, and mere mistakes in the proper construction of the Constitution, do not constitute an impeachable offense. Keep all of this in mind as we proceed and later as we discuss the charges against former President Donald Trump.

"On February 24, 1868 the House of Representatives impeached Andrew Johnson by a vote of 126 to 46. Seventeen members of did not vote. Eleven Articles of Impeachment were adopted. The 11th Article was the most significant. It accused the President of violating the Tenure in Office Act. Impeachment in this case meant an indictment.

"On March 5, 1868 the trial of Andrew Johnson began in the US Senate. Salmon Chase, the Chief Justice of the Supreme Court, presided. The trial would take 3 months. Though called, the President would make no appearance. Only his attorneys would represent him in the Senate. Ultimately, there would be 25 witnesses called by the Managers (the House prosecutors) and 16 by the defense.

"Overflow crowds wanted to watch the trial from the public gallery. To deal with this a ticket system was implemented. Only 1,000 color-coded tickets were printed for each day. They permitted use for one day. Some 20 tickets were given to the President, 4 were provided to each senator and to the Chief Justice, 2 to each member of the House, and 40 to the diplomatic corps. Leftover tickets were distributed to the general public. It was, of course, the hottest ticket in town. All members of Congress received hundreds of requests each day. News coverage was mainly by press and the telegraph. There was no Internet.

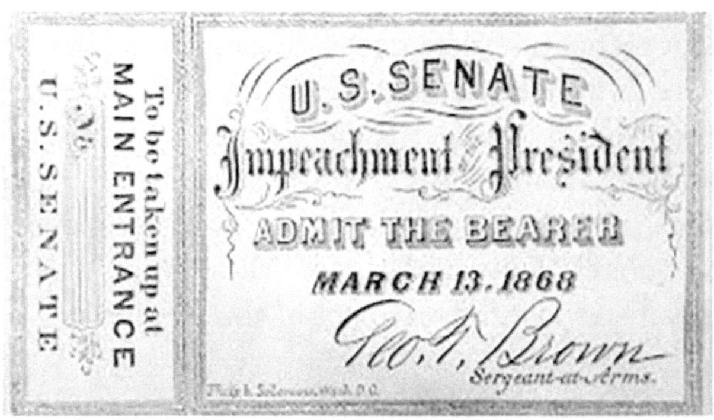

**THE TICKET**

"The improbability of the impeachment proceedings has influenced contemporary historians. As one stated:

*The ponderous two-handed engine of impeachment, designed to be kept in a cryptic darkness until some crisis of the nation's life cried out for interposition, was being dragged into open day to crush a formidable political antagonist a few months before the appointed time when the people might get rid of him altogether.*

"Cryptic darkness?"

"Juan, hidden in our constitutional toolbox is an immense power to be used only with the utmost propriety. As a society we must be cautious in removing a president. It must not be for petty charges or partisan grievances. It must avoid the appearance of a coup. The violations cited must be blatant and easily understood by the public. Fairness to the president must exceed the emotions to drive him (or her) from office. Though it lies in waiting, impeachment is a tool to be used with only the greatest discretion. That is why it slumbers in cryptic darkness."

"All that applies to Trump as well as Andrew Johnson?"

"Yes. Now, moving on…"

<u>Arguments, Pro and Con</u>

"On March 30, 1868 Benjamin Butler began stated the prosecution's case. Fifty-four senators listened to his opening arguments. Butler would speak for three hours. He delivered what some called a 'lawyer's plea with a dash of the demagogue.' He dismissed in a most contemptuous manner the defense's justification for President Johnson's view that the Tenure of Office didn't apply to Secretary Stanton. Unable to control his Radical Republican anger, Butler referred to Johnson as the 'accidental Chief.' He also called the President the 'elect of an assassin.' His disrespect seemed to have no end. In retrospect Butler was a poor choice as a Manager. Many wavering senators were put off by his disrespectful treatment of the President."

"Another Benjamin, this time Benjamin Curtis, delivered the opening argument for the defense. He was a former justice of the Supreme Court. His place in history was already marked by his dissent in the famous Dred Scott case. Curtis argued that Tenure of Office Act did not apply to Stanton. Why was this? His view was that Lincoln's term ended with his death. Johnson had not appointed Stanton and he had not succeeded in removing him from office. Furthermore, the Act was unconstitutional because it infringed upon the powers of the executive.

**BENJAMIN BUTLER    BENJAMIN CURTIS**

"Back and forth the final arguments went, April 22nd to May 6th. Legal arguments were heard. Technical issues were raised. And in far too many moments uninhibited hyperbolic language stole the day. From perhaps the most Radical Republican, Thaddeus Stevens, a torrent of anger flowed. He attacked the President as:

*… the wretched man, standing at bay, surrounded by a cordon of living men, each with he axe of an executioner uplifted for his just punishment.*

"John Bingham was also a Manager. He brought people in the galleries to their feet with his thunderous closing statement:

*May God forbid that the future historian shall record of this day's proceedings, that by reason of the failure of the legislative power of the people to triumph over the usurpations of an apostate President, the fabric of American empire fell and perished from the earth!*

"Continuing he said:

*I ask you to consider that we stand this day pleading for the violated majesty of the law, by the graves of half a million of martyred hero-patriots who made death beautiful by the sacrifice of themselves for their country, the Constitution and the laws, and who, by their sublime example taught us all to obey the law; that none are above the law…*

"William Groesbeck spoke for the President. He offered a spirited defense focusing not on the Tenure of Office Act, but rather on the President's view of Reconstruction:

*He was eager for pacification. He thought that the war was ended. It seemed so. The drums were all silent; the arsenals were all shut; the roar of the cannon had died away to the last reverberations; the army was disbanded; not a single enemy confronted us on the field.*

"Groesbeck then got to heart of the matter, President Johnson's lenient policy toward the Confederacy, especially that he was too forgiving, too kind:

*The hand of reconciliation (from the South) was stretched out to him and he took it. It may be that he should have put it away, but was it a crime to take it? Kindness, forgiveness, was it a crime? Kindness is the high statesmanship of heaven itself. The thunders of Sinai do but terrify and distract; alone they accomplish little; it is the kindness of Calvary that subdues and pacifies.*

"As to the Tenure of Office Act… William Everts' closing defense argument for President Johnson took on that issue. He said:

*They (the Radical Republicans) wish to know whether the President has betrayed our liberties or our possessions to a foreign state. They wish to know whether he has delivered up a fortress or surrendered a fleet. They wish to know whether he has made merchandise of the public trust and turned the authority to private gain. And when informed that none of these things are charges, imputed, or even declaimed about, they yet seek further information and are told that he has removed a member of his cabinet.*

"A moment... John I see your hand waving wildly. What's on your mind?"

"Two things... First, the language of the 1860's, it's so different than today. I think I'm finally catching on to it. It's so descriptive."

"That it is and it improves your vocabulary by at least 1000%. Your other point?"

"Johnson's defense... I was thinking of President Trump's impeachment. Some of Johnson's defense might have applied to his situation. Right?"

"Absolutely."

"The Johnson trial was so partisan."

"Julie, many historians would agree with you."

"Wasn't Trump's trial also partisan?"

"That argument is made and accepted by many."

"They just wanted to nail Johnson."

"Maria, that seems to be the case."

"Didn't the Democrats want to do that to Trump?"

"Again, many believe so."

"What do you think?"

"Impeachments are not ordinary trials. They're not *Law and Order* shows. They are political trials and a struggle for political power. They are a time for sharp elbows and overly zealous contentions when partisanship goes into overdrive."

"But what do you think?"

"As in any trial the defendant deserves counsel on his behalf and fairness in his peer's judgment, what we refer to as 'due process under the law.'"

"Did President Trump get that?"

"To a degree, yes. However, there are strong views in both directions, as you know. Shall we get back to the final vote?"

Three people let out their breath: Dr. Lopez, the Superintendent, and Mrs. Goldman. Had we been a bug-on-the-wall, we would have heard them say, "You conniving son-of-a-gun. You danced, sidestepped, and nuanced your way through those landmines. Thank God."

## The Vote

"Outwardly the Radical Republicans were confident. They believed the "great obstruction" was about to be removed. Inwardly, they were less optimistic. There were four or five undecided senators. One of them was Edmund G. Ross. They were spoken of as 'the recusants." One of them, James Grimes of Iowa, later said of his dissenting vote:

*I cannot agree to destroy the harmonious working of the Constitution for the sake of getting ride of an unacceptable President.*

"These senators were subjected to intense pressure. In his book *Profiles in Courage*, another slain president, John F. Kennedy, alluded to the pressure:

*Ross and his fellow doubtful Republicans were daily pestered, spied upon, and subjected to every form of pressure. Their residences were carefully watched, their social circles suspiciously scrutinized, and their every move and companions marked in special notebooks.*

*They were warned in the party press, harangued by their constituents, and sent dire warnings threatening political ostracism and even assassination. The Philadelphia Press reported 'a fearful avalanche of telegrams from every section of the country,' a great surge of public opinion from the 'common people' who had given their money and lives to the country and would not 'willingly or unavenged see their great sacrifice made naught.'"*

"*The New York Times* reported that Ross in particular was:

*… mercilessly dragged this way and that by both sides, hunted like a fox night and day and badgered by his own colleagues… His background and life were investigated from top to bottom, and his constituents*

*and colleagues pursued him throughout Washington to gain some inkling of his opinion. He was the target of every eye, his name was on every mouth and his intentions were discussed in every newspaper.*

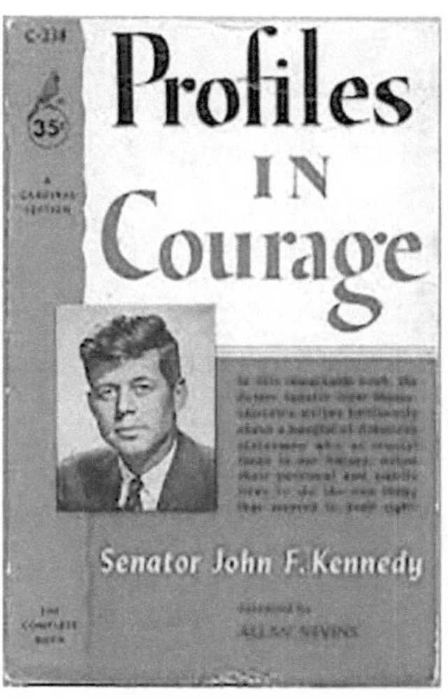


Their votes were needed. The impeachment math demanded that. There were 27 states represented in the Senate. That meant a total of 54 senators. Twelve of the senators were Democrats. Forty-two were Republicans. A two-thirds majority was needed for conviction. A 36 to 18 vote was needed. Anything less and the President would be acquitted. One thing was for sure; they would get no votes from the Democrats who leaned toward Johnson's approach to the Confederacy.

"An unexpected problem arose for the Radical Republicans. Who would take over if Johnson lost? There was no sitting Vice-President. The next in line would be Senator Benjamin Wade of Ohio, who was the president pro tempore of the Senate. This is, of course, the co-author of the Wade-Davis bill President Lincoln had pocket-vetoed. For many moderates in the party his stance on Reconstruction was too harsh. As an advocate for women's suffrage he was far ahead of many. Also, he favored soft-money (low interest rates) and was pro-labor to the distress of Northern businessmen. Wade put off any number of moderate Republicans who saw in General Grant as their best candidate in the upcoming 1868 presidential election. Living with Johnson a little longer might be acceptable.

On May 16, 1868 --- at noon --- Chief Justice Chase called the Senate to order. The galleries were packed. All members of the House were present.

Thousands lingered in the hallways or waited outside. Down the street thousands more waited in small groups. Every body waited for the vote.

A motion was made and adopted to vote on the eleventh article of impeachment. The Chief Justice said, "Call the roll." This was done. In time it became apparent that Ross' vote would be necessary to impeach the President of the United States.

## Ross' Decision

"Mr. Senator Ross, how say you?"

All previous senators had been asked the same question. A deafening silence existed.

"Is the respondent, Andrew Johnson, guilty or not guilty of high misdemeanor as charged in this article?"

"According to the records the Chief Justice bent forward, anxiety on his face. All the seated senators fixed their gaze on Ross. The public strained to see him, looking for some sign as how he would vote. It was as if people were listening to the "crack of doom.' And then the answer came, 'full, distinct, definite unhesitating and unmistakable:" 'Not Guilty.' Others heard the words and thought Ross had hesitated and was nervous.

The vote was 35 to 19. The President was saved. One observer of the moment said:

*The words swept over the assembly, and, as one man, the hearers flung themselves back into their seats; the strain snapped; the contest ended; impeachment was blown into the air."*

In 1892, long after the vote, Ross gave an interview to *Scribner's*. He relived the moment:

*Conscious that I was at that moment the focus of all eyes, and conscious also of the far-reaching effect, especially upon myself, of the vote I was about to give, it is something more than a simile to say that I almost literally looked down into my open grave. Friends, position, fortune, everything that makes life desirable to an ambitious man were about to be swept away by the breath of my mouth, perhaps forever."*

## The Students

"Dr. Goldman, that's quite a story."
"Richard, yes it is."
"My emotions are up in the air."
"Cindy?"
"I've never though a politician could be so brave. The country was lucky to have Ross."
"I feel the same way."
"Jake?"
"That guy Ross really had courage."

~

Time was fleeting and class was about over. The old guy needed to pull the loose ends together.

"I must admit to you that going against the current is never an easy things to do. You have lots of examples in American history of men and women who defied public opinion and stood by their principles. Ross, because of his vote, stands out. But he's not alone. Don't forget there were five other senators who stood with him. Now, as to your emotions, I have a suggestion. Write down how you feel and when we meet again I'd like you to form groups and discuss those feelings. No grade is involved. How could there be? There isn't a right answer.

The room was soon empty. The alphabetic groups of demanding adults dispersed, their views and feelings hidden away. In fairness to them, they had displayed extraordinary discipline. No one had gotten out of hand. The District TV camera was rolled out of the room to be used another day. The police officers waved goodbye and headed elsewhere. The old guy remained. He felt a hundred years old. He reached into his briefcase and pulled out two uneaten apricots. A moment later, having dried her eyes and gained some comportment, Dr. Lopez wandered over to Dr. Goldman.

"Harold, you did fine."
"Eleanor, would you like an apricot?"

# CHAPTER 22

# AFTERMATH

<u>June – Zooming Again</u>

It was almost 8:00 pm in the morning and already a bright, shining sun was hovering over the San Fernando Valley. Summer had arrived and it was going to be a triple digit day. The old guy sat before his computer at home. He hadn't felt like going to his classroom today. Fortunately it was a zoom day. He had earlier told his wife, "I'm feeling a little under the weather. Glad I'm zooming." She had nodded, saying, "I bring you some ice tea and a muffin. You can munch while you hold forth. Wasn't it nice that Dr. Lopez and your students agreed to this Saturday session?"

Earlier in the week the old guy had confessed to his boss that he was a bit fatigued, that his workload had knocked the stuffing out of him. Reading between the lines Dr. Lopez surmised the chemo treatments were behind his confession. Of course, she never acknowledged that point. Searching for a way to assist him, Dr. Lopez had suggested the early morning weekend meeting. The students, once they were given some inane bureaucratic explanation, went along with the deception. That's how he old guy ended up in his study. He gathered himself, clicked on his computer, plugged in the zooming coordinates, and said to the twenty some faces on the screen, "Good morning. Today we will deal with the aftermath of Ross' vote. Hang on to your remotes."

<u>William Cook Remembers</u>

Cook was the President Johnson's private bodyguard and a personal aide. He witnessed Ross' decisive vote. He heard the wild applause by many in the galleries, and the groans and anger of the disappointed Radicals in the Senate. Cook ran all the way to the Capitol to the White House. He was, as he later said, "young and strong in those days, and I made good time." He burst into the library. The President was seated with Secretary of the Navy, Gideon Welles and two other men. They were seated at a little table on which lunch had been served. Cook shouted, "You are acquitted!"

Along with others Cook shook the President's hand. Then…

*The President responded to their congratulations calmly enough for a moment, and then I saw that tears were rolling down his face. I stared at him; and yet I felt I ought to turn my eyes away. In a few minutes came a message of congratulation from Secretary Seward to "my dear friend." By that time the room was full of people, and I slipped away.*

<u>As for Ross</u>

After the vote Ross received a telegram from LD Bailey. He was a Kansas Supreme Court Justice. The telegram said: "The rope with which Judas Iscariot hanged himself is lost, but Jim Lane's pistol is at your service." Jim Lane was Ross' predecessor. He had committed suicide, thereby opening up his Senate seat for Ross.

A Kansas newspaper editorialized how a majority of Kansans felt about Ross' vote:

*On Saturday last Edmund G. Ross, United States Senator from Kansas, sold himself, and betrayed his constituents; stultified his own record, basely lied to his friends, shamefully violated his solemn pledge and to the utmost of his poor ability signed the death warrant of his country's liberty. This act was done deliberately, because the traitor, like Benedict Arnold, loved money better than he did principle, friends, honor, and his country, all combined*

The *New York Times* said Ross was nothing but "a miserable poltroon and traitor." *The Philadelphia Press* said that Ross and his fellow recalcitrant Republicans had "plunged from a precipice of fame into the groveling depths of infamy and death." Not to be out done, *The Philadelphia Inquirer* said of Ross and the others, "They had tried, convicted and sentenced themselves. For them there could be no allowance, no clemency."

Newspapers compared Ross to Benedict Arnold, Jefferson Davis, and Judas. Perhaps worst than that Ross, many argued, had sold his vote to gain wealth and control of patronage in Kansas. Patronage referred to the ability to appoint friends to various government posts in exchange for their support on some future day. Those charges stung Ross. In response he attacked his accusers and charged them with "orchestrating the whole impeachment campaign so as to get their hands on the controls of patronage." And so it went, charge and countercharges. Overtime various investigations found no evidence that Ross had been bribed for his vote.

In the midst of this torrent of criticism Ross wrote to his wife, pointing out:

*This storm of passion will soon pass away, and the people, the whole people, will thank and bless me for having saved the country by my single vote from the greatest peril through which it has ever passed, though none but God can ever know the struggle it has cost me.*

In 1955 Senator John F. Kennedy said this of Ross in his book, *Profiles in Courage:*

*In a lonely grave, forgotten and unknown, lies the man who saved a President, and who as a result may well have preserved for ourselves and our posterity constitutional government in the United States. By the firmness and courage of Senator Ross the country was saved from calamity greater than war, while it consigned him to a political martyrdom, the most cruel in our history.*

Kennedy went on to say:

*Ross was the victim of a wild flame of intolerance, which swept everything before it. He did his duty knowing that it meant his* *political death... **It** was a brave thing for Ross to do, but Ross did it. He acted for his conscience and with a lofty patriotism regardless of what he knew must be the ruinous consequence... He acted right.*

In retrospect Ross' vote was predictable. Before the trial began Ross spoke to another Senator. He wanted the President to have a fair trial. He said:

*The thing is here, and so far as I concerned, through a Republican and opposed to Mr. Johnson and his policy, he shall have as fair a trial as an accused man ever had on this earth.*

Certainly, Ross gave some indication of how he would vote. On the night before the Senate was to take its first vote for the conviction or acquittal of the President, Ross received a telegram from his constituents. It read: "Kansas has heard the evidence and demands the conviction of the President." The telegram was signed, DR Anthony and 1,000 others. The next day Ross replied:

*I do not recognize your right to demand that I vote either for or against conviction. I have taken an oath to do impartial justice according to the Constitution and laws, and trust that I shall have the courage to vote according to the dictates of my judgment and for the highest good of the country.*

It is fair to ask, what was Ross really afraid of? His reasoning, I think, went along these lines. If a president could be forced out of office by questionable, if no insufficient evidence, that was based on partisan disagreements, the presidency would then be under the control of any congressional faction in power. The delicate balance between the legislative and the judicial branches would be upset. Constitutional law would be jeopardized by temporary emotions and vicious judgments. Ross wanted to avoid that.

Senator Lyman Trumbull of Illinois reached the same conclusion as Ross to justify his vote to acquit. He said: "The main source of the president's political power --- the freedom to disagree with the

Congress without consequences --- would have been destroyed, and the Constitution system of checks and balances along with it."

Ross' action led to relentless criticism. Neither he nor any other Republican who voted to acquit President Johnson was ever reelected to the Senate. Ross and his family were ostracized in Kansas. The family faced poverty on their return to the state in 1871. Threats were made against Ross and his children. His business was burned to the ground.

"It doesn't seem like Johnson got a fair trial, isn't that so, Dr. Goldman?"

"Marsha, many people reached that conclusion based on the following:

- Evidence to support the President was arbitrarily excluded.
- Evidence existed that Senators had prejudged the President.
- Evidence exists that bribes were handed out to win votes.
- Tremendous public pressure was placed on Senators.
- Partisanship preempted a fair hearing.
- The Northern press was hostile to the President.

"Did some of these factors play a role in the impeachment of President Trump?"

"Good question, Sandra. With the exception of bribes, all of these factors were involved to one degree or another, as they were in the effort to impeach another president, Bill Clinton years before Trump. In other words it's difficult to hold a fair and impartial impeachment proceeding. Does that help?"

"I think so."

"Good, let's move on then."

Atonement

In 1926 a case came before the US Supreme Court. In *Myers v. United States* the Court affirmed the ability of the president to remove a postmaster without congressional approval. In a majority opinion the Court ruled that the Tenure of Office Act of 1867 was invalid.

This decision supported President Johnson's contention that he was entitled to replace Secretary Stanton without congressional approval.

Following Ross' death in 1907 F.H. Hodder, of the University of Kansas, wrote in the *Nation Magazine*:

*No man was ever more foully abused... If the people of Kansas wish to atone for the injury they did Mr. Ross during his lifetime they can scarcely do better than place his statue in the capitol at Washington, in the hall reserved for notable men of the states. Such a statue would commemorate a heroic act, a valiant soldier, and an honest man.*

William Carruth, who was also from the University of Kansas said:

*It goes hard with us to admit that he was wiser than the majority of us... Major Ross returned to his state, faced obloquy and slander, and earned the living of a poor but honest man, with the same silent endurance with which he met the stress of the great impeachment trial.*

In 1910 the Secretary of the Kansas State Board of Agriculture said this:

*For the vote cast by Senator Ross against the conviction of President Andrew Johnson, I was at the time bitter and indignant beyond expression. Now, forty-odd years later after, I am firmly of the opinion that Senator Ross acted with a lofty patriotism, regardless of what he knew must be ruinous consequences to himself.*

One of those consequences would have been his death. As Ross said later:

*I was aware at the time that I stood in personal danger... I was given a friendly intimation I stood in danger of assassination. One man voluntarily acknowledged to me after the trail that he had been connected with a plot to kidnap and take me to New York City.*

As with the others who voted to acquit the President, Ross found the courage to do as his conscience directed.

**ROSS OF KANSAS**

We must not forget the other Republicans who voted for acquittal. As Kennedy wrote of them:

*Not a single one of them ever won reelection to the Senate. Not a single one of them escaped the unholy combination of threats, bribes, and coercive tactics by which their fellow Republicans attempted to intimidate their votes, and not a single one of them escaped the terrible torture of vicious criticism engendered by the vote to acquit.*

## The Others

William Pitt Fessenden was from Maine. He was the first Republican to acquit the President. In explaining his vote he said:

*The public, when aroused and excited by passion and prejudice, is little better than a wild beast. I shall at all events retrain my own self-respect and a clear conscience, and time will do justice to my motives at least.*

He also said:

*I wish all my friends and constituents to understand that I, not they, am sitting in judgment upon the President. I, not they, have sworn to do impartial justice. I, not they, am responsible to God and man for my action and its consequences.*

**FESSENDEN OF MAINE**

Fessenden died on December 8, 1869 while still serving in the Senate. He was 62-years old. He rests in the Evergreen Cemetery in Portland, Maine.

John B. Henderson was from Missouri. He was one of the youngest members of the Senate. Though he was from a former slave state he showed political courage by introducing the Thirteenth Amendment to end slavery in the United States. Apparently, he made quiet efforts to avoid voting for or against Johnson. He considered resigning to appease his critics. That didn't work. There was a question as to whether or not a new senator from the state would be seated. After receiving an "insolent and threatening telegram" from Missouri, he found the courage and his sense of honor. He responded:

*Say to my friends that I am sworn to do impartial justice according to law and conscience, and I will try to do I like an honest man.*

Henderson died on April 12, 1913. He was 86 years old. He is buried in Green-Wood Cemetery in Brooklyn, New York.

**HENDERSON OF MISSOURI**

Peter Van Winkle was from West Virginia. Once Virginia left the Union, he help to found the State of West Virginia. He was elected the state's first United States Senator. After his vote the *Wheeling Intelligencer* declared "that there was not a loyal citizen of the state who had not been misrepresented by his vote."

**VON WINKLE OF WEST VIRGINIA**

Van Winkle died on April 15. 1872. He was 63 years old. He was buried in the River View Cemetery in Parkersburg, West Virginia.

Lyman Trumbull of Illinois had impeccable Republican Party qualifications. He had drafted a great deal of the major Reconstruction legislation, much of which President Johnson vetoed. Upon Stanton's removal, he had joined in censoring the President. No one expected him to protect Johnson. However, in his own words he explained his decision:

*Once set, the example of impeaching a President for what, when the excitement of the House shall have subsided, will be regarded as sufficient cause, no future President will be safe who happens to differ with a majority of the House and two-thirds of the Senate on any measure deemed by them important. What then becomes of the checks and balances of the Constitution so carefully devised and so vital to its perpetuity? They are all gone. I cannot be an instrument to produce such a result.*

For taking this position he was warned not to show himself on the streets of Chicago since there were some who would hang him from the nearest lamppost.

**TRUMBULL OF ILLINOIS**

Trumbull died on June 25, 1896. He was 82-years old. He is at rest in the Oakwood Cemetery in Chicago, Illinois.

Joseph Smith Fowler was from Tennessee and a former Nashville mathematics professor at Franklin College. His first inclination was to convict the President. In time he saw that the evidence against Johnson was "corrupt and dishonorable." He came to see Benjamin Butler as"

*... a wicked man who seeks to convert the Senate of the United States into a political guillotine.*

When he voted on May 16th he was extremely nervous. His voice faltered as he spoke. Many thought that he had said "guilty" and believed that Johnson was convicted. But then he answered again, clear and distinct: " Not Guilty." Later he defended his vote in a single statement: "I acted for my country and posterity in obedience to the will of God."

**FOWLER OF TENNESSEE**

Fowler died on April 1, 1902. He was 81 years old. He is buried in the Lexington Cemetery in Lexington, Kentucky.

James W. Grimes represented Iowa. He had been one of Johnson's bitterest critics in the Senate. In time he came to believe that the trial was intended to create "public passions through lies." Heaped upon him was unfair abuse and serious threats. He suffered a stroke two days before the vote to convict or exonerate. Paralysis set in. His doctor confined him to bed. Sadly, the Radical Republicans were overjoyed. A vote for Johnson, they thought, was stricken. They believed his illness would prevent him from voting. According to the records, in the galleries people sang: "Old Grimes is dead, that bad old man, we ne'er shall see him more." Grimes, however, fooled everyone. Four men carried the "pale and withered Senator to his seat. When it came time for Grimes to vote, the Chief Justice said he could remain seated. With the assistance of his friends, he struggled to his feet and "in a surprisingly firm voice called out, "Not guilty."

That "old man" left the country with a message that still rings true today:

*I became a judge acting on my own responsibility and accountable only to my own conscience and my Maker; and no power could force me to decide on such a case contrary to my convictions, whether that party was composed of my friends or my enemies.*

Grimes died on February 7, 1872. He was 55 years old. He is buried in the Aspen Grove Cemetery in Burlington, New Hampshire.

The focus of 1868 was President Andrew Johnson. He died on July 31, 1875. He was 66 years old. He was buried in the Andrew Johnson National Cemetery in Greenville, Tennessee. His body was draped in an American flag. A copy of the US Constitution was placed under his head according to his wishes.

**JOHNSON OF TENNESSEE**

As for Edmund G. Ross… He died on May 8, 1907. He was 81 years old. He was buried in Fairview Memorial Park Cemetery in Albuquerque, New Mexico.

~

The class came to an end. Happily, the old guy disconnected himself from the zoom world and the miracle of the Internet. Unlike the physical classroom where he drew energy from the interaction with students, zooming left him exhausted. Today, more so than in the past … Fortunately, the next class session would be at the school and that he looked forward to with joy. The school year was coming to a close, as was his life as a teacher. Retirement beckoned, but not before the Election of 1876 and the impeachment trial of former-President Donald Trump. Those topics would be his last farewell to those great kids he now considered family. And then it would be over. He would have served some purpose, altogether beyond his understanding.

# CHAPTER 23

# THE DISPUTED ELECTION

<u>June – Back in School</u>

"It's so good to see all of you in person. Today we have three goals: first, I need to collect your term essays on race; second, don't forget to pick up your last prep test for the final. I'm happy to again say you are all doing well. Third, we're going to discuss a disputed election.

"President Trump's impeachment?"

"That will be next week. So will the demonstrators, big time. Today, however, we will visit 1876 and possibly, as many historians have concluded, the most consequential election in American history when it comes to race relations."

The old guy felt good being back in the classroom. There was no doubt about that. His students seemed to reflect that feeling too. Even Dr. Lopez, sill sitting in her unobtrusive back seat, had a glimmer of a smile today. That the television cameras were strangely absent, as were the various activist groups, seemed to calm things down.

"Where's the TV bit today, Dr. Goldman?"

"Evelyn, I haven't the slightest. I guess the Election of 1876 wasn't catchy enough for the networks. But don't worry they're be here next week. The whole country, I think, will want to be in on our study of Congress' attempt to impeach Donald Trump. So dress sharply and groom accordingly. Who knows, perhaps there's a Hollywood-type looking for new talent."

"Before we get started, a question, Dr. Goldman. The class elected me to ask it."

"Okay, Thomas, but before you ask, I only accept bribes in non-traceable currency. Let me know if you want my secret Swiss bank account number."

"Is there a minimum amount necessary?"

"I'll bring copies of my sliding bribery scale next week. Okay?"

The class, certainly as one would expect, grinned and laughed. Even Dr. Lopez found herself chuckling. It was nice, she thought, to see the stress barometer falling for once. Of course, she knew it was only a temporary reprieve.

"Your question, Thomas?"

"Does the school district want to fire you?"

Talk about a shot across the bow.

"No, Thomas, not to my knowledge."

"What about some of the parent groups?"

"Some, I expect."

"Why?"

Bingo, another volley.

"Lot's of reasons, I guess. What do you think?"

"Because you raise issues and cover things others don't like?"

"Question or declaration?"

"Statement of fact."

Dr. Lopez was no longer chuckling.

"Some people think I'm indoctrinating you."

"That's a lot of hooey."

"Hooey, Susan?"

"You know, silly or nonsense. You always tell us to double-check everything you say. You know, jump on the Internet and get lots of opinions. That's not indoctrination, isn't that so?

"I certainly hope so."

"Some of the parents feel you're trying to make us feel guilty about what happened to the slaves, and to blacks since the Civil War?"

"Again, Charles, what do you think?"

"Hooey, lots of it."

At that everyone laughed.

"Any other questions?"

"I have one."

"Tim…"

"We heard you got into a brawl with a parent in the parking lot."

"I would describe it as a heated discussion."

"Tell us."

What could the old guy do? He checked Dr. Lopez. Her face radiated with curiosity.

~

"I was trying to get to my VW van of many years. This escapee from rational thinking was all over me; he was uncouth. He was using vulgar language, He smelled like last year's salmon. I tried to remain calm, you know, above it. I'm afraid I wasn't successful. I retorted."

"What did you say?"

"Claudia, I fell back on my Shakespeare."

"Shakespeare!"

"I quoted the good bard, *All's Well That Ends Well*" (Act 3, Scene 6). I called him:

*A most notable coward, an infinite and needless liar, an hourly promise breaker, the owner of no one good quality.*

My words fell on deaf ears, so I tried again. I quoted *A Midsummer Night's Dream*" (Act 2, Scene 1)

*I am sick when I look on thee.*

That came closer to his questionable intellect. That being the case I reared back and threw a last bolt. I quoted from *The Taming of the Shrew*." (Act 4, Scene 1)

*Away, you three-inch fool!*

"What did he do?"

"Miguel, he was stupefied, transfixed in place, an immovable blob, an ignoramus cluttering up humanity with a pea-size brain."

"You said those things?"

"And you are sworn to secrecy, young man."

"What happened next?"

"I left, enjoying as I did, my literary prowess."

"Where did you learn all those insults?"

"Phillip, it pays to have a wife who taught Shakespeare."

Dr. Lopez could hardly constrain herself. Where, she thought, have I hidden my complete works of the bard?

**WILLIAM SHAKESPEARE**

~

"Before you start, Dr. Goldman... Why did you give us the names of all those gravesites?"

"Gravesites?"

"You know, where Ross and others are buried."

"Marcus, when I travel I stop at a cemetery where someone of note is buried. I pause and consider his (or her) life. It sort of keeps me connected with the past and helps me to deal with the present. I did that with President Johnson, and, of course, Abraham Lincoln. Perhaps you'll consider do so yourself. Just don't tell all your friends. They might consider that ghoulish. Now on to 1876."

~

Lecture – The Results

"I will depart from our usual methodology. Today we start at the end and work our way back to the beginning. The year is 1876. Voting was over. The results were in for the presidential election. Victory required 185 electoral votes. Samuel Tilden was one shy.

Samuel Tilden (D)  184 Electoral Votes
Rutherford Hayes (R)  165 Electoral Votes

Tilden  4,300,500 Popular Votes
Hayes  4,036,298 Popular Votes

"The obvious winner was Tilden. But not so fast… It turns out the results in four states were open to question: Florida (4 votes), Louisiana (8 votes), South Carolina (7 votes), and Oregon (1). The tallies were close and there were claims that the results were tainted by fraud and intimidation by both parties. And, I should add, bribery. Now, get this. If all disputed votes went to Hayes, he would win the election, 185 to 184. Of course, to arrive at that count the disputes would have to be settled and the Democrats would have to give ground. And that's what happened. Hopefully, you're asking yourself how did this occur and what did it mean for the country? As you consider these questions recall our recent presidential election. So close… So disputed… Accusations flying fast and furious… People still upset… People challenging the results… Conspiracy theories blooming… Well, all of that happened in 1876.

**HAYES**          **TILDEN**

"Congress had a problem. How would it determine the winner? The Constitution didn't help. Nothing in it about this sort of problem… Plus, the Democrats controlled the House and the Republicans reigned in the Senate. It was divided government. The Congress was flying blind; something had to be done. On January 29, 1877, President Grant signed the Electoral Commission Act. It set up a 15-member commission composed of eight Republicans and seven Democrats to settle the disputed results. Essentially, he was asking the commission to reach a political decision as to who won the election.

"At 4:10 am on March 2, 1877 the winner was announced. Hayes was declared the winner. It had taken a stormy eighteen-hour session to reach this outcome. The Democrats went along with this decision with various degrees of support even though their man won the popular vote. That should raise a question. Why did they go along?

"A backroom deal was cut. The Democratic Party at that time was sectional. The Northern wing had supported the Union and the end of slavery. The Southern wing, once the war was over, wanted to restore political power to whites. Southern whites had to live with Thirteenth Amendment ending slavery, and with the Fourteenth that defined citizenship and due process, but they could not easily accept the Fifteenth giving all citizens the vote. To avoid threatened violence, possibly a mini-civil war, the Democratic Party went along with the final deal.

"Historians characterize the resolution of the crisis as the Compromise of 1877. The key to the deal was the removal of all remaining US military forces from the former Confederate States, which, as you might have guessed, included Louisiana, South Carolina, and Florida. What did that mean? Federal troops would no longer protect Republicans elected in those states. Nor would blacks that won elections be safe. Without the military to protect them, blacks would be at the mercy of states controlled by whites. They would also be subject to violence from the KKK and other extra-legal groups who wanted the black vote suppressed, along with black businesses and mostly small farms. The Southern wing of the Democratic Party supported this deal, since it meant the party would regain control from the Republicans. It was the beginning of what would soon be called the 'Solid South" and white supremacy. With little to prevent them, the Southern states would initiate Jim Crow laws. Again, these laws led to segregation in public facilities and housing, and in discrimination in every possible aspect of daily life. More to the point, by 1900 the black vote in the South was essentially eliminated. Black office holders were out. It would not be until the Civil Rights Bill of 1965 and the Voting Rights Bill of the same year were passed that black voters returned haltingly to the ballot box. Another President Johnson was involved in encouraging this. His name was Lyndon B. Johnson.

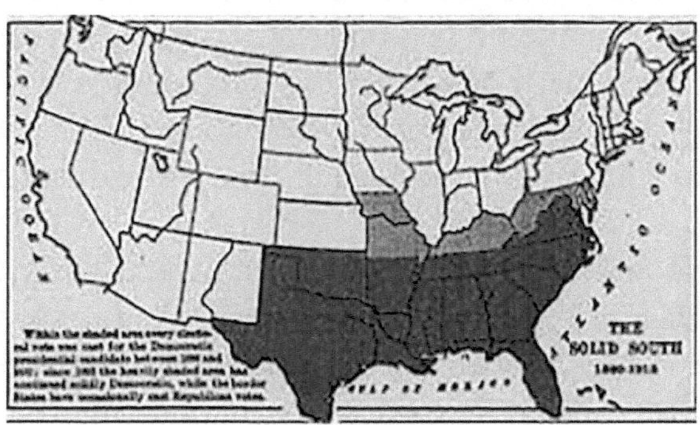

**THE SOLID SOUTH**

"The first act of Hayes' administration was to remove the federal troops. 'Home rule,' as it was called was restored. Federal troops would no longer interfere in Southern politics. Though the Southern

Democrats agreed to protect the freedmen, election-related violence increased, and over 3,000 blacks were lynched during the next four decades. There would be little Northern interference. As an aside, even today there is no federal law outlawing lynching in the United States.

"A second part of the deal was the appointment of a Southern Democrat to the Cabinet. This was done. David M. Key of Tennessee was appointed Postmaster General. At first glance, this seemed like an insignificant position. It was far from that. With post offices in every city, town, and hamlet, patronage ruled. Key could place his supporters throughout the South.

"Two other parts of the deal never came to pass. The construction of another transcontinental railroad through the South was desired. It was never built. Federal legislation to industrialize the former Confederacy through internal improvement (read that as infrastructure) was a promise not kept."

"Questions?"

"After all the bloodshed of the Civil War, why did the North accept this agreement?"

"Monica, a few reasons. First, the public did not want the country again divided by violence. Second, the Republican Party wanted to stay in power in the North and continue to reign in the White House. Third, it is difficult to maintain a crusade. The Civil War was over. Slavery was no more. The three key amendments had become law. The country wanted move on. The same thing happened to President Woodrow Wilson after World War I. The crusade to "make the world safe for democracy' was over. The battle over the League of Nations was done. The country wanted to return to 'normalcy. It did so under President Warren Harding. The same challenges faced the civil rights movement of the 1960's. It too had a short span. That may also be true of the 'Black Lives Matter.' Only time will tell."

"As I see it, the blacks got the raw end of this deal. Am I right, Dr. Goldman?

"Hal, no question about it. Many blacks then, if not now, feel that the former slave was betrayed by the demand for white supremacy in the South, and Republican political control in the North. It's still an issue we're working out today."

"It would be nice to rewrite history."

"To create a better ending, Ellen?"

"Yes."

"Historians do that to a degree. They can't change the facts, nor can they alter what happened. They try to understand and explain from different perspectives. We sometimes refer to them as revisionists. There is, of course, a danger in all of this. It is always a challenge to superimpose your values on an earlier generation. Equally so, danger lurks in trying to make the facts fit to what is pleasing to you. Recall, if you will, that the North called the conflict, the Civil War. Many in the South referred to it as the War of Northern Aggression. Having said that, recall what Napoleon said about history. 'It is the story the winners tell.'"

"Is that why people disagree about the attack on the Capitol?"

"Drew, to a degree, yes. But remember that, whatever your view is, most probably we're too close to the event to have perspective and a greater degree of objectivity."

"Is there anything true in history?"

"The facts possibly…"

"What if people disagree on the facts?"

"Then we have a problem."

～

"It was time to end the class. The old guy passed out a two-page article. He said, 'Read this. It is, I think, one of the best speeches in American history, yet unknown by most citizens. We'll review when next we zoom."

The students departed and, as was now her ritual, Dr. Lopez strolled over to the old guy. Once at his desk, she said, "Do I get a copy?"

～

## Zooming – The Speech

Rutherford Hayes toured the South in September 1877. He was not yet installed as President. He made numerous speeches in which he announced his plans to end the federal policy of Reconstruction. That meant he would remove the last Union forces in Louisiana, South Carolina, and Florida. He wanted to end the post-war iniquities of he North continuing to dominate the South politically. He also hoped that Southern whites would stop using violence and intimidation to deny blacks their constitutional rights. He wanted to unite the nation by bringing together Northerners and Southerners, Democrats and Republicans, and blacks and whites. On September 24, 1877 he delivered a speech in Atlanta, Georgia that expressed these themes.

He first talked about slavery.

*What is there to separate us longer? Without any fault of yours or any fault of mine, or of any one of this great audience slavery existed in this country. The colored man was here, not by his voluntary action. I think it is fair to say that it was by the crime of our fathers that he was here.*

Hayes next pointed out what the country had been through.

*Both sides found in the Bible confirmation of their opinions, and both sides finally undertook to settle the question by that last final means of arbitration --- force of arms.*

He then asked the question of the hour.

*Now, shall we quit fighting? Is there any reason, then, why we should not be a peace forevermore? We are embarked upon the same voyage, upon the same ship, under the same old flag. Good fortune or ill fortune affects you and your children as well as my people and my children.*

The future president then stated his philosophy of government and the hopes he had for the country.

*I believe it is the duty of the general government to regard equally and alike the interests and rights of all sections of the country. I am glad you agree with me about that. I believe further, that is the duty of the government to regard like and equally the rights and interests of all classes of citizens. That covers the whole matter. Let us wipe out in our politics the color line forever.*

Hayes then stated the problem still haunting the country.

*What troubles the people at the North, what has troubled them, was that they feared that these colored people, who had been made freemen by the war, would not be safe in their rights and interests in the South unless is was by the interference of the federal government. After thinking over it, I believe that your (Black's) rights and interests would be safer if this great mass of intelligent white men were let alone by the general government.*

Perhaps naively Hayes ended his speech with a fervent call to unity, and to what President Lincoln had called, "the better angels of our nature."

*Now let us come together. Let each man make up his mind to be a patriot in his own home and place. You may quarrel about the tariff, get up a sharp contest about the currency, about the removal of state capitals and where they shall go to, but upon the great question of the Union of the states and the rights of all the citizens, we shall agree forevermore.*

<u>Dr. Goldman's added note:</u>

Hayes' speech was of import years ago. It still has significance in our own time. Partisan differences abound.

That we accept. However, differences that destroy the fabric and unity of our society and endanger our constitutional form of government, that, I believe, we should never accept. Keep that in mind when we consider the impeachment of Donald Trump when next we meet.

# CHAPTER 24

# TRUMP

<u>June – Back in the Classroom</u>

"As I say your essays were great. My comments, you will find, should be viewed in a favorable light. You should know that copies of your work were made for Dr. Lopez and the Superintendent. They are also available for viewing online. They did not include my comments or any grade mark. Also, your names have been blocked out. I'm sure you'll have no trouble recognizing your own work."

The old guy had joyfully passed back the essays. As he did so he observed that again representatives of different community groups were seated in the back row, along with Dr. Lopez. The television cameras were once more lit up for the expected action. Outside of the room, he knew, were two husky District police officers. There was also one officer in the room. On the street in front of the school demonstrators were, as they say, demonstrating. The old guy had driven through their gauntlet of placards and chants, and various gestures that would put a Navy semaphore signalman to shame. At home his wife would be listening, as well as a highly polarized country. He knew that. The students knew that and from their sharp outfits and exquisite grooming they were prepared for television exposure. Of course, the old guy wasn't prepared for what happened next.

"Dr. Goldman, were our essays copied as part of a deal with the District to keep you as our teacher?
"Philip, it seemed prudent to do so."
"You were under the gun?"
"Some things we must accept in life."

"You're hedging."
"I'm mindful that many things are in play today."

After almost twenty weeks with Dr. Goldman his students knew pretty well how to read him. Much like a radar station little got by them.

"I think we should begin. Today we will take a hard look at what led to the impeachment proceeding against former-president, Donald Trump. At our next meeting we will delve into the Senate trial. Recognizing as we do the controversies swirling around these topics, we will try to focus on factual information that seem beyond question."

**PRESIDENT TRUMP**

## The Facts

"On January 3, 2021 the House impeached the 45th President of the United States. This fourth impeachment of an American president occurred on the week before Trump's term of office expired. It was the second effort to impeach this president. The first failed. In its second effort the 117th Congress adopted one article of impeachment against the President. He was impeached 'for incitement of insurrection.' It was argued that he had 'incited the January 6th attack on the US Capitol in order to overturn the 2020 presidential election.' Again, it was argued that the President:

*Made willful statements that encouraged and foreseeably resulted in imminent lawless acts at the Capitol.*

"The House contention was that the President's statements on social media pushed a voter fraud conspiracy that led to a mob unlawfully breaching the Capitol and engaging in 'violent, deadly, destructive, and seditious acts.'"

"Was this a coup, Dr. Goldman, the rioting? Some people call it that, isn't that so?"

"Monica, here our choice of words becomes difficult. Yes, some call it a coup. Others describe it as sedition. Many consider what took place as domestic terrorism. A good many people prefer the words rally or protest."

"What do you think?"

"All these words convey various ways of looking at what happened. Words are chosen to support points of view. They can only approximate what took place. For right now it's best for us to just stick to the facts that are generally accepted."

Again, the old guy's students could read between the lines.

## The Attack

"On January 6, 2021 some 2000-2500 people invaded the Capitol. They were supporters of the President. They were opposed to Joe Biden's victory. They wanted to overturn the 2020 presidential election results. In the face of this mob the Capitol Police attempted to lock down the complex. The police were attacked. Some 138 police officers were injured. The lawmakers in the building were evacuated. Not one was of them was injured. That, of course, raises a question. Had our representatives been harmed, perhaps even killed, would that have altered the public's perception of what took place? How would the later debate as to what happened and why been different? Would law enforcement been more aggressive in dealing with the rioters?

"Prior to the riot then President Trump had encouraged his supporters to come to Washington. He wanted them to protest his false claim that the election was 'stolen.' He blamed left-wing Democrats for doing this. His exact words were: 'Big protest in DC on January 6th. Be there, it will be wild.' He also said: 'f you don't fight like hell, you're not going to have a country anymore." Why January 6th? That was the day the Congress would certify the election results."

**ADDRESSING THE CROWD**

"What did he mean by that, 'you won't have a country anymore?'"

"Howard, as in the case of many things the President said various interpretations were made. Given what his followers were saying, and the signs they carried, plus the fact that almost all the protesters were white, only one conclusion, I believe, is possible. Our population's diversity was a threat to them. White nationalists were, as they saw it, losing control in what they considered a 'white man's country.' A point of view had become a grievance and this led to frustration and anger. The photographs and film of that day showed Nazi emblems and Confederate flags shown and waved for the world to see. To have Hitler's flag in our Capitol was an abomination. Not once during the Civil War did a Confederate flag wave in the Capitol. That flag symbolized slavery and the later brutal oppression of the freedman."

**AN ABOMINATION**

"Was all of this planned, I mean the attack?"

"Yes, the weight of evidence suggests that. The rioters brought tools to pry open doors. They had spray cans used against animals.

They wore helmets. Some had flak jackets. A few had smuggled guns into the city. Pipe bombs were later found near both the Republican and Democratic National Headquarters. Molotov cocktails were discovered in a vehicle near the Capitol. There was a strong current of premeditation to the attack on the Capitol."

"But didn't many demonstrators just want to assemble and express themselves peacefully?"

"Tim, of course. But there were also chants of 'Hang Mike Pence' and 'Pelosi is Satan. And let's not forget the gallows erected to hang the Vice President…"

**The Big Lie**

"What's this business about the 'big lie?"

"Jaime, once the polls closed President Trump declared victory. He demanded that all vote counting stop. He began a campaign to subvert the election outcome. After ten days of investigation even Trump's lawyers agreed that there was no 'factual basis' or 'legal merit' to challenge the results. Over time sixty lawsuits, including two before the Supreme Court, reached this same conclusion. There was no proof to nullify the election results.

**THE BIG LIE**

"Why do people believe the 'big lie?"

"The simplest reason is sometimes the best one. Trump's supporters wanted a victory. They needed a justification for the loss. The 'big lie' was, I believe, a way to scapegoat Biden's success. What could account for Trump's loss? Only one thing; he had been robbed. That being the case, the question emerged: who had robbed Trump of a second term? The only possible answer was people of color; that is, non-whites. Diversity in key states had tipped the scales for Biden. That's what was at the heart of all this, a changing America."

"How can you prove that, Dr. Goldman?"

"For once, Daniel, I have an easy but objectionable answer. Since the 2020 election numerous states have enacted new voting regulations that focus on 'people of color voters.' Gerrymandering has attempted to dilute that vote. Potential voter fraud is cited for these discriminatory changes. One other things comes to mind… Trump's supporters never adequately explained how well the Republicans did across the country in what are called "down ballot elections." If the opposition was cheating, it really didn't do a good job."

## A Personal Note

I have been voting since 1960. That's when you had to be 21 to fill out a ballot. Over the years I've won some and I've lost some. Some of the elections were close, others were landslides … Regardless of the outcome, I always accepted the election outcome. I never claimed I was cheated even when there were some questions in my mind. At all levels of government the losing candidates were generous when they conceded. They didn't call on their supporters to march on the Mayor's Office or the Governor's Mansion, or the home of the winning candidate. Occasionally, there were court suits, but little more. People respected the system with all its imperfections. We recognized that voting was messy, highly political, and very personal, sort of like rooting for your home team. But once the game is over you go home, saying, "We'll get you next year." A great many of Trump's supporters couldn't do that."

## Combat

As the Old Guy finished his sentence an adult from MAG leaped to her feet and charged toward him. As she did her hands balled into tight fists and her eyes narrowed into tiny dots. Unabated anger cloaked her face even as salvia dripped from the corner of her mouth. As she approached the old guy she screamed, "Stop indoctrinating these students with your poisonous far-left propaganda. You want them to hate President Trump, the man God sent to protect our Christian country! You should be locked up, you dirty Jew."

The police officer started toward the woman. The old guy put up a hand to keep him in his tracks. With the television camera beaming live coverage the old guy surprised everyone with his response.

"Madam, you drive a somewhat tarnish brown Ford, don't you?"

"You stinking creep, why do you ask?"

"When I was parking I saw you leave your car. I saw the Confederate flag sticker and one for Charlottesville. You were there?"

"Damn right, you sinful bastard. I was there protesting the removal of a statute of General Robert E. Lee."

"And, along with neo-Nazis, white nationalists, Klansmen, neo-Confederates, and various right-wing militias, you were yelling racist and anti-Semitic slogans, were you not?"

"I was you child-pornographer. I was there to say, 'You won't replace me!'"

"Who won't replace you?"

"Them!"

"Them?"

"Who do you think, you worthless creature? The blacks, the Mexicans, the Asians, and those rag-heads from the Middle East... This is a white-Christian country. We've had enough of this racial pollution."

"And what would you do if Trump had won?"

The woman gasped for breathe before responding. She gazed intently at the television camera, and then, realizing that this was her moment, she blurted out the vindictive grievances torturing her soul.

"We'd get rid of affirmative action for the blacks. All questions of reparation would be ended. Books about race in our schools and libraries would be censored. Newspapers with leftist leaning would be shut down, as would television news shows not to our liking. There would be no more permits for Mosques. Synagogues would be monitored. The Christian Bible would be in every classroom. Immigration would be limited to acceptable Nordic-type people. And that's just the beginning…

"In other words you want an authoritarian government that controls and censors?"

"Yes, you miserable creature."

"You would use the police and military to enforce your views?"

"Good patriotic people would rally to do that."

"In other words you would throw away our constitutional rights?"

"To bring God's work to our country, oh, yes."

**THE KLAN**

**AMERICAN NAZI**

**CONFEDERATES**

The enraged woman had enough. She turned from the camera's blinking eye and moved toward the old guy, hatred blistering her face. No doubt about it… She was going to attack the teacher. Before the officer could stop her, three students leaped from their chairs and surrounded the woman. Philip Reilly spoke for them. "Get back in your seat and shut up, or we'll going to physically remove you from the room, you nut case!" Unable to speak, the flabbergasted woman retreated from the room, yelling, "You've been brainwashed, you dummies." As she left the students stood up and applauded. In the back of the room Dr. Lopez settled back into her seat, thankful that she hadn't needed to restrain the woman with the karate skills she learned in college. She also thought under her breath, "You deceiving rascal. You turned that woman's ranting into a teachable moment." In his downtown office the Superintendent reached for a bottle of aspirin, saying as he did, "I need to check out my retirement benefits."

<u>Looking Back</u>

Dr. Goldman continued. "Where does all this leave us? One historian attempted to pull the loose ends together:

*President Trump declared that he would never concede the election; he criticized the media; he called for Pence to overturn the election results; he repeated many falsehoods misrepresentations that inflamed his followers. He did not overtly call on his supporters to use violence or enter the Capitol. His words, however, were filled with violent imagery. He suggested to his followers that they had the power to prevent Biden from taking office. He called on his supporters to "walk down to the Capitol" He said, "We can't let that happen. Biden, he said, would be an "illegitimate resident." He added, "Something's really wrong. He told his base that they should go to the Capital and "try to give Republicans the kind of pride and boldness that they need to take back our country." He reminded them that, "You'll never take back our country with weakness. You have to show strength and you have to be strong. You have to demand that Congress do the right thing and only count the electors who have been lawfully slated."*

"That does it for today. At our next meeting we'll get on with the trial. Hopefully, there will be fewer fireworks. And thanks for helping me out today."

Chapter 25

# THE DEFENSE

<u>The Last Meeting</u>

All teachers have experienced the joy and sadness of the last class meetings before finals. On the one hand, they're glad the semester is ending, even more so if its just before summer vacation and a chance to rest and travel, to be home with your kids, and to grab a tan by the swimming pool if you live in Southern California. On the other hand, there's always that class that made teaching a joy, those special students with whom you experienced a unique relationship. Of course, that was true of the concurrent class. The old guy had to fight back his conflicting emotions as he spoke to his class.

"Well, here we are. Today is our last class meeting. Your essays have been returned. Your 100-multiple question final is over, and returned to you. The grades are in and you know how you did. That being the case there's no need for another meeting. I must assure you that it has been my honor to be your teacher. If you feel so inclined please leave your e-mail address with me. It would be nice to stay in touch."

"Dr. Goldman…"
"Yes, Sid."
"We have a proposal."
"The hamburger bribe business?"
"Not exactly. We'd like to have a class party at a different spot."
"And where would that be?"
"Brent's Deli… We understand you like the food. We've contacted the manger and reserved a backroom for our class."
"You did, did you?"

"It's our way of saying, 'Thanks.'"
"I can bring my girlfriend?"
"Naturally. We've already spoken to Mrs. Goldman."
"And what about my boss?"
"Dr. Lopez and the Superintendent have been told."
"This smacks of a conspiracy."

Of course, the television cameras captured all this. Those who teach probably missed a heartbeat as they applauded the old guy's students. Secretively, they all cherished such a moment and looked forward to one. Regardless of their political leanings, the adults in the back of the room were quiet. MAG had replaced the 'nut job' with one less so. Again, outside of the school the demonstrators did their thing, watched carefully by LAPD, who kept the two main groups moving and separate.

"Well, let's get on with our last lecture, the Second Trial of President Donald Trump." Before we begin we will hear once again from our old friend, Edmund G. Ross. What he said about the Johnson impeachment bears strongly on ex-president, Donald Trump.

*Conditions may, and are not unlikely to arise, some day, when the exercise of the power to impeach and remove the President may be quite as essential to the preservation of our political system as it threatened to become in this instance destructive of that system. Should that day ever come, it is to be hoped that the remedy of impeachment as established by the Constitution, may be as patriotically, as fearlessly, and as unselfishly applied as it was on this occasion rejected.*

It would be wise of us to keep Ross' words uppermost in mind as we progress.

<u>Lecture - The House Managers</u>

"On January 25, 2021 nine House Mangers (prosecutors) delivered the charges (indictments) to the Senate. The singular Article of Impeachment accused former-President Trump of:

1.  Inciting an insurrection.
2.  Inciting the January 6th attack on the Capitol.
3.  Attempting to overturn the 2020 election results.
4.  Inciting lawless action at the Capitol.

"The trial began on February 9, 2021. This would be a first in American history; a departed president was being placed on trial. Chief Justice John Roberts did not preside. That honor went to Patrick Leahy, a Democrat. He was the president pro tempore of the Senate. Eventually, 57 senators voted "Guilty;" 43 senators voted "Not Guilty." Some 67 votes were needed for conviction; that is, 2/3rds of the Senate. On February 13, 2021 Donald Trump was acquitted of all charges."

"Didn't the House vote for impeachment just one week before Trump's term ended?"

"That is correct, Monica."

"Well, then why have a trial? Seven days and he would be out of office."

"Good question. There are two reasons. First, our laws and norms must be protected. That demands accountability. That's why all Democrats in the House, along with ten Republicans chose to impeach. The focus of their argument was this: it was unwise to allow any president to commit crimes shortly before he left office, which he might do if there was no fear of punishment."

"What's the second reason?"

"If found guilty the president is removed from office. He (or she) is now disqualified from holding 'any Office of Honor.' As one political scientist put it:

*Impeaching an official even after he has left office provides a fundamental element of conviction. It protects the Republic from people who would abuse their power.*

"Dr. Goldman, I didn't think Congress could impeach a former president. Am I correct?"

"The answer is, I'm afraid, a little muddled. First, the House voted for impeachment while the President was still in power. Most political scientists believe the Senate could hold a trial even after the President left office. To quote one academic:

*If impeachment does not apply to former officials, then Congress could never bar an official from holding office in the future as long as that individual resigned first.*

"How was the military involved in the impeachment?"

"Jack, the short answer is this. Following a long tradition of staying out of domestic politics the Joint Chief of Staff issued a statement on January 12th 'condemning the attack.' The statement reminded military personnel that 'Biden was about to become their commander-in-chief.' Moreover, the statement included this:

*The rights of freedom of speech and assembly do not give anyone the right to resort to violence, sedition, and insurrection.*

The Joint Chiefs ended with this promise:

*As we have done throughout our history, the US military will obey lawful orders from civilian leadership, support civilian authorities to protect lives and property, ensure public safety in accordance with the law, and remain fully committed to protecting and defending the Constitution of the United States against all enemies, foreign and domestic.*

"Did Trump get a 'fair and impartial trial?'"

"Ray, that's a difficult question to answer. Technically, yes. He got a fair trial. His political peers in the Senate judged him and found him innocent of the indictment. As in the case of Andrew Johnson, impartiality was difficult to discern. The Democrats wanted Trump out of office, now and forever. The Republicans wanted him acquitted. It was, as you will recall, the complete reverse of 1867."

"Then he got away with inciting the storming of the Capitol."

"In a legal sense, yes. In the court of public opinion a rift in views existed. Most Democrats and Independents felt Trump was guilty. Almost all Republicans took a different stance. That divide continues down to today. Again, as in Johnson's case, historians will continue to evaluate what took place, reaching conclusions that today we may have difficulty seeing."

"What did the defense say on Trump's behalf?"

"Susan, the defense provided, as you would expect, a partisan legal defense of the President. The important thing is to understand how Republicans justified their 'Not Guilty' vote. In their own words let's see what they said:

Senator Mitch McConnell (R, KY), who was the Senate Minority Leader voted to acquit the President. He said, however:

*Former President Trump's actions that preceded the riot were a disgraceful, disgraceful dereliction of duty. There's no question --- none – that President Trump is practically and morally responsible for provoking the events of the day. There is no limiting principle in the constitutional text that would empower the Senate to convict and disqualify former officers that would not also let them convict and disqualify any private citizen… The Senate's decision today does not condone anything that happened on or before that terrible day.*

**MINORITY LEADER**

Senator Rob Portman (R-Ohio) also voted to acquit. He said:

*What President Trump did that day was inexcusable because in his speech he encouraged the mob, and that he bears some responsibility for the tragic violence that occurred. I have also criticized his slow response as the mob stormed the US Capitol, putting at risk the safety of Vice President Pence, law enforcement officers, and others who work in the Capitol. Even after the attack, some of the language his tweets and in a video sowed sympathy for the violent mob.*

Senator John Thune (R, SD) said:

*My vote to acquit should not be viewed as exoneration for his conduct on January 6, 2021, or in the days and weeks leading up to it. What former President Trump did to undermine faith in our election system and disrupt the peaceful transfer of power is inexcusable. But he is no longer president. The Constitution is clear that the primary purpose of impeachment is removal from office.*

Senator John Cornyn (R, TX) said:

*The trial reminded us that too many public officials, including the President, have used reckless and incendiary speech… The arguments of the House Impeachment Managers that the Constitution permits the impeachment of a private citizen, the free speech protections of the First Amendment don't apply, the due process clause of the Fifth*

*Amendment is optional, and that the trial may include a presiding officer who also serves as a juror all were a bridge too far.*

Senator Mike Lee (R, UT) voted to acquit. He said:

*No one can condone… President Trump's word, actions, and omissions on that day… The fact is that the word "incitement" has a very specific meaning in the law, and Donald Trump's words and actions on January 6, 2021, fell short of that standard. The House rushed its impeachment without an investigation, charged President Trump with a crime it failed property to allege, and then sat on its poorly worded Article until after he left office.*

"Dr. Goldman, all these arguments have merit, isn't that true?"

"Howard, you're correct. But here again we must be careful in evaluating what was said. First of all, the Republican senators were in a difficult position. They couldn't be seen as condoning what happened and Trump's involvement. At the same time they wanted to protect the President. Most, as former lawyers, nuanced a semi-legal response, thereby placing them in the middle of this political morass. Secondly, these senators did not want to infuriate Trump's base with a guilty vote. Senators, as do all politicians, are always thinking about the next election and the constant need for campaign contributions. Those two demands, as you can see, placed them in an awkward spot. That was also true in 1867. A constitutional crisis is never an easy thing to navigate.

"There was no Edmund G. Ross?"

"Here you are mistaken, Howard. That's okay. Most Americans have forgotten that seven Republican senators voted with the Democrats, making the impeachment the most bipartisan in our history. Let's find out why they voted as they did.

Senator Richard Bird (NC) said:

*The evidence is compelling that President Trump is guilty of inciting an insurrection against a coequal branch of government and that the charges rises to the level of high Crimes and Misdemeanors.*

**BYRD OF NORTH CAROLINA**

Senator Bill Cassidy, of Louisiana said:

*Our Constitution and our country is more important than any one person. I voted to convict President Trump because he was guilty. It was clear that Trump wished that lawmakers be intimidated while they counted votes, and that Trump didn't act quickly to dissuade the violent mob.*

**CASSIDY OF LOUISIANA**

Senator Susan Collins of Maine said:

*The impeachment trial is not about any single word uttered by President Trump on January 6, 2021. It is instead about President*

*Trump's failure to obey the oath he swore on January 20, 2017. His actions to interfere with he peaceful transition of power --- the hallmark of our Constitution and our American democracy --- were an abuse of power and constitute grounds for conviction.*

**COLLINS OF MAINE**

Senator Lisa Murkowski of Alaska said:

*The evidence presented at the trial was clear; President Trump was watching events unfold live, just as the entire country was. Even after the violence had started, as protestors chanted "Hang Mike Pence" inside the Capitol, President Trump, aware of what was happening, tweeted that the Vice President had failed the country. Trump had set the table for months, saying that the "election was rigged." He did everything he could to stay in power.*

**MURKOSKI OF ALASKA**

Senator Ben Sasse of Nebraska said:

*In my first speech here in the Senate in November 2015, I promised to speak out when a president --- even of my own party --- exceeds his or her powers. I cannot go back on my word, and Congress cannot lower our standards on such a grave matter, simply because it is politically convenient. I must vote to convict. Those lies had consequences, endangering the life of the vice president and bringing us dangerously close to a bloody constitutional crisis. Each of these actions are violations of a president's oath of office.*

**SASSE OF NEBRASKA**

Senator Mitt Romney of Utah said:

*President Trump incited the insurrection against Congress by using the power of his office to summon his supporters to Washington on January 6th and urging them to march on the Capitol during the counting of electoral votes. He did this despite the obvious and well- known threats of violence that day. President Trump also violated his oath of office by failing to protect the Capitol, the Vice President, and others in the Capitol. Each and everyone of these conclusions compels me to support conviction.*

**ROMNEY OF UTAH**

"You see, Howard, Ross was alive and well. These six senators put principle before party. They were willing to take the heat from their colleagues and their constituents. While we may disagree on other issues with these six, on the question of protecting our Republic they stood tall. Never forget that."

"Ross and others never won another election. Will that happen to these people?"

"If they choose to run for reelection, we'll find out, won't we?"

"So should Trump have been impeached?"

"That is the question, isn't it, Philip?"

~

It was time to close shop. The old guy knew it. His students knew it. All things, it seems, come to an end. One by one the students left, but only after first shaking hands or providing youthful hugs. All said two things: "Thanks and see you at Brent's. In his heart he knew he would see them one more time. Under intense public pressure, the Board had scheduled a special meeting this Saturday in the Monroe High auditorium. His students, he felt sure, would be there. They knew too much about impeachments to miss it.

Minutes later the adult observers left, the television camera blinked off, and was rolled out of the room. Again, he was left alone with Dr. Lopez. She quietly approached him. It was then that she saw the tears. His job now done the old guy could no longer withhold his emotions. No words were spoken. Dr. Lopez embraced him. The old guy offered no resistance.

~

What was not said in those closing moments in the classroom? On Saturday, just three days from now, the Board would determine the Old Guy's fate. Those opposed to him wanted his credential stricken. They wanted his retirement pension revoked. They wanted him disgraced and humiliated. They wanted to send a message to wayward teachers. "Don't talk about race. Don't attack Trump." They didn't care about that the semester was all but over. They wanted retribution.

Others, including past and former students, would stand and defend the Old Guy. That was to be expected. Whether they could talk over the expected loud shouts and boisterous behavior was another question. Four people in particular had already determined what they would say.

## The Superintendent – Dr. Benjamin Wetzel

The Board should know that Dr. Goldman's students passed the District exit exam in flying colors. Higher scores have never been seen. A special examination provided by our Office of Instruction was given in the blind. Dr. Goldman's students showed remarkable success. The average was 98%. That score was highly correlated with his own examination. There the students achieved a 99% score on the average. Please note that the essays he assigned were submitted to history professors a UCLA and USC, and Cal State Northridge. The common response was, "We wish our students could research and write as well. His students did a remarkable job." That being the case I recommend that he retire with full benefits. He has earned them."

## The Instructional Supervisor – Dr. Florence Williams

"At the request of the Superintendent I was given an unusual task. I was to monitor a veteran teacher. What did this mean? Dr. Goldman would submit duplicate lesson plans each week. One copy went to me; the second copy went to his principal. In addition, all testing materials would also be reviewed, as would the results. Additionally, an adult would always be in the classroom when classes were held in the high school. When zooming, all meetings would be recorded and made available to the public. Initially, as an Instructional Supervisor I was highly skeptical of Dr. Goldman's unorthodox teaching methods. This was particularly true when he was discussing controversial subjects such as war, race, and impeachments. That said, he complied with all State and District regulations, as well as with the requirements already discussed. It is fair to say that no teacher has ever been under greater scrutiny. In summary, there is no compelling reason to challenge his credential or to withhold his pension. He has done nothing wrong."

## The Student

My name is Philip Reilly. My family is very conservative. My mother is the president of MAG. This semester has been difficult for me. I wanted to please my parents. In time I came to understand that there are many ways to look at things. Dr. Goldman helped me to see this. In a private conference with me he explained the necessity of honoring our parents, while being true to our own beliefs. Though I love my parents I no longer accept without question what my parents tell me when it comes to politics. Of course, I apply that same concept to what Dr. Goldman said in class. He insisted on that. This insight will never show up on a test or my GPA, but it was possibly the best thing I learned this semester. I expect the Board to treat my teacher and friend in a "fair and impartial" manner."

## The Principal

"My name is Dr. Eleanor Lopez. I have given considerable thought to what I should say about my colleague, Dr. Goldman. Leave it at this. I have two children in the public schools. If possible I would want Dr. Goldman to be their teacher. I am so proud he taught in our school and I would rehire him if he chose to continue teaching."

## The Teacher

"At this moment words escape me. Permit me to just say this. Teaching is an honorable profession with a unique obligation to do right by our students. That I have always tried to do over the past 40-years… I have no regrets about that. I leave it to the Board to decide my fate."

# Epilogue

The old guy got lucky. Better heads prevailed in spite of the angry shrieks of self-appointed vigilantes who would have strung him from the highest tree on the Monroe High campus. The School Board voted to save his hide no matter the political costs. As one member said, "There was absolutely no cause for dismissal. Dr. Goldman was a testament to dedication and scholarship in the classroom. We could ask no more of him or any teacher."

The old guy would retire with a well-earned pension. He wouldn't lose his teaching credential. As Dr. Lopez had hoped her feisty teacher left the profession with his principles uncompromised in the face of irrational calls to censure and control what was taught. The Superintendent was also pleased. His old friend would leave teaching with his pride intact. There was a quiet dignity in that that all teachers seek.

Four months after the old guy retired he received a phone call from his oncologist at Kaiser Hospital. The fickle gods were not yet done with him. Dr. Chou told him that the CDC and the FDA had just approved a new treatment called immuno therapy. Though still in the experimental stage this approach to treating cancer worked by getting the body to fight the cancer. On an emergency basis Kaiser was selecting some patients. He had been selected. It meant coming into the hospital every month for treatment, perhaps for the rest of his life. Immuno therapy might not get rid of the cancer, he learned, but could keep it a bay. That was good enough for the old guy and his wife.

Of course he received e-mails from his students as time passed. They began, "Hope you're feeling okay." It turns out this was more than "make talk." Apparently, the students had known about his cancer for months. One of the supportive parents had seen him getting "chemo" during that difficult semester and put two and two together. Soon a few parents knew and remained silent. That's how Monica, quite by accident, learned about the cancer from her mom. Naturally, she shared this with her peers. As a group they decided not to say anything. They would support their dying teacher. To their post-class inquires he had a stock, purposefully non-committable answer: "Doing okay. Thanks for asking." And then he would change the subject. "How's college?" Or: "What's happening with the job you took?"

Occasionally, he heard from Dr. Lopez, who brought him up on the latest school gossip. She asked, of course, how he liked retirement? Again, he had a prepared answer: "I'm acclimating." About once a month she came by on a Sunday after church to say hello. She and Lynn had hit it off. It didn't hurt that Dr. Lopez wanted to learn how to quilt and Lynn, pretty much a master quilter, offered to teach her the ropes. On one occasion Jaime and the children also came over. The kids hit the pool. The men fired up the BBQ and life was good.

The old guy slipped easily into his AARP life with hardly a misstep. He worked in the garden, always paying special attention to his tomato plants. With time on his hands he was able to carry on extended conversations. As you would expect he took good care of Pomp now that he had time to wash and polish, as he always wanted. And, yes, he did engage in car talk with the van.

*"How are you doing, Old Buddy?"*
*"I'm not that old, Pomp."*
*"Well, if that's the case, how about a bit more elbow grease on my hub caps and tires."*

With his wife Lynn he considered renting a small RV. They began planning a national park trip, beginning with Yosemite and ending up with Mt. Rainier in Washington. If this first venture agreed with them they just might purchase a rig.

Each day the old guy retreated into his study where he worked on what he called "his secret project." On a large desk he had copies of the essays his students wrote. Comments were written on them, but not the usual corrections or suggestions. When asked what he was doing he always gave a vague reply: "Just doing a little something." His wife wasn't the nosy type, but she was curious. She affectionately pestered. Always concerned about his next meal, the old guy eventually caved.

"I pulling together an anthology of sorts, tied to a lot of history. The student essays will be highlighted, since they are at the heart of what I intend to write."

"You'll give the students credit in the footnotes?"

"More than that. With each chapter I'm enlisting their assistance where their essay is involved."

"Collegiality… You old rascal, you just want to spend time with them, don't you? You're having trouble letting go?"

"Dr. Lopez is a kind of co-author."

"You are a wily one, and at your age."

"The Superintendent wants to add his ten cents, too."

"And what about me?"

"I'm in need of a proofreader. You know I can't spell to save my life."

"Your distortion of grammatical rules is also well known."

"Well, then, want the job?

"Only if you tell me the opening line."

*See that vintage VW Camper exiting the 405 Freeway at Devonshire Street in the San Fernando Valley? That's where our story begins. The Old Guy driving the 1987 van will be 65-years old in a couple of weeks. He's also within three months of finally retiring from the Los Angele School District.*